What can one woman ~~do~~ with a little magic on her ~~side?~~

In the picturesque Pacific coast town of Avening, it's hard not to believe in magic. This is a town where the shoes in the window always fit, where you can buy a love potion at the corner shop, and where local lore seamlessly mixes with the supernatural.

And then there's Autumn, Avening's most beloved resident, shopkeeper, and guardian of the Jaen sisterhood. When she receives word she's been promoted within the order, Autumn must undertake the unenviable task of selecting her own replacement. But who in Avening is magical enough to take Autumn's place? Is it shy Ellie, who is used to thinking of herself as invisible? Perhaps it's Stella, the clumsy loud-mouth whose grandmother trained her in Appalachian healing. Or Piper, the mother of two teenage girls, whose serious illness has suddenly given way to a surprising and disconcerting ability. Autumn has a list of thirteen women who just might have what it takes—but can she get them to open their eyes to the magic in their lives?

This endlessly surprising and heart-warming debut is the story of the magical things we take for granted everyday—our friends, our community, and, most of all, ourselves.

When
Autumn
Leaves

🙵

When Autumn Leaves

A NOVEL

AMY S. FOSTER

THE OVERLOOK PRESS
NEW YORK

First published in the United States in 2009 by
The Overlook Press, Peter Mayer Publishers, Inc.
New York

NEW YORK:
141 Wooster Street
New York, NY 10012

Cataloging-in-Publication Data is available from the Library of Congress

Book design and type formatting by Bernard Schleifer
Printed in the United States of America
FIRST EDITION
9 8 7 6 5 4 3 2 1
ISBN 978-1-59020-255-5

For the first Ellie,

my grandmother.

When
Autumn
Leaves

Calendar of Pagan Holidays

Winter Solstice

Dec 21

Samhain
Oct 31

Imbolc
Feb 2

Fall
Equinox
Sept 21

Spring
Equinox
March 21

Lunghasadh
Aug 1

Beltane
May 1

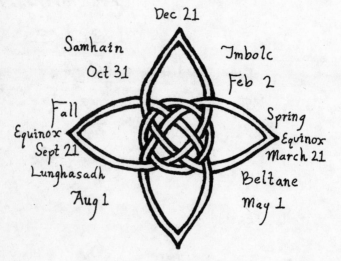

Summer Solstice

June 21

Here We Are

THERE IS A SMALL BRONZE PLAQUE IN AVENING HEATH among the brush and wildflowers, shining like new even though it's been there for a century and a half. People walk by it in every season (the people of Avening are not the type to let a little thing like the weather keep them from going out of doors). But who knows how many of those citizens have actually ever read it?

This is what the plaque says:

> August 1, 1859. "We have found our Garden at last. But there will be no apples or serpents, no shameful exile for being the creatures God made us. Here there is a promise of a truer Eden, despite the exquisite imperfections that abound. There will be sanctuary and protection for all who have need of it."
> —Serafina Avening

Both the ambiguity and the biblical—or is it heretical?—tone of the words on the plaque have only added to the legend of Avening. As with all creation stories, ask anyone on this island about the town's beginnings and they will each give you a different story. Some claim Avening was set-

tled by a different sort of pioneer: a collaboration of matri-
archs looking to escape the religious rigidity of the time.
They traveled the length of the continent, east to west, guided
only by a vision of Serafina Avening, who led them through
blue-black waters to a land of cedars ringed by snow-capped
mountains. Others claim Serafina's intents were less noble,
that she and her followers came in search of fabled West
Coast gold. Others still say it was shamans of the Salish, a
tribe of First Nations peoples, who shipwrecked Serafina
Avening's boat here during a thunderdance. There are non-
believers who doubt that Serafina Avening even existed, or
believe that she is an amalgamation of many different
women. But Autumn Avening, who claims to be Serafina's
very direct descendent, has always insisted the woman was,
indeed, real.

Like Serafina promised all those years ago, Avening is a
haven and a refuge from so many of the troubles that circle
other small towns and hover over the concrete sorrows of big
cities. Most everything begins with a good intention. But too
often those intentions, lost to greed and politics, become simply ideals, irrelevant to progress. Not so for Avening, cradled
on a piece of lush Pacific coast. The town's founders, whoever they were, their ideals, their framework and forward
thinking, created a foundation that stuck.

Serafina Avening was the one who instituted the
pagan holiday system. Not because she was a witch, like
some people have called her. It was because those holidays
center around the seasons, the harvest, night and day, tangible things that people could see and count on, a common
thread that united them all. Not everyone may believe in

the same thing, but everyone can believe that even the darkest, coldest winter will move over and make room for spring. And so they all celebrate together, and it's enough to create the shared community that a town needs to thrive and bustle.

It is true that only a certain kind of person feels comfortable living in Avening. People are drawn to it or repelled by it like a magnet. Those who fit will stay; those who don't move as soon as they're grown, or pass it by when planning a holiday. One could say (and many do) that the town itself chooses whom it wants.

How Avening came to be isn't what matters. All you need to know is that Avening, beautiful and enchanting, nestled off the coast of British Columbia, began with a secret. But even the secret isn't really important, not anymore, or at least, not yet. So we won't begin there. This is a different beginning.

𝒞

The morning of December 12th was wet, the sky a heathery gray. Autumn Avening opened her eyes and rolled onto her back. If she hadn't known any better, she would have sworn that she was in one of those kitschy motel rooms with the vibrating units in the beds. But Autumn knew it wasn't her mattress that was vibrating; it was her spine. She groaned. All the tingles in her brain, the humming in her nervous system, were signals. Something—or more accurately, someone—was coming.

Autumn had been in Avening for a long time. For a while, she'd fought the suspicion that she was on borrowed time. Now—she just knew it—they were going to make her leave.

Life callings are strange. Many, many years ago, Autumn was just an ordinary girl, who led an ordinary life. Then she was called to join the Jaen and she began to lead an extraordinary one. She did a lot of interesting, often dangerous work. Then it all seemed to come full circle; for the last little while, her life had become fairly ordinary again. And while what was normal everyday stuff for her would be fairly wondrous for anybody else, Autumn had grown accustomed to a life of relative peace, safe and smooth and lovely.

Autumn tried to ignore the buzzing in her spine all day, but later that day, as she sat at her desk, she knew. She didn't hear the gate opening, but knew a gate had opened somewhere in her house, because she felt the presence of a visitor, one of her own, in her house. A couple moments passed, and Autumn sat unproductively at her desk, fighting down a mixture of sorrow, anticipation, and annoyance.

"Halloo," she heard from the bottom of her stairs. Autumn knew the voice; it was Sister Neal. At least they had sent someone she actually liked. Technically she was meant to love all her Sisters in the Jaen. And she did love them, in theory. In reality, there were many that she couldn't stand.

"Sister Neal," Autumn called with genuine pleasure as she met her old friend on the stairs. The two embraced and touched foreheads, as is the custom of the Jaen. "Let me look at you," Autumn said brightly. "It's been too long, Sister."

Neal raised her eyebrows by way of an answer. She had aged; her hair was almost completely silver. Before too long she would take her place as an Elder. "The years have caught up with you as well, Autumn," Neal said in her thick Irish brogue. "Keep that in mind before you say something cheeky."

Autumn laughed. She should have known better than to think too loudly around Sister Neal. "Let's go through to the kitchen and I'll make some tea. I had a hankering to make soda bread yesterday, so you're in luck." Autumn hooked Neal's arm through her own and led her to the kitchen. The kitchen was not in fact part of her living quarters, but down on the ground floor in Demeter's Grove, Autumn's store. Demeter's Grove was a "new age" kind of store, as they were calling them these days, and Autumn sold everything from incense and candles to especially elemental stones to clothing to books. She was used to inviting all kinds of strangers and friends into her kitchen; demonstrations—cooking, baking, tincture or poultice-making—were another dimension of her business.

Autumn motioned for Neal to sit at the old table in front of the stone fireplace, under the drying herbs suspended from the ceiling. "Well, this is a treat," Neal said playfully. "And I see you're as prescient as ever, my dear."

"You sound surprised." Autumn flicked on the electric kettle and pulled out just the right kind of tea from a canister sitting on an open shelf.

"Well, I am, honestly." Neal smiled, but Autumn noticed a hint of caution in her eyes. "You must know why I'm here."

"Of course, yes. They sent you to tell me it's time for me to leave. You're here to give me my year's warning." Autumn swallowed her unhappiness. "But we've been friends a long time, Neal, and I believe I owe you one or two. Did you think

I'd shout the house down?" Autumn asked, leaning against the dishwasher.

"Hardly," Neal assured her. "But . . . we expected you to be on the defensive." Autumn bit the inside of her lip. It was an unconscious move, one she did to keep herself from speaking. "We know, we really do, how much Avening means to you."

"And you know why, Neal, and why this situation is unique," Autumn said slowly, turning her attention to the kettle, which had popped. She poured the steaming water into the teapot. Neal said nothing, just waited for the tea to be poured, for the bread to be cut and buttered. She waited for Autumn to sit down so she could face her.

"You're not the first, Autumn, nor will you be the last to play such a central role in a community. Things change, technology, wars, politics. The Jaen changes accordingly. Other Sisters will do what you have done." Neal took a sip of tea. "Oh, this is lovely."

"Yes, I realize things change. It's just hard, to let go." The Jaen knew Autumn respected Neal too much to ever lie to her, or be disrespectful; that was surely why they'd sent Neal, specifically, so Autumn couldn't put up too much of a fuss. This irritated the hell out of Autumn, that they could be so calculating.

Neal took a bite of bread, wiped her fingers off on her napkin, and reached into a pocket sewed on the bottom of her tunic. She pulled out a piece of paper and slid it across the hardwood of the table.

"What's that, then?" Autumn asked, her fingers lightly touching the item in question.

"Oh, I think you know," Neal said seriously.

Autumn picked up the paper, unfolded it carefully, and read the names. "This has got to be some kind of a joke."

"You know that it is not," Neal answered, her smile completely gone.

"Well, you lot have made a mistake," Autumn blurted.

"You know that we do not make mistakes," Neal said tightly. "The Vedea has been the Jaen oracle for thousands of years. It is never wrong. Sometimes it is hard to accept, hard to understand, certainly, but never wrong."

Autumn had to tread lightly. Neal was her friend, her Sister, but also her superior. "I don't even know some of these people. Never even heard of them. Ellie Penhaligan? Who in the hell is that?" Autumn took a deep, seething breath, trying to calm herself. "I assumed I would be choosing from a pool of women that I've been working with. Some I have even been grooming, personally, for years."

"Well, you assumed too much. You knew this wasn't only your decision to make. You made a vow, Sister Autumn, to serve the Jaen, as it has served humanity since before humans even knew how to record their own history. And so you will serve." Neal took a sip of tea. She exhaled and softened her face. "Look, I'm sure there is some leeway here. This is a guide—but a guide you cannot ignore. These women must be included in your decision-making process. And after all, you get the final say. I cannot for the life of me imagine why that's not enough for you."

A bureaucratic loophole! Autumn felt some relief. "I'm sorry. It's just that . . . actually, I thought I wouldn't be given a choice at all. I thought the Vedea would know, somehow, who I had in mind, and that would be the end of it. I thought I could use my year's warning to prepare that person. I didn't think I would have to use that year to choose." That new thought—that she'd only have a year to make this decision—suddenly made Autumn a little frantic.

"So now you don't want the choice at all?" Neal's eyebrows rose. "I could go back and ask the Vedea to come up with something more . . . concrete," she suggested.

"No, no, of course not." Autumn clasped her hands together solemnly. "I will use the list. I'll investigate all the candidates with due diligence. I'll make the right choice."

"Of that I have no doubt. You have the added advantage of having so many talented women to choose from. There really is no other place on earth like Avening. You have been blessed."

Autumn nodded. She didn't want Neal's kindness. She didn't want to hear how wonderful Avening was. She knew. And it hurt.

Neal reached across the table and took Autumn's hand. Her grip was gentle and wise. "We are Jaen, but we are also human. We need change. It keeps us vibrant, helps us grow and makes us better. You need the change, Autumn. You have another chapter in your life to begin. And Avening needs a change, too. Fresh blood. A new perspective. It's time."

"I know," Autumn agreed. "I'm just being nostalgic. It's hardly productive; don't mind me."

"It's fine, dear. Things are happening, moving forward. You'll think on many things now, not just the decision before you. That's the way of it," Neal said as she stood. "I have to go. I'm sorry, Autumn. But thank you for the tea."

Autumn nodded, unsure herself of whether or not she wanted Neal to stay.

"Goodbye, Sister," Neal said before her gate opened. "Please, please call me if you need to talk about this. If you need some objectivity. We worry sometimes that you've grown too used to being on your own. And like it or lump it, we are family, Autumn."

Autumn embraced her friend and promised that she would call, that she would keep them involved in her progress. It was a promise she meant at the time. Autumn closed the door so she wouldn't have to hear the gate. She put the note in her pocket, never wanting to look at it again, but then yanked it out only a couple of hours later. The Winter Solstice was approaching, the time when the winter's longest and darkest nights subsided and gave way to light and sun. Autumn knew she should be taking advantage of this particular celebration to start her own life-changing process, her moving on and forward. Besides, there was just no point in avoiding it any longer.

Like the first time Autumn saw it, the list seemed wrong. But wrong simply wasn't a possibility. Each name on the list was there for a reason, just like Neal had said. The problem was that she personally knew women who seemed far better suited to the task than some of the women on the list. Maybe the Vedea hadn't gotten it wrong per se; perhaps it had simply overlooked a few. Or maybe this was all part of some bigger test. That particular idea made her stomach flip. She was too damn old for such things.

If only she could have an interview process, like with any other normal job: take out an ad in the paper, just put it out in the universe. Then, possibly, the universe would take care of what the Vedea may have overlooked. Autumn bit the end of her pen and looked up at the ceiling. Why not an ad in the paper? This was her call, and Avening was a different sort of town. The people here thought she was a witch (which was hardly the case, but let them think it) and plenty of them had seen her Book of Shadows.

That afternoon, Autumn came up with a plan. If she said she was looking for a protégé, if she made it almost like a contest and had the interested candidates write an essay, then she could really see where their heads were at, where they stood spiritually. The idea that these women would be participating in such an important choice also made her feel good, less deceptive. It seemed so much more modern and egalitarian for women to step up on their own, to voice that they themselves were ready for their lives to change, than to receive some ominous Jaen tap on the shoulder. Would people understand she was leaving? She doubted it. Even if she were to come out and say so, she feared no one would believe her. She was so much a part of that town.

Autumn made her arrangements—she dialed up Tucker Bradshaw, a devilishly handsome reporter at the *Avening Circle*, about an article she hoped he'd write on her search for a protégé. Less than an hour after she hung up the phone, it rang again. On the other line was Ellie Penhaligan, who turned out to be the *Circle's* researcher. That was a laugh—one of the names on her list that she hadn't recognized, and the universe was already sending her avenues of communication. One of her candidates was now helping to set the wheels of her plan in motion.

By the time the Winter Solstice celebration came around nine days later, the word had spread around Avening like wildfire. Autumn was looking for an apprentice. But she wasn't, not technically. What Autumn really needed was a replacement.

December 21:
Winter Solstice

LLIE PENHALIGAN WAS A SLOW WALKER. IT WASN'T that she was unwell, and she wouldn't have called her ambling "philosophic." It was just that Ellie knew exactly how long it would take to arrive at any given destination. That's the kind of person she was.

On December 21st at 8:15 a.m., there Ellie was on Brigid's Way, making her slow and deliberate steps, one foot in front of the other. If you were an average person walking down that same street on that very same crisp morning, you probably wouldn't notice Ellie at all. Even if you were acquainted with the woman, more likely than not you still would fail to see her. Invisibility was Ellie's own special magic.

When she was younger, Ellie used to believe that her invisibility was a metaphor for something else, assuming it was her awkwardness, her fear of saying or doing the wrong thing. She had thought as she grew older, more confident, wiser, she would outgrow this not being noticed. But lately, Ellie really felt like a ghost. She would be in a place, but not really there. People looked through her, past her. Her invisibility had taken on a life of its own. It wasn't a metaphor anymore, or a defense mechanism or eccentric little tic. She was actually invisible. At least, that was how it felt to her.

Ellie wondered whether her parents were to blame. They were, after all, children of the sixties who had met at a love-in or lie-down or something of that sort, about which Ellie knew little except that a lot of drugs had been involved. Could Ellie's lack of physical presence be a genetic mutation caused by acid or mushrooms? Ellie grew up on their hippie commune among the highest, densest redwoods, where they dug their hands deep into the soil and grew their own food, made their own clothes. So perhaps it is there that the mystery is solved. Ellie indeed was a child of the earth, a baby of beiges and taupes and browns and muted greens. Nature doesn't scream and shout, demanding constant attention, and neither did Ellie. Maybe her invisibility was just her blending right in.

Ellie pulled her long camel coat close and shoved her hands deep into the pockets. Even with gloves on, she could feel their tingling. It was desperately cold, too cold even to snow. She needed the jolt of caffeine as much as she needed to wrap her hands around something warm for the remainder of her walk. She stepped inside Hallowed Grounds, the coffee shop, and stood momentarily to let the heat of the colorful little café find its way into her bones. Besides the selection of tea and coffee, Sean sold an assortment of baked goods made by his wife, Rona. And although Ellie could never quite taste it, she figured Rona must use an abundance of cinnamon in all her creations, because the smell of it always stayed in Ellie's hair and on her clothes long after she had left the coffee shop.

Ellie was pleased to see Sean today. There was something about him, something that made her feel like she'd been given a big cat tranquilizer. He wasn't handsome in any kind of conventional way; truth be told, he was not even that friendly. But she could tell that he liked who he was. "Hi Sean. I'll have a latte, please."

Sean looked at Ellie and his mouth curled into a half-smile. She knew this smile all too well. It was the relay of a spinning brain, a brain working to figure out who she was and how he knew her. Ellie had come to accept it in her everyday interactions with people. She was unremarkable, though her stomach flinched a little as she thought so.

"Uh, Sally, right? No, let's see, Lori?"

"Close enough. It's Ellie." Ellie smiled to let him know that he was entirely blameless.

"Right, sorry about that. A latte, was it? Is it cold enough for you then, Ellie?" Sean punched some buttons on his cash register. "Or are you one of those strange birds that love being at the very heart of winter?"

Ellie beamed at him. "Yes."

Sean's eyebrows rose. "Yes, you love winter? Yes, it's cold enough for you?"

"Uh, yeah, I, yes, I do. Yes, it is."

Sean shrugged and turned to make her latte. How had she managed to screw up casual barista banter? She closed her mouth and waited for her coffee. Sean handed it to her after taking her exact change and looking over her shoulder to the next customer.

Despite her rather clumsy answer to Sean, she was thinking how much she really did love winter as she slipped out the door. Walking down Brigid's Way, Ellie noticed how many lights were already strung. Before the night was over they would cover every roof and tree. Tonight, Avening would honor the season with its traditional Solstice Lighting ceremony. Every shop and storefront would decorate in its own special way. There would be nothing mundane or predictable about these lights. Some would be white, some pink. There would be glittery snowflakes and plastic reindeer. Avening would come alive with the stamp of each individual character, and there were a lot of characters in this town. Ellie and her coworkers at the *Circle* had a tradition of throwing their own Solstice party. In doing this, those who ran the paper were immensely relieved that they'd avoided the gauntlet of political correctness—"Happy Winter" was so inclusive that it sidestepped offending anyone. Ellie was excited to go; she liked being in the spirit. But first, she needed a pair of shoes to wear.

It only took her two minutes to get to Justy Bluehorn's shop. Justy was a cobbler, a real, honest-to-goodness cobbler. Rumor had it he had been a fairly famous actor way back when, had traveled all over the world performing in exotic locations. He gave it all up to be a shoemaker. Ellie believed it. She'd seen his shoes, and there could be no doubt that he was indeed an artist.

She'd been in his shop only once, about a year after she first moved to Avening, to drop off a pair of shoes to get resoled. Immediately upon entering his shop, she was mesmerized by his display. Ellie knew that she didn't have a clue when it came to fashion—no one saw her anyway, so it didn't matter what she wore—but Justy's shoes were, without a doubt, the most beautiful shoes she had ever seen. They were delicate, and yet there was a solidity to them. They felt heavy in her hands when she picked them up. And the colors! Hues she had never seen before, that she could not have imagined. She had been tempted to splurge, but when she found the particular pair she liked, a soft brown Mary Jane, she felt suddenly unworthy. They seemed too perfect. She put them down but resolved to come back and buy a pair when she had an occasion or lifestyle worthy of them. As of that morning, she still didn't.

She was, however, dropping off a pair of shoes. They needed to be redyed, or fixed, or polished, or something. They were the only dressy shoes she owned, and she'd owned them long enough to be embarrassed by their age. She had called Justy yesterday and asked if there was anything he could do on such short notice, since she wanted to wear them for the office party.

Justy had said that he was sure they could figure something out. So with twenty-eight minutes left before she had to be at her desk, Ellie Penhaligan entered the Dutch door of Justy's workshop with her fingers crossed.

Ellie was surprised to find the shop exactly as she had remembered it in her mind's eye. The walls were the same velvety maroon, the shoe display possessed that same magnetic draw, the low counter still looked as if Justy had assembled it from a piece of old barn siding. She was about to call out, but at the very moment her mouth began to open, Justy emerged from the door leading to his workshop.

Justy wiped his hands on his apron. "Oh hello, Ellie. I thought it might be you."

Ellie's mouth shot open. She quickly shut it again, but she was sure the man had seen it. Something was wrong. Firstly and most obviously, Justy had recognized her even though he hadn't seen her in years. The way he said hello wasn't like he had just happened to surmise from a phone call that it must be her. He had greeted her as if he knew exactly who she was. As if he not only saw her, invisible Ellie, he knew her.

"Ellie? Everything all right, dear?"

Ellie felt the flush of pure embarrassment spread and warm her already rosy cheeks. "Oh. Yes, Justy. It's just I can't imagine how you would remember me. It's been such a long while since I've been in here."

"Well now, I suppose I have a thing for faces, especially those that are as pretty as yours. No, now don't go looking away. Your virtue is safe from me, my dear."

Again Ellie was horrified. How was it that she had no control over her face? "Oh no, Justy, I didn't think that . . . I know you weren't . . ."

Justy chuckled warmly. "I know, I know. I was just having a bit of fun. So let's see what you've got in that bag. There isn't a pair of shoes in this world that I can't work the Old Bluehorn magic into."

Ellie pulled her old shoes out of her tote and put them into Justy's hands.

"Well, they may look worse for the wear, but these are good, solid shoes, here." He laughed, and turned one of the shoes around to examine the heel. "I think you understand what I'm saying, don't you? About the way something looks different from how it really is?"

Ellie wanted to speak to this strange old man who remembered her name; she wanted to tell him, "Yes! Yes! I know exactly what you mean, look at me! No, don't look at me, close your eyes and imagine who I might be and that would be closer to the truth of it!" But of course she could not get the words out.

Justy must have sensed this. "Well, they will require a bit of work. You sure you don't want to give them a proper burial and choose something from the shop? I'll give you a discount."

"Oh no, Justy. That's very kind, I don't really think . . . I just . . . maybe next year." How could she tell him that she thought his shoes were too beautiful for her without sounding like she was fishing for a contradiction? "Um. Isn't there anything you can do with these old ones?"

"Yes, I think I can figure something out. Don't you worry. I understand you'll be wanting these for tonight?"

"That would be great, if you could manage it. I was hoping to pick them up after work. I'm sure you're really busy, and I feel terrible for asking you to do this on such short notice."

"Don't you worry a bit, Ellie my dear. I'm always up for a challenge. Tell me, this isn't your first Solstice Lighting, is it?" Justy leaned toward her almost conspiratorially.

"Oh no, I've been going since I moved here." Ellie was suddenly aware of the time. If she didn't leave soon she was going to be late for work.

"And how long is that? If you don't mind me asking."

"No, I don't mind." She twitched, though, and realized she was running her fingers over her watch. "I guess about seven years, since I graduated from college."

"Why Avening? Why not Vancouver or Seattle or even New York City, for that matter?"

Again, Ellie was startled by this conversation. "Well, let's see. I went to Victoria for university. After I graduated, I was going to drive to Arizona to visit my dad. He moved there after my mother passed. I thought I would maybe stay with him a while, see what my next move was going to be. I loaded up the car and somehow . . ." Ellie momentarily placed her fingers over her mouth, not to stop the words from coming, but out of habit. It was often something she did when she was thinking. Her eyes widened and she looked at Justy square in the face. "You know? I don't even remember how I got here. God, that's weird. Anyhow, I . . . I stopped and got some coffee, and I suddenly felt like . . . like . . ."

Justy smiled knowingly. "Like you were home?"

"Yes! It was almost as if I couldn't imagine being anywhere else in the world at that moment. And I just . . . I just decided to stay." Ellie half-smiled, but it was more to herself than to Justy. She could not have explained why it had felt so right in Avening. It wasn't like she was living the life she had always wanted there. It wasn't as if she had a great circle of friends, or even, God forbid, a boyfriend. But at the end of the day, Avening had more to offer than anywhere else. A good job, great restaurants, beautiful scenery, and nice people.

Justy saw Ellie struggling, and cocked his head. "That was pretty brave. I don't imagine you knew anyone else who lived here."

"No, but that didn't really bother me. I don't really know anyone anyway." As soon as Ellie said the words she wanted to suck them back inside her mouth. She couldn't believe she had said something so private to a stranger. "I . . . I meant, you know, I don't really know anyone really well, I mean, the way that I suppose a lot of other people do."

"And why would you suppose other people know each other better?" Justy raised an eyebrow at her.

Ellie felt herself get flustered. "Well . . . my parents, for example. They each knew what the other was thinking most of the time."

"So we're talking about the idea of true love, then?"

"No, not entirely. I've met good friends, siblings, people who are just able to read another person absolutely. I . . . just never found that I had that connection with anyone else." Ellie eyed the door, wondering how she could cut the conversation short.

"Maybe you're just a very complex person, Ellie, and you haven't met anyone capable of understanding you." Justy smiled. He suddenly seemed to decide to back off. "Yes, well. I'm sure you'll figure it all out. You're young yet. You have loads of time. Come back around five-thirty and I'll have your shoes done for you."

Ellie breathed a sigh of relief. And yet as she backed away from the counter, she found that there was a huge part of her that wanted to stay. What was it about this odd, wizened man that inspired such intimacy? Why did he see so much of her? Why did he even care? But then again, why shouldn't he? What have we become, she wondered, that we care so little about those around us, in our community? She was ashamed of her cynicism. But she glanced at her watch, knowing with an inward groan that she was going to have to get a move on it if she didn't want to be late.

"Yes, thank you, Justy. I'll see you then." Ellie headed for the door, turning its great black iron handle with little effort.

"Bye, Ellie. Have a good day."

"Bye!" Ellie pushed herself outside, where the weather had taken a turn for the worse. A great wind was blowing down Brigid's Way, creating mini cyclones of old newspaper and loose garbage down the normally clean street. She quickened her pace, trying to climb outside of her own head and the words that Justy had put there. "Nothing is ever easy," her mother often said when her day had not gone in the direction she thought it should have. No, nothing is easy, Ellie thought. But does it become easier? Ellie couldn't imagine herself as an old woman, silver and shriveled and still not knowing anymore about how to turn her brain off, how to stop caring about all the questions she knew she'd never find the answers to.

Before she knew it, she found herself in front of the *Avening Circle* office. The old building had seen better days, but Ellie couldn't imagine what it must have looked like new and unworn. The walls sagged a little, not quite dilapidated, but with an easiness of sorts that made everyone feel comfortable upon entering. As often as Ellie had felt uncomfortable in her life, she never felt truly out of place in that building.

She climbed the familiar groaning steps up to the second floor. The heat from the old radiators made the windows steam from floor to ceiling like abstract canvases. Here she moved ghostlike past the maze of mahogany desks. If her coworkers took any notice of her arrival, they might have called out a greeting, but Ellie slipped into her invisibility and moved past them all without being seen.

Quiet was the excuse she gave for needing her own small office. Ellie was the paper researcher and often had to make phone calls. The separate office didn't prevent her from overhearing her coworker's phone calls and chats. She was a serial voyeur. It wasn't spying, not exactly. Only her way of feeling included, like she was part of something other than her own small life.

Ellie opened the door to her office and sat down at her desk. She felt foggy, like she hadn't slept well, except that she had. Justy's face with its deep lines and his perfect long fingers swam behind her eyes. Normally, she loved her job. She would have never believed that something like research on a small town paper could ever be satisfying, but it turned out Ellie loved a great story, playing detective, pulling those stories out from dusty books. Today, though, she was just lacking energy. She turned on her computer and looked despairingly at her inbox. Some of those memos would have to wait until after vacation.

Vacation. She suddenly remembered today was her last day of work until after the new year. She rolled her eyes, irritated that she had not made any plans at all. She had just plain forgot. She supposed that she could go away, but this time of year was one of her favorite parts of living here—the lights, the trees, the excitement and happiness everywhere. No, she would definitely stay. Nothing in that moment seemed more blissful than the idea of all the movies she could watch, the books she could read, the organizing she could do. She might even finish that embroidery project that she had started two years ago.

She smelled Stella before she heard the knock. The sickening sweet smell of Shalimar was made bearable only by a hint of rain and mud.

"Well hey there, Sugar. I didn't see you come in!"

Of course Stella hadn't seen Ellie come in; no one had. No one ever saw her come in. "Hello, Stella," Ellie muttered. It really was too early in the day to deal with all of that energy. She didn't dislike Stella Darling. More than anything Ellie felt a twitch of pity for her. At just under five feet, Stella could barely contain herself within her clothes. Ellie wasn't sure if they were too small for her, or if she just happened to own one of those unlucky bodies nothing seemed to fit right. Her hair was an unnatural red that flew out in every direction and she wore too much makeup.

At the paper, Stella's specialty was weather and farm reports. She also knew a fair bit about natural remedies for everyday problems. She always had great tips for things like curing earaches with a hair dryer and various surefire stain removal techniques. Truth be told, Ellie often felt like she had more in common with Stella than she did anyone else. She recognized the invisibility magic wrapped around Stella's uncontrollable curves. But unlike Ellie, Stella fought it with everything she had. She tried too hard, and although she was not invisible physically the way Ellie could be, she slipped the minds of those around her. She invited herself loudly, brazenly to be included. It was that brazen energy that Ellie wasn't always keen to deal with at nine in the morning.

"Don't take this the wrong way, Ellie, but you don't look so good," Stella chirped in her thick Southern accent.

"I'm just tired," Ellie said, fighting the urge to roll her eyes.

"No, I don't think it's that." Stella walked her way right into the office.

"Really? Well, what do you think it is then, Stella?" Ellie asked the question even though she really didn't want to hear the answer.

"Hmmm." Stella tapped a purple fingernail on Ellie's desk. "It looks like Puppy Brain to me."

"Puppy Brain? Wow! Is that dangerous?" Ellie grimaced at the edge of condescension she heard in her own voice.

"Now, Ellie, just hear me out. That's what my Granny Pearl called it, Puppy Brain." Granny Pearl starred in most of Stella's quirky anecdotes. They had become so increasingly bizarre that Ellie wondered if her Granny wasn't just a device Stella had invented. Maybe she thought an eccentric mountain woman somehow added credibility to her various diagnostics. "It happens when you think yourself out. Every thought and idea chasin' its own tail." Stella patted Ellie's shoulder in a way that was probably meant to be comforting. "Relax, you're almost out of here, right? Just hold steady."

Ellie felt her skin was thinning out. After Justy's conversation this morning she couldn't deal with anyone looking so closely at her. She felt like crying. She could just imagine Stella's version of comforting, wrapping her lily arms around her, patting her gently like a grandmother would, that smell of hers permeating everything and sinking down into her own pores. No, she wasn't going to cry. "Yeah, Stella. I really do need some downtime. So, did you need anything?" Ellie hoped she didn't sound dismissive.

"Well, I was hoping that you checked out that patent thing I dropped off a couple of days ago." If she was offended, she didn't show it.

"Oh right, the Idlewilde patents. Well, the info is all right here. I was about to go and drop all these off to everyone's inbox, but you might as well take it now."

Stella took the packet from Ellie but didn't leave. "So . . ."

"So what?"

"So I mean . . . were they real? The inventions?"

Ellie was tempted to tell her to just read the report she had worked half a day on. But it was obvious by the way Stella had both her feet rooted into the hardwood planks that she wasn't going anywhere. "Well yes, according to the patent office. Jamie Idlewilde did hold the patents for such things as the 45-Foot Beanstock Seed Cure, The Phantom Messenger Service, and the Happy Horse Hypnotizer. But I couldn't track down any evidence that says that these inventions actually worked."

"You think they didn't?"

There was a moment of silence as Ellie eyed her coworker. She couldn't tell if this was Stella's way of making a joke, or if she was actually serious.

Stella clucked her tongue. "Geez, Ellie, I didn't take you for such a skeptic. How long have you lived in Avening now?"

Ellie surprised herself by blowing out an exasperated sigh. First Stella told her she looked bad, now this! "What's with people today? That's the second time someone's asked me that question today! I've lived here over seven years, and today's the day everyone wants to know!"

"Well, if you've lived here that long, how can you be so skeptical?" Stella said brightly. "I thought that was against the rules or something."

It was true. While living in Avening, Ellie was aware that some things defied logical explanation. Illnesses were cured, visions were seen. You could even get actual potions from the drugstore. But nothing happened directly to her, and she grew to accept the bizarre anomalies as normal. People get used to the spectacular; whether or not this was a good or bad thing, Ellie still hadn't figured out.

"I'm not skeptical, I'm just jaded," Ellie said with a smile. "Besides, if you knew all the answers, I'd be out of a job. So there you go."

Stella surrendered by way of a shrug. "You got me there, Sugar. Hey listen, you make any plans yet? To go away or something?"

"No."

"No, you haven't made plans? No, you're not going away?"

"No . . . I mean neither."

"Well, you should come down to my house. I'm having a Welcome Winter party in a few days. Make lemonade outta lemons kinda thing."

"That sounds nice. But I really haven't thought about what I'm going to do over the next couple of weeks." Ellie knew that Stella was hoping for a more definitive answer. But she couldn't face committing herself to another party. "I'll call you, okay?"

"You know what? I'm just gonna count on you coming. You call me if you decide not to, all right?"

Ellie could feel her irritation in her toes as they scrunched up inside her shoes. "All right, Stella. I hope you don't mind, but I've got a ton of work to do . . . "

"I'm already gone." Stella headed for the door.

Ellie settled into her work, ignoring the fingerprints of dread that wound their way around her stomach. She couldn't put her finger on what was wrong today. At 1:00 sharp, Nina Bruno made her daily appearance at Ellie's door. Nina stood there, in all her former beauty queen pageant glory, tall and slim and panther-like. Nina's dark hair always seemed to capture whatever available light there was, and her skin, much to Ellie's annoyance, was flawless. Today she was wearing a black wraparound dress that accentuated every curve and parted in just the right place to show off the best part of her legs.

"Ready?" Nina said in her casual way.

The morning had trudged by, and Ellie was more than ready for lunch. "Yep, just let me grab my bag."

"Avalon? Or Icky's?" Nina started walking before Ellie got out the door.

"Icky's. I don't feel like waiting."

"Good call, El. I'll meet you there. Gotta go pee first." Nina veered to the toilets.

Of course, Ellie knew the reason Nina had to go to the bathroom before they started their short walk to the restaurant—not to pee, but to touch up. Outside there was a whole new crop of people for Nina to present herself to. Ellie didn't mind Nina's preoccupation with her looks. Nina used her beauty like a talent. If her personal presentation looked like a piece of art, it was only natural that people would enjoy looking at her.

Ellie made her way to Icky's by crossing the street and turning down Mabon Road. As Ellie walked, she prepared herself for lunch with Nina. She guessed, correctly, that people wondered why Nina kept her so close. Nina was a magnet. Men wanted to marry her, or at the very least, sleep with her. Women wanted to be like her and hoped a little of Nina's casual self-confidence would somehow transfer onto them. But Ellie, being a keen observer of human nature, knew exactly why Nina felt the need to have Ellie in her life. With Ellie, Nina talked and talked about herself and her life, never asking Ellie for her opinion or feedback. It was as close as Nina could possibly get to being by herself, which Ellie suspected she preferred over anyone else's company. Ellie supposed this should bother her, but somehow it didn't. She was amused by Nina's outrageous self-love, but Ellie also knew Nina's friendship forced Ellie into human interaction, which she knew was good for her. Nina was always inviting Ellie to openings or parties. They had even vacationed together in Cabo San Lucas one year.

The weather had warmed up a bit since her cold walk to work, but the sky looked one-dimensional, like a big white curtain had been stretched across it. Maybe it will snow, Ellie thought. That would be nice for tonight's ceremony. In this part of the world, rain was the norm, but it always got at least one or two good snowfalls a year. The timing couldn't have been better.

Ellie got to the door of Icky's and stepped on her tiptoes,

lifted her arm, and touched the worn wood of the sign above—a diehard habit. Icky's was really called Icktome, for the spider in First Nation mythology. The sign was a carved and painted dream catcher along which Ellie couldn't resist running her finger.

Icky's was crowded with its usual lunchtime customers. Ellie spotted a table in the corner and immediately nabbed it, putting her coat and bag on the chair. The place was really more of a cafeteria than restaurant. There was no waitstaff; you ordered your food at the counter, and after awhile your name was called out. Before long, Nina walked in the door, causing the usual amount of head-turning as she did so.

Nina joined Ellie in line just as she was about to order a tuna sandwich. "Good timing. Hey, Bob, what's happening? I'll have my usual salad, please."

"Hey, Nina!" Bob grinned good-naturedly over the counter. "Just the salad? Is your friend gonna have anything?" Nina must have introduced Ellie to Bob about a dozen times.

"Ell, know what you want?"

"The tuna sandwich, please."

"No problemo. That will be $10.65, ladies. I'll call you when it's ready and tell you what—I'll get Freda back there to make it a priority, 'kay?" Bob leaned over the counter a bit towards Nina.

"Bob, you're a sweetheart and a gentleman," Nina replied. They paid for lunch and sat down at the table Ellie had staked out.

"He's so nice, that guy. He's always rushing our orders through."

"Gee, I wonder why, Nina?"

Nina ignored the comment and started taking off her layers of winter accessories. Today, Ellie didn't feel like hearing about any of Nina's usual unhinging personal crises or philosophical revelations. She was actually thinking that she should have simply gone home early, before lunch even began. But here she was, so she slipped into her half invisible mode. "I'm a duck," she thought, "A green and purple mallard. Everything Nina says is water off my little feathered . . ."

"Hey, you know Tucker's story about Autumn Avening?" This was a rhetorical question, of course, because Ellie would have to know as the paper's researcher. Tucker had written a story about a contest Autumn was having; apparently she was looking for some kind of apprentice. Ellie wondered why Nina cared. "Yes, of course I know about the story."

"I think he likes you, you know." Nina said, suddenly switching gears.

"Whatever, Nina," Ellie said dismissively. "Really, why would you even say that?" Too late, Ellie realized she had been baited. She hadn't meant to ask the question, but her mouth settled around the words before she had a chance to rearrange it.

"Well, let's just say . . . I've heard things." Of course Nina had heard things; she was an incurable gossip. "And besides, what about the way he looks at you when he thinks you're not looking? And his body language . . . please. Come on, Ellie, are you, like, completely blind?"

Ellie hated her condescending tone. But there were too many variables in Nina's argument to either accept or reject it.

It was too much for Ellie to think about. She decided to dodge the issue. "Humph. Maybe. Anyway, what about his story?"

Nina shrugged and tucked her hair behind her ears in a perfect gesture of conciliation. "You know. The contest. What do you think? You going to enter?"

Ellie knew this was Nina's way of telling her that she herself was going to enter Autumn Avening's bizarre contest. Autumn was one of the more colorful residents of Avening; Ellie had talked to her just recently while doing some preliminary research and fact-checking for Tucker. Although she had never met Autumn formally, she'd seen her a few times around town. Autumn Avening was best described as the good witch of the north grown older (but not old old) and retired to the Pacific Northwest. It was fairly common knowledge that Autumn was indeed a witch of the very good kind. She ran a bookshop out of her home and gave various lectures on a variety of health, self-improvement, and empowerment tactics. But she was getting old—or so she said on the phone, although Ellie felt like she was talking to a woman her own age, full of vitality and a sharp wit. The contest was Autumn's way of passing the torch, so to speak. Besides the long career profile Tucker had written—and boy, had Ellie come across some strange information when she was researching that one—Autumn had also taken out ad space in the paper, a prominent space already booked in the first Sunday edition of each of the next twelve months. Apparently, she was pretty serious about tapping a protégé for her difficult-to-explain business.

Autumn had a Book of Shadows, a very famous Book of Shadows everyone seemed to know about and precious few had seen. Supposedly, in this book was a journal that not only recorded Autumn's incredible life but also contained secret spells for everything from curing a variety of illnesses to shape-shifting to, some said, flying. Or at least that's what the gossip was around town. The Book was quite an alluring prize to compete for.

Now, Ellie didn't really buy all the occult stuff, but she'd been in town long enough to know that there was often a kind of truth in even the most outrageous stories. But the whole contest thing didn't seem right to Ellie. It didn't seem . . . mystical enough. Her instincts told her there was more to the story. But she was a researcher, not a reporter; it wasn't her place to get involved.

The contest itself, she had to admit, was intriguing. All those interested in being considered for successorship had to write an essay. This essay had to explain why she (yep, *she*— the contest ad didn't specifically exclude men from entering, but it did make heavy use of the female pronoun) felt like she was the most suited to work with Autumn. Autumn had been strangely vague about what the exact specifics of this work would include. And no matter how hard Ellie tried to steer the conversation to a job description, Autumn verbally crawled around it.

Ellie thought it sounded suspiciously high schoolish and sexist, but she also figured that Autumn must have a reason for such an unusual approach. Of course, Ellie was not going to enter. Even thinking about it—like, what if she were forced at gunpoint to write an entry? what kinds of things would she have to say?—made her feel like throwing up. How could she explain to this wonderful woman that it was highly unlikely anyone would come to Ellie for any kind of guidance? They probably wouldn't even be able to find her.

The fact that Nina seemed interested in the contest baffled Ellie. Nina wasn't exactly the kind of person who could open herself up to whatever earth energy Autumn and her ilk commanded. Nina was singularly the most self-involved person Ellie had ever known. Ellie got the feeling that whoever took up ownership of the Book would also eventually take over as unofficial patron to the off-center spirituality that guided Avening; in that job, Nina would last five minutes.

"No, I'm not going to enter," Ellie answered neutrally. "I really don't have the time or desire to devote myself to something like that. Why, are you?"

"Me? Oh God, no!" Nina laughed. "Can you imagine me in a pointy black hat and striped knee-highs racing around town on a shriveled old broomstick? Not likely."

Ellie gave Nina a skeptical look. "I don't think that's exactly how it works, with the broomstick and stuff, Neen. And I'm sure the uniform has changed in the last three hundred years or so."

Nina shrugged. "I just thought, I don't know, it might be something you'd be interested in, like a new hobby. Or a hobby, since you don't have one at all, to the best of my knowledge."

Ellie sucked in a breath; that seemed like a bit of a slap. "I do have a hobby. My garden, remember? And I embroider," she added weakly.

Bob called out their names and Ellie went to go and collect their lunches from the front. She couldn't help but smirk when she noticed the forced smile on Bob's face as he realized it was Ellie and not Nina picking up the food.

They both ate their lunch, which was, as usual, very good, and talked about the party and plans for their vacation. Nina was going home to Forks, to spend the time with her parents. When lunch was over, they both walked back to the office. Nina, in a rare gesture of real affection, slipped her arm into Ellie's and pulled her close.

"Things are changing, Ell. I can feel it."

To this, Ellie had no response or defense. She felt like nothing was ever going to change in her life. Maybe the something dark that had been nagging her all day was the realization of this, of one day pulling into the next.

℘

That afternoon, Ellie made a few brief and unrevealing phone calls and pushed around a lot of paperwork on her desk. The goings-on of the office outside her door were a kind of ever-present buzz, like clothes turning over and over in a dryer.

At 5:15 she was ready to call it a day. She turned off the computer and straightened up a bit, because she knew she wouldn't want to walk back into a messy office come January. People were already starting to get ready for the party. The caterers were setting up a huge buffet table. Max Moore, the local DJ, was bringing in speakers, and those brave few who had offered to do the decorating were stringing paper from ceiling fans.

Ellie was walking towards the door when she noticed Tucker Bradshaw still on the phone at his desk. He happened to look up as she was passing and she threw him a smile. He put up an index finger and she stopped. He covered the mouthpiece with his free hand.

"You coming tonight?" he barely whispered.

"Uh, yeah."

"Good, see you there," he said, and turned his attention back to the phone.

Maybe there's something to what Nina said today, Ellie thought to herself as she headed up Brigid's Way. She liked Tucker; he was handsome in a very unassuming manner. He was tall and a bit lanky, but not in that now popular junkie look kind of way. He had a head full of not-too-closely-cropped black curls and lovely blue eyes. He was originally from North Carolina and had that Southern gentleman charm going for him. Every time Ellie asked Tucker a question, he answered with a "Yes ma'am!" that always unhinged her spine momentarily. But it wasn't like she thought about him seriously.

Ellie didn't know much of love, but she knew enough to know her love life was pretty sad. Any relationship Ellie had attempted in the past was, unsurprisingly, a failure. She had to go out of her way to get a man's attention, because, of course, men didn't notice her otherwise. The ball never came close to her court. This always seemed to put her at such a disadvantage that the emotional investment eventually seemed too big a burden for Ellie to handle. She concentrated on making her life full without a partner, and it worked. Mostly.

Brigid's Way was beginning to come alive. It wasn't just that the decorations and various lights were out to signal the celebration of Solstice, but the citizens were out as well, talking, laughing, offering warm cups of cider and coffee. The smell of burning logs hung in the air, and Ellie began to feel somewhat restored after her empty and demoralized day. She dodged the various ladders standing against trees half strung with lights. Before she knew it, she was at Justy's indigo door.

The shop was dark except for the light coming from his store's elaborate Solstice window display. Ellie laughed at the twinkling oversized boots, obviously belonging to the North Pole's most famous resident, framed by two layers of white and blue fairy lights. The smell of cloves and citrus floated in the air. On the counter, a brown paper bag stood with its top neatly folded down in one perfect pleat. On the bag was a note:

> Ellie,
> Hope you enjoy the shoes. They certainly were a challenge. I felt so inspired that I found myself overcome with a desire to feed the muse. I'm working in the back like one of the big guy's elves. You can pay me later.
> Justy

Ellie found herself strangely disappointed that she couldn't see Justy in person. She felt a little sad at the thought of him all by himself tonight, working away. She was tempted to go ahead and find him back there and at least thank him, to make sure he knew his work didn't go unappreciated. But then she thought better of it. Ellie knew the value of privacy. She took the bag and walked out the door.

The sky had turned to full night. There was a crescent

moon that shone hazy through low clouds, and at about five minutes away from her house, the first few hesitant flakes of snow began to fall. This was her favorite type of snow, the type that made its way down to earth in perfect round balls like little bits of cotton candy. Despite the snow, the night was clear, with little wind and barely any moisture. It seemed like the perfect night for a Solstice Lighting, and Ellie resolved to enjoy it.

Ellie made her way up the familiar twist of Wicker Road. Even with just the porch light on, her house looked inviting and settled. The single oak that took up the majority of her front lawn was already beginning to collect the first measures of snow. She quickly walked up the three steps and went in.

There was nothing grandiose about the place, but it was a perfect fit for Ellie. The house looked a little like an old English cottage. It was tiny, reminding her of a dollhouse. Which suited her perfectly. Any bigger and the place would have echoed, and Ellie would have been aware of how acutely alone she was. She filled the walls with various pieces of artwork, and her queen-sized bed with pillows she made from pieces of vintage fabric. There were two fireplaces and wall-to-wall hardwood floors with perfectly worn-in wainscoting. The back rooms were all windows that could be opened up so it seemed almost a part of the garden. Ellie's study was lined with bookshelves on every wall except the alcove, in front of which she had placed an old secretary. She even had a small balcony off the master that looked over the garden and was a wonderful place to read.

She flicked on the light in her bathroom just long

enough to light some candles and started to run a bath in her claw-footed tub. She headed into her bedroom, unloaded her coat and scarf on the chair and went into her closest. Her clothes came in two varieties: dark and darker (or in the summer, beige and beiger). She supposed she'd settle for the tunic ensemble she wore last year. Then she remembered the new eggplant shirt she'd bought on sale a couple of months ago. Suddenly revitalized, she took the outfit and laid it on her bed. She then emptied out next to it the brown paper bag Justy had put her shoes in. Her breath caught in her throat.

She could hardly believe these were her shoes; she had to double-check the manufacturer label to see that they were. Where once the leather had been sagging and scuffed, it was now supple and flawless. Justy had cut the front down so that the cleavage of the toes could be seen. He had taken that sturdy but rather chunky heel off completely and replaced it with a thin stiletto. Justy seemed to know the exact height to make the heel sexy, but not so terrifyingly high that Ellie would have to worry about tripping and breaking her neck. Along the front, just above the toe, was a black suede strip flourished with an elaborate suede flower and a metal bud, making it look both modern and feminine.

The shoes were gorgeous. They looked haute couture, although Ellie knew they had come from the village shoe shop. She would have to wear her boots and take them with her in her tote. They were too precious to expose to the weather.

After her bath, Ellie dressed quickly and blew out her hair. She had little makeup, but what she did have she applied. She wore her grandmother's Edwardian drop earrings and overall felt pleased with how she looked. She was even more pleased to realize she cared how she looked. She pulled her coat on, rewrapped Justy's special shoes, and walked downstairs. Ellie opened the door, frisking herself while still inside to make sure she had everything. Satisfied that she did, she made her way to her car.

Brigid's Way was heaving with people and the snow continued to fall in perfect white tufts. The sidewalks were filled with folding chairs and tables covered with an array of vats of cider and huge coffee urns. Luckily, Ellie had a parking space in the lot behind the office. She locked her car and headed up the small alley that spilled onto the street. She heard voices, soft and beckoning, caroling a winter song. The spirit of Solstice seemed a tangible thing Ellie could pull from the air. This was happiness, she thought. The senses connected, from everything and everyone around her.

The door to the office had been left partially open. Ellie pulled off her boots and stuffed them in a plastic bag, which she stowed on a shelf above the radiator. She pulled Justy's shoes, her shoes, gingerly out of her tote. She marveled at how comfortably they fit. He must have put a liner in there or something, she thought. She stood, taller than she had been moments earlier, and felt put-together, finished. She walked up the stairs confidently.

Ellie was later than she had anticipated. The party was in full swing. Max had on some stellar 70s tune, and the buffet table had been picked over more than a few times. Ellie wasn't all that hungry, but she was thirsty. As she walked to the bar, she noticed that the volunteer decorating committee had done a great job. Hanging from the ceiling were dozens of individually cut snowflakes, decorated with a colorful variety of sparkles so that they glinted from each desk light below. She poured herself some warm cider into a silver paper cup.

There had to be a good fifty or sixty people there. A pretty good turnout. She knew most of the people, coworkers and their families. From the corner of her eye she saw Tucker, talking with another man she didn't recognize, probably a date of someone's. Tucker looked in her direction and noticed that she had been staring at him. Tonight, Ellie thought, I will not be mortified by how completely obvious I am. Tonight we are celebrating. I will let winter reinvent me. There's nothing wrong with looking at someone.

During this inner dialogue, Tucker had excused himself from his conversation and was making a beeline toward her. By the time she looked up, he was a foot away from her. "It looks like you're the last one to arrive, Ellie. Did you plan a big entrance or what?" Tucker said sweetly as the song began to fade from Max's speakers.

Ellie opened her mouth to reply, but she wasn't the only one who was surprised by what came out. **"Oh! You got me! I knew everyone was waiting for me to arrive so they could start having a good time!!"**

Every head in the room turned to her direction. Ellie's hand flew to her mouth as she realized she had just sung out at the top of her lungs. Tucker's eyebrows rose and his mouth turned into a smile. "Watcha drinkin' there, Ell?" he asked.

"Oh my God!" she warbled operatically. The drama in her voice made her feel like she was in a low-rent Wagner piece, done very badly.

49

The entire party was staring at her in mixed expressions of amusement and concern, not sure yet if this was some kind of party game. **"I don't understand . . . I can't stop . . . I just can't stop singing!! Help!"** Ellie sang as she backed away from him and into the wall.

She had lost all control over her mouth. Had she fallen asleep in the bath? Was this some horrible nightmare? Something in Ellie broke, she felt small and trapped. Tears began to pool around her eyes. This is what crazy is, she thought. I am an insane person now. She tried desperately to gain control of her words and thoughts, but they slipped away from her, dancing circles around her head. When Tucker saw that Ellie was now in serious distress, he moved toward her.

"Ellie? Are you okay?"

"Do I look like I'm okay? Do I sound okay?" What had before been a simple explosion of song, ridiculous and grandiose, was now tempered into a kind of rhythm. Ellie's voice was sultry and oddly intimate, phrased like an old jazz standard.

Tucker looked into her eyes and she knew he could see her terror. Maybe if this had been any town besides Avening, somebody would have called an ambulance and Ellie would have been strapped down and drugged within the hour. But in Avening, and most especially on the night of the Solstice, people had been known to go through odd transformations.

Their coworkers begin to gather and show concern for Ellie, who had backed herself up against the wall, her palms and fingers pressed into it, looking ready to spring. But instead of flying forward, Ellie slid down to the floor, her breathing irregular and rapid. Stella, with surprising efficiency, went to Ellie's side at almost the exact same moment as Nina Bruno. In a gracefully executed move, Nina squatted close to Ellie's ear.

"Ellie," Nina hissed. "I don't know what you're doing, but this isn't the place for it. Pull yourself together, for chrissakes. People are trying to enjoy themselves here, and you're turning it into West Side Story."

Stella glanced at Nina crossly, and Ellie felt her shame swap itself for anger. Nina's insensitivity lit a match in her belly and shot through her like a fuse. Could Nina really believe that Ellie would do such a thing purposely? Ellie Penhaligan, who had never in her life asked for any kind of attention? If she believes that, she doesn't really know me at all, Ellie thought.

"**What!? No, just get out of my face right now, Nina!**" Ellie belted in a Janis Joplin kind of way, without an ounce of control. Her coworkers looked at Nina hard enough for Nina to tell that she had uncharacteristically done the very worst thing she could have done. Nina opened her mouth to make a joke or diffuse the situation, but she must have sensed the crowd could not be won over to her side, so she backed away. However, unlike Ellie, Nina Bruno didn't have any practice with not drawing attention to herself. She very obviously stomped away, fists clenched, her body rigid and awkward.

"Okay, Ellie. I want you to breathe, Sugar," Stella said sweetly. "There's no real reason to get yourself into a panic."

Ellie was still holding on to the anger that she hadn't completely released on Nina. "**No reason to panic?!**" she sang. "**Listen to me!! This isn't me! I would never in my life**

. . . I have never . . . done anything like this! Somebody . . . has to help me!"

"No, what I meant is, okay, this is alarming. But you're in a safe place here. Nothing bad is going to happen to you. These are your friends . . . right, guys?" Stella looked to everyone for backup.

Ellie expected a murmur, but instead there was a steady chorus of encouragement from everyone that had gathered around them. Ellie looked up, and saw on their faces not horror, not even indifference, but real concern, some even smiling in a supportive way.

"Now get up. That's it. Everything is fine," Stella said soothingly. "By the way, you have an amazing voice. It reminds me of my Mama's porch songs. Yep, she would sing every night after dinner." Stella drawled on distractingly as she coaxed Ellie up and out towards the door. "She'd just sing and sing her whole life out loud. It was always the last thing I would hear before I went to sleep. No matter what kind of day I had, I would hear Mama sing as she knitted or mended clothes, and I would know that everything was all right." She took their coats and bags from the coat rack and just kept talking.

Tucker, who was following them, called out to the party, "Now everyone, we're going to take Miss Ellie home, and we're going to figure out what's goin' on. Don't none of you worry. Just go on and enjoy yourselves." A varied chorus of good-byes and well wishes followed the three of them out the door. The cadence of Tucker's and Stella's Southern accents made the whole thing seem even more surreal. Did Tennessee Williams ever write a musical? *Cat on a Hot Tin*

Fiddler's Roof? The idea made Ellie smile involuntarily, which she immediately stopped. She seemed crazy enough already.

"Where are you taking her, Stella? You want me to come?" Tucker asked sincerely.

"Aw, no, Tucker, that's awfully sweet of you, but I think this might be girl stuff. Right, Ellie?"

"**Probably**," Ellie sang, holding onto the last note. She was no longer embarrassed, just kind of resigned and maybe a little sad that her life might be reduced to a Broadway musical.

"Ellie," Tucker said, "I can't pretend to understand what's going on here, but you and I have seen weirder shit, excuse my language, happen in this town. And if it means anything to you, which all things considered right now I'm sure it doesn't, I just want you to know, that I . . . I don't think this is something you should be, you know, embarrassed about. I've always thought you were something special."

Ellie looked at him, their eyes locked. She stepped forward, putting a hand to his face, pulled him close and softly, in the nature of a lullaby, sang him a thank you.

Suddenly the lights from every tree down Brigid's Way were lit up in Winter Solstice colors. The crowd cheered, and Ellie knew that at that moment things were bad, but maybe not as bad as they could be.

Ellie surrendered her keys to Stella, who got into the driver's seat and pushed it as close to the steering wheel as she could. "Don't worry, Sugar. I'm an excellent driver."

"**Whatever. Just get me home, please**," Ellie sang.

"Funny. I would say at least you still have your sense of

humor, but I'm not even sure you had one in the first place. Did you?"

Ellie responded by rolling her eyes and giving Stella a little smile.

When they arrived at the house on Wicker Road, Ellie felt a look of complete relief settle over her features. Stella sat Ellie on the couch and lit a fire, then disappeared to the kitchen. She emerged several minutes later with a tray bearing a pot of chamomile tea and a joint. Stella handed over a cup of tea and then lit the joint, taking one long drag. She held out her hand, gesturing for Ellie to take it. Ellie shook her head.

"Aw, come on. This could help. You never know. At least you'll relax a bit, and then the figuring out might be easier."

Ellie tentatively took the joint from Stella's hands, shrugged, and inhaled. She felt her spine drop down into her toes and she placed the joint in an ashtray above the mantle.

Stella was watching Ellie carefully. "Ellie, stop thinking about how this all happened, and think about why it's happened, 'kay?" Stella's hands waved wildly enough to land an airplane. "You think I care if you sing? Hell, sing your heart out. Maybe this is the only way everything you've held back has to come out. Now just tell me the first thing that pops in your head."

Ellie didn't know what was in her head. She looked at Stella and wanted to cry. This woman, who she always thought of as someone to simply put up with, had come through for her. She felt humbled, and stupid. **"I'm sorry, so sorry, that I haven't been nicer to you. You're a good person,"** she sang.

Stella cocked her head and chuckled. "Well, aren't I the lucky one? All this going on and the first thing you think of is my feelings? I don't think so, Ellie. It's not that easy. By the way, you've always been nice to me. But this isn't about me. This is all about you. Or maybe that's the problem."

Ellie squirmed in her seat, suddenly uncomfortable with her limbs. She realized she was no longer—and after tonight never again would be—invisible. Part of her felt the familiar terror sweep over her, and yet part of her was relieved to know she finally could be seen, however it had come about. "**I'm scared, Stella,**" she sang. "**Maybe this is just some Solstice fluke, but what if it never goes away? I can't live a life like this.**" Ellie wanted to press her hands into her chest to stop it from heaving, but she knew that with the singing the gesture would seem over-the-top, so she pressed them into the couch on either side of her instead. "**I feel like promising something. Like I'll try harder to be part of things, if this is the lesson my body is trying to teach me. But I don't even know where to begin.**"

"Ellie, what are you talking about? You're part of things. You're part of my life, every day."

"**No. I'm not. You and Nina and Tucker, you can see me, right? But no one else can. No one sees me. I'm not here.**" Ellie sobbed and sang all at once.

"You are here. Ellie . . . Sugar . . . you think people don't see you? Or notice you?" Stella seemed perplexed momentarily, and then she narrowed her eyes and bit her lip. Ellie could tell Stella was thinking and connecting the dots. She knew Stella was remembering and understanding that there was something to what Ellie was saying.

"See? You know I'm right, so maybe there's a reason why . . . why nobody really notices me. It doesn't just happen . . . you're born to it. So maybe I would be going against some great plan if I suddenly change who I am." Ellie sounded overly show-tune-y. It sang so wrong, not even she believed it.

"I hate to use a cliché here, but everything happens for a reason. Maybe this is the big plan, Ellie." In that moment, Stella didn't seem silly or eccentric. Ellie knew that she might believe that she was invisible, but she wouldn't believe Ellie couldn't be seen if she wanted to.

And wasn't Stella right? Was this the big plan? The season had shifted. Tonight they celebrated this shift, accepting that all things change, but then eventually they end at the very place where they begin. Ellie was part of this circle. She felt a calm take hold, she smiled, and then she started to cry.

To Stella's credit, she did not rush over to console her. She did not wrap her arms around her, as Ellie had imagined her doing just that afternoon. Instead, she walked over to her bag and pulled out her iPod. She slipped it into a set of speakers on the mantel and pressed play. The music diffused whatever was left of the situation. Who cared if Ellie sang, when Aretha Franklin was singing already? They switched the pot of tea for a heady Merlot. Then both women sang and drank and got thoroughly pissed out of their skulls, because really, what else was there to do?

Over Ellie's winter garden, the gray sky was about to turn over. Neither one of them could remember the last time they had stayed up all night. It made them both feel ridiculously (and gloriously) young. They were drunk and high and happy. So when the doorbell rang that morning, their first reaction was to laugh. Ellie doubled over on the couch, in hoarse hysterics, her voice battered from all the singing. Stella staggered to the door, teasing Ellie that it must have been Tucker wanting some early morning luvin'. But when she opened it, Autumn Avening was on the other side, looking far better than anyone had a right to at that time of day.

"Hello, Stella. I just thought I'd come round, check on Ellie. Hope that's okay?"

Stella blinked and nodded, stepping away so Autumn could come through.

"Come in . . . come in . . . come oooon in," Ellie sang.

Autumn gave her an appraising look. Perhaps getting Ellie shit-faced would not have been her approach to the problem, but she didn't seem to disapprove, either. Autumn had heard, through various sources, what had transpired with Ellie Penhaligan the night before. She had also heard . . . what Ellie could do. Why she hadn't known of her skill before this was unsurprising—invisibility is a tricky sort of gift. And Autumn had so many people to look after in Avening, it was hardly surprising that the one person she would have actual difficulty looking at would slip through the cracks. At least now she understood why Ellie was on the list.

At that moment, however, Ellie was noticeably . . . present. Autumn touched Stella's arm and Stella stood back, knowing she was totally outranked.

"Ellie, dear . . . Stand up for me, please."

Ellie wasn't sure why Autumn was in her house. And truthfully, she was a little too buzzed to really care all that much. The whole night had been too bizarre anyhow. So she stood, swaying a little and squinting one eye. Autumn crossed her arms and examined Ellie from head to toe.

"Ellie, those are lovely shoes."

"Thank you!" Ellie sang. **"And you and you and you . . ."** How naturally it became the *Sound of Music* number!

"Are they Justy Bluehorn's work, by any chance?"

Ellie paused. She had forgotten that she was even wearing them, they were so comfortable. She opened her mouth to answer yes, but she decided to nod instead.

"Take them off, will you, please?" Autumn asked this the same way that she would have asked a child. Ellie complied easily enough. "Now speak," Autumn ordered.

"What would you like me to . . . oh! I'm not singing. I'm cured!" Ellie leapt up, thrilled.

"Justy Bluehorn is a cheeky bastard. Ah well, I suppose he's done some good. You are . . . better? Right, Ellie?"

"I guess. I don't know. I just . . . I have this problem," Ellie heard herself saying. Here she was with the town witch standing in her living room the day after Winter Solstice. If there was ever a time to get it off her chest, it was now. "I mean, at least I think I have this problem. This will sound crazy, Autumn, but I'm pretty sure that I can make myself . . . Or maybe I just am—"

Before Ellie could continue, Autumn cut her off. "I know, Ellie, I know. And we'll have to work on that, but it's not important. I mean, it is important, but not right now. Things have changed for you. They'll be easier now, or possibly more complicated, but . . . well. Just know that for the time being, you'll have a much better handle on . . . your ability."

Ellie's head swam. She felt drunk again on Autumn's words. But then again, maybe her fatigue was messing with her. She stood there, with her mouth half open, feeling like an idiot, like she should be asking a million questions but was unable to form them.

"Right, well. I'd best be going. You two need some sleep." Autumn might have read Ellie's mind. She turned and headed for the door, but before she opened it, she turned again. "It's really not my business to say, Ellie, but . . . Nina Bruno . . . is she a friend of yours?"

"I think so," Ellie said, remembering Nina's reaction at the party.

"She's so very pretty, isn't she? Beautiful, really. That perfect skin, those long legs. And that hair! It's so black. Black as a raven's feather, that's what my mother used to say. Do you know, Ellie, what a group of ravens is called?"

Ellie shook her head, unable to tell where this was going.

"It's called an Unkindness. Isn't that strange? An Unkindness. Well . . . it's something to think about. And by the way, both of you should enter my contest. Goodbye." The door slammed and the two left behind jumped at little at the sudden noise.

Autumn thought about what had really happened on her drive home. There were three women in that circle (literally and figuratively, all three worked at the *Avening Circle*). Two were on Autumn's list, one was not. But Autumn had a pretty good theory as to why.

Stella had handled Ellie's extraordinary situation exceptionally well. It was odd that Stella had steered clear of Autumn before now, considering what Stella was and her odd refusal to embrace it. When Autumn looked past the horrible clothes and the grocery list of everything else that made Stella so unappealing, she could recognize the amazing potential there. But could she, or anyone else, look beyond what they saw or felt?

Autumn stopped the car at a light, dismissing her doubt, because her mind was already made up. Stella had been brilliant with Ellie. She was in the running, for now.

Ellie Penhaligan was more of a problem. Autumn knew what she was and knew what she could do, but just because she had talent didn't mean she was right for the job, especially given her temperament. Still, Autumn couldn't dismiss the gift. It was strong.

The light turned again, and Autumn softly pressed her foot into the gas. The universe was providing her with plenty to deal with. Her biggest problem yet was Nina. Nina was incredibly powerful, possibly too powerful. She didn't know enough yet to gauge whether Nina was simply born a bitch or made one by circumstance, and that made all the difference. But her abilities would have to be dealt with one way or the other, so she too was in the running.

Autumn passed Justy's and considered pulling in just to give him a piece of her mind. He knew the rules. But it had started to rain, and the rain was washing away the snow, which made her feel a little sad, and annoyed. Besides, Autumn was tired. It was only the first day of winter. She rolled her eyes. It was definitely going to be one of those years.

March 21: Spring Equinox

STELLA DARLING AWOKE WITH THE FAMILIAR RUMBLE of a hollow stomach. It was the ghost of hunger, of too many childhood nights going to bed without enough food; dreaming always took her back.

Stella kicked off her blankets and pulled back the curtain with one brisk movement. She tasted the metallic tang on her tongue before she saw the clouds, low and outlined in a purplish gray. Stella ran down the hall, through the kitchen, and out the back door, her cats leaping behind her. She stepped out into the small patch of concrete that made up her patio and closed her eyes, taking in a big breath through her nose. A storm, maybe two hours away. Stella's face broke into a wide grin. She threw her eyes upward in a silent thank you to the heavens and raced back inside.

Stella's heart pounded with both excitement and relief. For years she had waited for a stormy Spring Equinox, and today, finally, the Gods, the Universe, Jesus, or whatever, had rewarded her patience and vigilant prayers. Today was going to be her day. In less than two hours, Stella Darling would catch lightning in a bottle.

In her small, outdated kitchen, she put the kettle on the stove, then turned to her pantry for two tins of breakfast for Lucy and Ethel. After she emptied the cat food in their bowls, she walked briskly to the bookshelf that lined one full wall of the living room and pulled an aging scrapbook from the top shelf. It was the one true legacy of the Darling family, her grandmother Pearl's *Journal of Remedies and Miracles*. She carefully turned the pages until she came to the one she wanted.

Stella stared at her grandmother's neat and careful hand. Beside the directions were pencil sketches of various bottles. Stella mentally raced through her inventory: yes, she had the perfect one, an identical match to the bottle Pearl had put a bold asterisk beneath. She could do it.

More than thirty years ago, Stella had seen her grandmother catch lightning. Up above the blue grasses of Kentucky, in the dense mountains of her childhood home, in a place called Look Pass, Stella had been groomed from a young age to take over for her Granny Pearl. It had nothing to do with her genetic makeup or her heritage, or order of birth, or physical attributes: a mender was born and called so within the first few hours of her arrival in the world. It was something in babies' eyes, in the calm acceptance of their mother's breast, in the energy that swam around them, making a hand tingle when placed on their tiny heads. Stella, it turned out, was one of those babies, just like her Granny Pearl had been.

Looking back, Stella would have called her family dirt poor. Not the kind of poor portrayed quaintly on TV or supermarket paperbacks, but real poverty. Stella's father was a coal miner with a gaggle of daughters and two sons too young to join him in that dark, black mouth of coal mine that seemed to swallow so many other husbands and fathers whole. And so Stella's mama made do on that single paycheck. She kept those boys in school so eventually they could go on and do something else. She despised that mine as much as she hated the devil himself.

Still, it wasn't the Darling way to focus on everything they didn't have. Stella knew that this wasn't because they were better people or closer to God; it was just that they didn't have enough exposure to the rest of the world to make any kind of real comparisons. They were ignorant, plain and simple. There was too much to do, or make, or stretch in order to accommodate the ever-growing Darling family for them to have any contact with or concept of the world beyond their piney, secluded town. In the handful of hours Stella found herself without work to do, she would sit and watch the clouds thunder by, or listen to the wind shake through the trees. She was so grateful for the rest, boredom simply didn't occur to her.

She went to school some, but she was the second oldest and a mender to boot. School was a luxury; she was lucky if she could go two days a week. The boys of course went every day, rain or shine. And Stella understood her mama wanted something different for them. Still she kept up with her studies, and what's more, she enjoyed them. Even from a young age, Stella knew if she hadn't been born on the mountain, if she'd been the daughter of a banker or a shopkeeper even, she would be a different person, the kind of person that had more choices.

Stella also understood what her life would become eventually when she took over from her Granny Pearl. In her poor mountain community, a mender wasn't simply an eccentric character; a mender was a real necessity. Not everyone who lived in Look Pass could afford an actual doctor—in fact, the majority couldn't—and getting up and down the mountain on roads poorly kept and unprotected by tax dollars could be a treacherous business even if they had the money. So women like Pearl served as physical and spiritual healers, healing broken bones and hearts in equal measures. Not a day went by that Pearl wasn't tending to someone, or making preparations for something she somehow knew would soon be needed. Stella would watch her with a rapt adoration, marveling at the speed of her hands, her almost photographic memory, and her musical voice, which changed depending on the seriousness of the situation. Stella watched and learned, knowing that one day she would be the one to whom the folks would come.

When Granny Pearl caught the lightning, Stella was only twelve. Technically, it was still winter, but the mountain was unseasonably warm and the air heavy and cumbersome. Pearl spent the previous afternoon writing laboriously in her scrapbook, taking moments here and there to catch just the right word. Stella was sitting on the porch, watching the dull overcast sky and waiting for her baby sister to wake up from her nap.

"You hear somethin'?" Pearl said through the open door.

"Nope, too hot even for the birds to sing, Granny."

"Hear somethin' now?"

Stella turned her head to look at her grandmother, but she could only see her elbow moving in a lazy rhythm. "No. You expectin' someone?"

"Maybe," Pearl replied. Stella closed her eyes and tried to throw her ears out along the dirt path that led to their small little house. Sure enough, she soon heard the sound of footsteps dragging towards them. She waited for a moment or two, until Granny Pearl's guest emerged from around the bend of pines. Stella cocked her head in surprise. She didn't recognize the young woman, who was wearing an obviously store-bought, light pink dress and floppy straw hat that shaded her eyes from the mountain's haze. As she came closer, Stella could see that despite her clothes, she had a somewhat mousy complexion. Her cheeks were flushed from either the weather or the walk, or both.

The woman stopped dead in front of Stella and, in a small, quiet voice, said, "Oh, hello. I'm looking for a woman named Pearl Darling. Does she live here?"

"You walk all the way up here?" asked Stella.

"Oh no, I drove most of the way, but then . . . the road just ended, and . . . "

"Yeah, 'cause them's not very good shoes for walkin'."

"I'm sorry, I hate to be rude, but I'm just about dyin' of thirst. Could you please tell me if Pearl Darling lives here?" The young woman did look awfully faint, and Stella felt a stab of guilt that she hadn't acted more hospitably. Just as she was about to call out for her grandmother, Pearl appeared in the doorway. She could be a fierce-looking woman when she wanted to, and she was coolly reserved when it came to city folks. It all depended on who sent them to her, and whether or not they could make peace with the mountain. The mountain was an excellent judge of character, repelling those who weren't strong enough, clinging to those who were. The stranger blanched at the old woman's unflinching appraisal.

"Humph, who sent you here?" Pearl asked.

"Marj Pennybaker." The city woman's face cracked into a tentative smile. "She also said you'd be as mean as a pole-cat till I told you it was her."

At that, Pearl smiled widely. Marj was Pearl's first cousin, who had grown up on the mountain but married a preacher from town. "She's a hoot, that ole lady," Pearl said. "I tell ya, that Billy Pennybaker married our Marj so he could love the heathen ways right on out of her, and she married him just to prove that God didn't live in no church."

The woman, looking a little embarrassed, smoothed out her dress over her knees. "Ahem. Mrs. Darling, I don't want to take up too much of your time. I understand you're a very busy woman, but Marj suggested you might be able to help me, and truth be told I'm at my wit's end."

"Well, if Marj sent y'all up here, it must be important. She don't usually send no one up this way. Jis go on an' tell me what's weighin' on you so heavy. Don't worry, I save the judgin' to God."

"You don't know me, Mrs. Darling . . ."

"Call me Pearl."

"Well, Miss Pearl, I'm very pleased to meet you. My name's Dolores, Dolores McDonald." The woman smoothed her dress again, a little nervously. "You don't know me, Miss Pearl, but if you did, you'd know that comin' up here is just about the bravest thing I've done in my whole life."

Dolores looked up at Granny Pearl, as if for encouragement, but Granny Pearl just stared back. Dolores would have to spit out her whole problem on her own.

"The thing is," she said tentatively. "I feel like . . . Well, I feel like my whole life is a movie and I'm just watchin' it happen. I try to get involved with things but . . . I don't fit right. It's like . . . like I'm not too good at makin' decisions, and then before I know it other people make 'em for me. I just kind of let life spill around me, and then nothin' quite goes right."

Granny Pearl gave Dolores a shrewd look. "What do you mean, darlin'?"

Dolores chewed on the corner of her mouth. It took a second or two before she began again. "Well . . . the truth is I don't feel comfortable in my own skin. Especially when it comes to men. Whatever I say, sounds right in my own head, but ends up comin' out totally wrong." Dolores leaned back after that, obviously close to tears. "I know this is going to sound crazy, but I feel like I'm trapped where someone else is supposed to be, someone who could fit right into my shoes. Like there is someone out there who's livin' my life, and I'm livin' theirs. That make any sense to you at all?"

Pearl said nothing for a moment, taking a long, hard look at the woman before her. "Well, I don't rightly know if I can help you, Sugar. But if I had it to give, I'd give you a good hard dose of courage. I know when people don't make their own decisions it's usually because they don't reckon they're smart enough or good enough to make the right ones. But everybody gets it wrong sometimes. That's just part of life. We have to be strong and give it a go anyway."

Dolores's eyes looked pleadingly toward Pearl. "Don't you have anything that's like that?"

"Like what?"

"Like a dose of courage?"

Pearl gave out a great hoot of laughter. "Nothing but a big ole jug of moonshine out back there." Pearl took Dolores's hands, pulling her up from her seat. "Now wait a minute, don't go lookin' like someone shot your dog." She stood there, holding her hands for a moment, deciding. "Now, I think I can help you, but I can't promise you nothin'. You know the first day of spring is tomorrow? Well, if the Lord sees fit to give us a storm on that day, well, then, I can give you what you need. If not, you'll have to wait for next year. All right?"

"Okay," Dolores croaked." But . . . I don't understand . . ."

"Don't reckon you need to. If everything happens in our favor, then I'll give you your dose of courage. I'll give you back the cord that connects you to your body, and it'll jolt you right into the place you wanna be."

"Sounds like lightning, Miss Pearl," Dolores said with half a laugh.

"That's exactly what it is, child: lightning in a bottle."

Stella, who had watched the whole dialogue curiously from the doorstep, had never heard of such a thing. She figured it might be one of Pearl's placebos. Sometimes, just the suggestion of magic was enough to help people make their own magic. But Stella that afternoon saw her grandmother move with determination, gathering the rarest of herbs and checking and then rechecking her journal, and began to think otherwise.

Stella crawled into bed that night too excited to actually sleep. She lay there, in that small space, listening to her grandmother's slow and patient prayers for rain from down the hall, like a familiar song that she did not know the words to. Stella could not be sure, but she thought she heard the distant drum of thunder south of her open window.

In the gray hours before full morning, Pearl gently brushed a strawberry blonde curl from Stella's face, and then bent down to whisper in her ear, "Come on, Sugar, get dressed and meet me outside."

Stella blinked in the twilight. She slid out of bed and dressed quickly in the hall, pulling on the pair of overalls she had slung over her chair the night before. She opened the screen door that led to the backyard. There was just enough light to see her grandmother marking out a circle about nine feet in diameter.

"Whatcha doin', Granny?" Stella stepped toward the circle, but her grandmother stopped her with a raised hand.

"Don't go walking in here till I build you a door."

"A door? What do you mean? And what is that stuff?"

Pearl held a small iron bowl in one hand, and a knife in the other. "For heaven's sake, child. I'm throwin' a circle, and this here's salt. Keeps the hobgoblins out. That's all you need to know for now."

Stella's eyes widened. "Granny, that there's witch stuff! I done heard you tell about a million folks you ain't no witch." Pearl looked at her granddaughter with noticeable exasperation. Stella had seen her grandmother set a bone, lay her hand on a sick person and heal them. In fact, Stella had seen her do any number of things that defied logic or explanation. But this, whatever Stella was seeing, didn't look organic at all. It was a ritual, and nothing like the ones she had seen in church. Looking at her grandmother, she had a feeling that what she was witnessing wasn't anything Jesus talked about.

"Well, I ain't no witch, child," Pearl said with a great deal of force. "This is a trick passed on from my grandmama and from her grandmama before her, 'til, well, back to the beginnin' of the Darlings. Ain't nothin' evil here. This is to help someone. Folks down in the church may not like it. But since when did I give a hoot what other people think? Besides, you think Jesus cares about a circle made a salt? He got more important things to be busy with."

Stella took a step backwards. Pearl was transformed in the dim light, like someone else, a wizened old lady from a fairy tale. It sent a shiver down Stella's spine.

"Sugar, look at me." Pearl said it, knowing it was the last thing in the world Stella wanted to do. "It's me, your Granny. Baby girl, you listen to me, this here's earth magic. You get a handle of all that energy, and ya got to make sure you don't bring the bad in with the good. I promise I'll explain later. Don't be afraid, Stella. You were born to this, it's part a you. If you can't trust me, trust that. You must feel it, the magic pullin' at your belly."

Stella closed her eyes, and she did feel it. It was like her ears were in her feet, a steady hum coming up through her shoes and winding around her chest. "Granny?" she asked. "What do you mean, build me a door?"

Try as she might, Stella could never recall in detail exactly what happened inside that circle. She could say the words: "It got darker," or "The wind picked up and raced through our hair, and our clothes," or "The hole that Granny dug for the bottle seemed to glow," but she could not really remember the images. There was a moment when Pearl called down the storm, corralled it with her arms, and a streak of lightning hit the ground. That moment flashed clearly in her memory, but beyond that, she could not remember, as if her young mind had willed itself to forget, as if this thing was too big for her to carry around in her small body.

Stella never did see the bottle full of lightning. That afternoon when Dolores McDonald returned to the mountain, Pearl immediately pulled her into the house and closed the door. Stella tried to put an ear up to it, to hear what was going on. When that didn't work, she snuck around the perimeter of the house, standing on her tiptoes to get a peak through a window, but she saw nothing. Dolores emerged a little while later. At first she looked the same, but then Stella caught her eye and was trapped there. The woman kept her in her gaze for a handful of seconds and then let her go. Stella felt strangely disappointed. She was not clear about what she saw there: wisdom, surely, and kindness too, of a sort, but most of all it was defiance, a look as determined as a brush fire. And then Dolores smiled, walked erectly down the stairs and down the path until she disappeared around the bend.

Stella thought about those fleeting moments for years. Was Dolores truly transformed? Was it only wishful thinking?

She never saw Dolores McDonald again, but they received a Christmas card every year, and each year it was from a different place. All that moving around troubled Stella, because she thought the whole point was for Dolores to find her place in this world. But Pearl explained to her that it made a whole lot of sense, because after all, lightning never strikes the same place twice.

As she grew older, Stella's restlessness baffled her family and friends. They loved her, they liked her, but they did not understand her, though they didn't really try all that hard. A chasm grew that began to separate her from the others.

At least once a month she invented an excuse to go into town. She would walk around the wide streets, go into the stores with fluorescent lights and beautifully dressed mannequins, and then lose herself in at least two showings of the film playing at the old movie house. But when she brought a magazine home, filled with gossip and pictures of the stars she had just seen, her friends would give her an odd look with narrow eyes.

There was a boy, a young man really, Bailey Thomas, for whom she always had a special fondness. In fact, just about everyone thought they were going to marry. They weren't perfectly suited but there were so few boys her age that were suitable at all. Stella liked Bailey, with his wide shoulders and hair the color of husked corn. Even his hands, so calloused and rough, felt good on the parts of her skin that were smooth and soft. But then one day, he simply stopped courting her, stopped really talking to her at all. When finally she walked the short distance to his house to ask him why, he simply said, "I like you, Stella. Hell, I might even love you. But you got a way of makin' me feel small, like I don't have enough of what you need. Couldn't bear a lifetime of that." Stella knew enough about herself not to protest, and liked Bailey Thomas enough to know that he deserved more. Eventually he married one of her sisters.

By the time Stella was twenty-one, she had all but taken over her grandmother's position as mender. It was seductive, what she could do, reach out with her hands and pull sickness out of a body. Pearl did a lot of teaching and explaining, but there were no words exactly for what happened when Stella laid her hands on someone. She felt the essence of who they were jump up to her fingertips. Their energy ran hot and cold on the surface, easy for someone like Stella to read, and sometimes if that energy was wrong she could push it away with her hands.

It wasn't as if she laid her hands on everyone, every minute of the day. Most of what she did required good old-fashioned herb remedies and tinctures and teas. She had memorized almost every plant on the mountain, and she remembered what she had seen her Granny do in that circle. Stella wanted to do it all, try every bit of folklore. She knew what Granny Pearl had been capable of: spells. And she had a feeling she was capable, too. She really didn't think she was a witch. She knew she was different, but after all she did for the community, she was surprised at how wary the townsfolk were toward her. It was as if they could all read the secret longings of her heart and it made her feel smothered.

At the same time, Stella felt like an old woman. Every

day she woke up and found it harder to get out of bed, and when she did she moved a little slower than the day before. She was tired: tired of working for nothing, tired of the struggle. It wasn't things, possessions, she yearned for, but the idea of living a life of swimming with the current instead of against it.

When Pearl began to die, Stella ministered to her faithfully. One day, near the end, when she was in and out of consciousness, Stella was bringing her grandmother's head up to get some water past her parched lips when Pearl grabbed her arm. She grabbed it so tightly that the tin cup flew out of Stella's hands. She studied Stella's face with narrow eyes.

"Good Lord, child! What are you still doin' here?" Then she fell back into the pillow, into yet another coma-like sleep.

Stella tried to rouse her. She wanted to yell, "Wait! Wait! What do you mean, here? In this room? Or in this place? And where will I go? What will I do?" But Pearl would not wake. Stella sat on the narrow bed, crying tears of grief and helplessness.

Something happened soon after, though. Finally letting go of all that water, all those tears, inside her, she could see the light. Whatever her grandmother had meant, she was still there, in the very last place on earth she wanted to be. She knew the town needed her, or someone like her. But she was no martyr. She wasn't afraid of hard work, but she was fed up with being unappreciated. She was tired of feeling like an outsider. The world was so very big, somewhere there was room enough for a different kind of girl like Stella to be happy. So she packed her bags, grabbed the $183 she had saved over the course of her lifetime, took Pearl's book, wrote a note to her family, and walked down the mountainside without looking back even once. Pearl was gone, and Stella was too.

She worked at a diner, renting a single room from an old widow who needed the extra cash. She scrimped and saved until she had enough money to buy a car. It was really a piece of crap, rusted inside and out, no windshield wipers. Its old radio only ever got two static stations. When she bought it, she quit her job and started driving west, making her way from town to town, eating peanut butter and white bread for breakfast and dinner. She would often sleep in her car, working odd jobs when she saw ads, picking crops when farmers needed seasonal labor, or selling remedies she would concoct from roadside plants to strangers she could just tell would need them.

One day, having crossed the entire country, she stumbled onto the car ferry to Avening. When her old car died half a mile from the dock, she took it as a sign. She'd been in Avening ever since.

Stella felt more at home in Avening than she ever had in Kentucky, which was amazing, since when she'd lived in Kentucky she'd had no way of knowing she didn't feel at home. She knew that this was a place that was right for a person like her. Stella was one of those people with odd talents and special gifts. That energy that she felt when she laid her hands on someone floated through the air in Avening. The town buzzed and hummed and purred. It felt alive.

She enjoyed her job at the *Circle*, the local paper. She felt she helped people, even if it wasn't on the personal level that she was trained for. The thought occasionally crossed her mind that she should get back into the business of mending. But it reminded her too much of home. It made her feel guilty. It just didn't seem right that she would abandon her own kinfolk to tend to a bunch of strangers. So she helped out here and there where she could. She used her gifts, but she turned away from what she really was.

Eventually, though, that decision took its toll. Lately she had begun to feel that something was off. It was hard for Stella to be objective about much of anything, let alone herself. How could Stella have known, when she left home, how much of herself the mountain would take as a sacrifice? The years and time had revealed the gaps in Stella's character. The mountain took that part of Stella that used to make others gravitate towards her. Out of fascination or fear or awe, she had drawn people to her. But now she forgot the rules of being social, so she blundered along, trying to be bigger than life in hopes that no one would miss her.

Stella knew she could never go home, for many reasons, but most important because home had irrevocably become Avening. Now she was caught in a place where she knew she belonged and yet which didn't belong to her at all. Even if she did go back to haunt the former places of her childhood, she knew that in truth all she would find would be the ghosts of her former self. The mountain had let her go, and now she needed something solid, something she could hold onto.

There wasn't really any particular aspect of her life that was totally wrong. And sometimes she wondered if maybe everything was in place, if maybe this is what it was like to be an adult, to constantly feel like she was waiting for something, or searching for something. Perhaps nothing was missing at all. Was happiness a thing? Something to be measured and defined? There were moments when Stella found herself thinking, yes, I am happy now. But in just thinking those thoughts, she drove them away, as if happiness itself was not a thing to be acknowledged. So she ignored it, hoping that somehow happiness would just settle on her. So far, that particular approach hadn't worked.

*Last year, Stella had recalled her grandmother's Equinox spell, and she realized that she felt exactly the way Dolores McDonald had described herself all those years ago: disconnected, somehow, like her life was happening to someone else. Lightning had worked for Dolores; it would work for Stella.

Looking at Pearl's book these thirty-odd years after she'd first seen lightning collected, Stella ran her fingers over her grandmother's words and almost heard Pearl's lively cadence in her head. She closed her eyes and smelled, faintly, Pearl's scent of mint and lavender, as though her grandmother had just walked by and was sitting in another room. She felt her grandmother close, her spirit watching and guiding her through the steps.

Stella's cellar was a small space, but far more organized than the rest of her house. Between the washer and dryer were two tall bookshelves. One held the results of hours of canning, everything from jams and jellies to peaches and cherries. On the other set of shelves were rows and rows of small glass bottles, carefully labeled, full of roots, herbs, and flowers she always kept on hand, even though she seldom used them for anyone other than herself. Now, she found she needed many of them, and she said a silent prayer of thanks to Pearl, who had taught her this very thing by example.

Stella, who could feel the storm drawing nearer, began mixing the ingredients with her mortar and pestle feverishly. It was a curious combination, everything from goldenseal and blue cohosh to ginseng. She mashed it all together, Lucy and Ethel watching with obvious boredom. She then went to a small cabinet in which she stored extra bottles. She moved them around noisily until she found the one that matched Pearl's description of what was required. It stood about ten inches tall, with a fat, round neck: an old milk bottle.

After bulldozing up her narrow stairs and dumping these things on her kitchen counter, Stella flew to the back-yard. There were a few ingredients that she needed fresh, and she had all of these growing in her small garden. With a small pair of cutting scissors she took early spring cuttings of elder flowers, marigolds, chamomile, and rose hips. Stella looked up to the sky and noted the gathering clouds. The air smelled musky and sweet and there was the metallic taste on her tongue again, but much stronger. The storm was moving in more quickly than she had thought.

Back inside she added the ingredients to the granite bowl and began to pound them together. She spat in it twice, and added water gradually. With a funnel she poured it into the bottle. That part of the preparation accomplished, she moved outside. Birds called to one another, and Stella hoped it wasn't some kind of animal warning system. She tried to dismiss the thought from her head. It wasn't like she knew exactly what she was doing.

For her circle, she would use a flowerbed that she had been planning on turning into a pumpkin patch. Mentally she calculated the diameter; the space was just big enough for her to throw the circle. She began to dig smack in the center. The hole had to be large enough to fit the bottle completely, so that not even the neck was visible.

In her dirt-covered frenzy, Stella suddenly began to laugh. If anyone could see her now, digging frantically at nine o'clock in the morning, still in her nightgown, her hair unbrushed — even Lucy and Ethel were eying her like a crazy person. Stella gently covered the bottle with earth so that it stood upright without any chance of moving, the open neck visible only when she stood directly above it.

Stella took a moment to glance at Pearl's book where she'd left it on a little wrought iron table. She took a large wooden bowl filled with salt and an old walking stick about half her height. Walking clockwise, she outlined the perimeter of the circle with the salt. She had never thrown a circle before, had never needed to. But she knew that this was more symbolic than anything else; she needed to feel safe in order to open herself up to the energy. Then she stood square in the middle, over the bottle, and began to speak in a loud, somber voice.

"I call upon the four directions to be present in this circle. North, the element of earth, be with me here, Mother, let your properties ground me and guide me. East, the element of air, I have called you to my purpose, bring forth your charge." Stella tried to ignore how ridiculous she felt. "South, the element of fire, join me in this circle, feed it with your power. West, element of water, I ask you to come inside, nurture this place, help me direct the storm."

Stella closed her eyes then and drew down the power. She visualized the sky, the purple-gray clouds gathered above her. She imagined a thread, made from the atoms of the cosmos: atoms both she and the clouds shared, atoms they traded back a forth. She pictured this thread winding around the sky and then down to the earth to her hands, curling about them like a snake. With her arms extending outwards and her head thrown back, she began to call to the storm.

The ritualistic aspect of calling lightning had intimidated Stella, but not this part. Like her Granny Pearl had said, she was born to do it. She felt like she knew what to do in the same way you know your address or phone number, an unconscious knowing you don't think about. It was earth magic, and Stella imagined herself at the end of a long chain of ancestors who had been working with it since the beginning of time. Stella was made hollow, an empty vessel for the energy to consume. To her, it felt like a dance. She swayed in the directions of the heavens, charming the energy down to the place she wanted it to go. When she opened her eyes, she saw the daylight had almost entirely disappeared. The clouds above her spun violently, the color of a new bruise. With her stick, she cut a doorway through the circle and walked just outside it. She could not be too close when the lightning struck.

The storm hummed through her teeth. She was no longer scared, no longer wary; she had become part of the violent process. "Now! Now!" she screamed. She slammed the stick deep into the earth, and at that very moment, the clouds shifted and a bolt of lightning struck the bottle. The force brought her to her knees, and she felt the strings of atoms flying from her body as she cut the mental cord connecting her to the storm. Still on all fours, she crawled back into the circle. When she stuck her hands into the earth, relief washed over her. It was the same feeling as that you get when you cry for hours: a calm exhaustion settled into her bones. Stella grabbed the bottle, covering the neck with a cork stopper she had stuck in one of her boots. Her body released the four directions with gratitude, thereby banishing the circle.

It was done. But had it worked?

Back inside the house, Stella put the bottle on the kitchen table without looking at it. She filled the kettle again and lit some candles. The rain had come in an angry downpour, blocking the sun and rattling the windows. Stella went to her bedroom to get dressed in an old flannel and loose jeans. She removed her muddy boots, replacing them with fleece slippers.

She padded back out into the kitchen and made tea. Both Lucy and Ethel had crawled up onto the table, sitting erectly on either side of the bottle, reminding Stella of an Egyptian hieroglyph. She was scared now, scared it hadn't worked, and a little scared it had. Still without looking, she took the bottle in her hands. There was something in it. The heat bled into her palms. Gingerly she held it up to the dim light. Apart from the herbal concoction she had mixed, something swirled in the bottle. Iridescent sparkles danced throughout the liquid and leapt up to the neck.

Stella had no idea what lightning in a bottle was supposed to look like, but whatever was inside her bottle seemed to be alive. There was only one sure way to test it, though, so she carefully lifted off the cork top. A few of the sparkles escaped and landed on her skin. It wasn't painful, exactly, but it was shocking, like being splashed with ice water. As Stella's breathing grew more rapid, she lifted the bottle up to her lips. "Ohh shit," she muttered. Hardly poetic, she knew, but what else was there to say? She closed her eyes and drank the liquid in one swift gulp. Her head swam, the room began to pulse, and Stella Darling rather ungracefully fell off the chair and passed out.

Autumn felt the storm gathering that morning. She had been up early, but Stella's loud, rather obnoxious spellcasting would have woken her up anyway. She'd had no idea at the time that Stella was capable of calling the storm.

Autumn wished she had been given some warning so, at the very least, she could have monitored the situation. It was wild magic, and possibly dangerous. But it was better this way; Autumn needed to get a sense of how things would be in Avening when she was no longer there to put out every fire. She needed to see how whoever had worked the magic would deal with its aftermath without her help. It was part of the vetting process, however much she disliked it.

She looked up at the stormy March sky, churning as it was with electric clouds, and sighed. She wondered if Stella Darling had any idea what she'd gotten herself into.

When she came to, Stella wasn't sure of where she was, or what she was doing on the floor. It wasn't until she stood that she noticed the difference. As soon as her feet touched the ground, she felt the swell inside of her. Her body was calmly indifferent, even though her mind raced. She felt dangerous and powerful. The spell, the lightning, had pulled her together. She had been a puzzle, scattered, pieces every-where. Drinking from the bottle had made each piece of her fit, had kicked and punched and fused them into place. Deep down inside, this fierce woman had always existed, but had been smothered and hidden out of duty and sacrifice. No longer.

When Stella looked in the mirror, she saw with sad efficiency how the weakest aspects of her personality had been allowed to make almost every single one of her choices. Her environment was that of a woman of a certain age who lived alone. Stella, who felt she was at her best when she was help-ing others, had tried to create a home that felt warm and inviting, but which in fact did the total opposite. It was stifling in there and claustrophobic.

Stella was a whirling dervish, a tornado. She cleaned and gutted. She threw things away that she didn't need or want, or could no longer bear to look at. The clutter was overwhelming, it hurt her brain, made her clench her eyes and fists together. She wanted space, clear, empty space, to breathe. In the kitchen she got rid of every bit of food that contained fat or processing. At the end of it, it looked like Old Mother Hubbard's. Oh well, she thought. I'll just go to the store later. The thought of an errand with such purpose thrilled her.

In her bedroom, she went through every article of clothing she owned. What on earth possessed her to buy such things? Sweatshirts with cats on them, sweaters with sequins, leggings . . . with stirrups! In the end, her closet was barer than her kitchen. She resolved to go into town and buy new clothes that actually fit.

When the cleaning was done, the garbage bags were taken out and sorted as actual garbage and charity shop give-aways. Better, much better. At the kitchen counter, she ate a sandwich out of the few tolerable things that were left in her refrigerator and made a list while standing. She tapped her toe on the hardwood and wrote out all the things she wanted and needed in two categories. She would repaint the house—pink simply no longer applied to her. Eventually, she would need all new furniture, but she couldn't buy it all at once. She would do it room by room, until the house was completely made over. "I mean really," she said out loud. "I can't imagine what I was thinking."

Bullshit, she thought to herself. She knew exactly what had made her furnish what was essentially a lovely old house with cheap, ornate furniture; if ever anyone had come for a visit (which they hadn't so far) they would have thought she was living the high life. Pathetic. She shook the thought out of her head and focused on how to fix it. Years of growing up in poverty had made her a hoarder. She had a chunk of money saved up, and could easily find $10,000 to use on redecorating. But at that rate it would take her years to finish the whole house. She would have to find a way to make extra money. She wrote "money" down on her list under the category of "needs."

She knew it would take months, if not years, to get her house and her body into decent shape, but she could do something immediately about one thing, at least. She picked up the cordless phone and dialed four doors down, to Dottie Davis's.

It could be said that Dottie was Stella's best friend. Dottie did hair in her kitchen. This arrangement suited her perfectly, as she could entertain and make money at the same time. Dottie was a round, black woman, Stella wasn't exactly sure how old (Dottie offered up the same number every birthday). The fact that her skin was practically flawless without a wrinkle in sight didn't help much with guessing.

When Stella knocked on her door ten minutes later, Dottie yelled, "Come in!! I'm in the kitchen!" Stella stepped through and exhaled deeply.

"What in the hell happened to you?" Dottie demanded.

"What do you mean?" Stella put her bag on the kitchen counter. "Hey, where's Jack?" Jack was Dottie's grandson, though she called him her "godsend." Dottie had full custody and she truly loved Jack to pieces. He was such a kind and good and smart boy, he made it easy.

"He's got a cold, but it's not bad enough to keep him from reading. Don't dodge the question. What happened?"

Stella shrugged her shoulders. "Nothing, really. I just tried something out of my grandmother's book. It's like . . . courage. A dose of courage. Can I sit?"

"A dose of courage." Dottie looked at her with one eyebrow raised and her lips pursed. Stella had told Dottie about her Granny Pearl and the things she'd seen her do. It wasn't like Dottie thought Stella was lying, but she didn't quite believe her, either. "What exactly could you mean?"

Stella decided to change the subject. "The truth of it is, I can't stand my hair a minute longer. I know you've been telling me for years to give up the henna, and I'm finally ready. I want to cut it, too, but I think I may be too fat for short hair. What do you think?" Stella said this without taking a breath.

Dottie eyed her up and down. "Stella, it's not that easy. Red is the hardest color to get rid of. I'm going to have to bleach it out and you may end up being more blonde than you want to be."

"Like platinum?"

"Yep."

"Perfect. I mean, if I had it my way, I see it as being almost white, you know? But a very light blonde will do."

"Okay." Dottie seemed wary, but Stella knew she would go ahead. That was Dottie's way. She got her point across in a secret code of teeth-clicking and hip-holding with some eye-rolling and arm-folding thrown in for good measure. Stella decided not to read this body language and to follow her own instincts ahead. Dottie put a black plastic smock over her friend and began applying the bleach. While she was doing this, Stella couldn't sit still. She was either tapping her fingers on the table, bouncing her knee, or shaking her foot.

"Sweet Jesus, Stella," Dottie groused into Stella's scalp. "Stop moving. You're making me nervous." Stella heard her friend's teeth click several times before Dottie paused for a moment, holding the black application brush in her hand. "Stella, are you on drugs?"

"No! Why would you say that?"

"Come on. You can tell me." Dottie put one hand on her hip.

"Dottie, I'm not on drugs, I swear." Stella was amused at the idea she was so transformed her friend thought it chemical. And maybe it was, but it was all her own brain doing the mixing.

"Yeah, well, I could swear that you're on speed. Diet pills are drugs, you know."

Stella sighed. She didn't want her best friend to think she was in trouble. "Dottie, I'm not on anything, I promise. I just saw things clearly today, is all. I had a . . . revelation."

"A revelation?"

"I've been all this time living with furniture I can't stand, buying clothes to impress other people, deliberately making myself look . . . what's the word. Like an impostor. No, more like I'm in disguise, hoping no one will recognize me. I looked at myself in the mirror today, really looked. And you know what I saw? A big ol' clown, that's what I've become. A joke." Saying the words out loud to someone made them feel more real, and Stella felt a curious rush of relief and anger all at once.

Dottie stopped what she was doing. "Stella, I'm glad you've been takin' a good, hard look at yourself, should've done it a while back, I suppose. But you can't dismiss yourself as . . . I don't know. Fraudulent." She applied the last of the bleach to Stella's hair. "I mean, the way you put it, it's almost as if you're telling me you've been living someone else's life."

"Oh, but I have. That's just it, Dottie."

"Stella, that's impossible. Are you trying to tell me you were possessed?"

How could Stella convey that that was absolutely how she felt? Completely explaining how she got from there to here would involve more talking than Stella was willing to do that night, or maybe any night, so she said simply, "The past can be a demon, the past can get inside and change you for the worse." Dottie rolled her eyes, but that was all she did, which meant to Stella that at the very least she half believed her.

The morning after Equinox was totally unlike the day before. The sun came through Stella's window like a gentle slap, but a slap nonetheless, and Stella opened her eyes furiously. She leapt out of bed, cursing herself for not shutting the curtains. Then she realized that she had to go to work that day anyway and headed off to the bathroom for a shower.

It wasn't until she fed the cats, had some toast, got dressed, and left the house that she noticed that, for the first time in her adult life, she had not woken up hungry. It was a good feeling, almost as if her body was telling her something important.

She pulled her bike away from the side of the house and pedaled down Keltia Avenue to work. Stella always biked the three or four miles to the *Circle* offices when the weather permitted. That morning, it didn't feel like a chore. The motion of her feet, the sound of the spokes whirring, and the wind that pushed her hair back off her face were liberating. She felt years younger.

When she reached Brigid's Way, Stella slowed down and cut into the sidewalk. She pulled her bike up to a nearby rack and locked it in. And although she could feel her thighs rubbing against each other in her drawstring pants, it was a relief to not have to deal with the constricting support hose that she usually wore everyday, even with slacks.

Stella made her way up the stairs and to her desk, not noticing the looks, the hushed whispers as her coworkers muttered to each other at her altered appearance. Her mind was too focused on writing. In fact, she doubted that her fingers would be able to keep up with the speed of her thoughts.

Nina Bruno's inspecting eyes made the hair on the back of Stella's neck stand up on end. "Stella? Oh my God! What happened to you?"

Normally Stella would have loved the attention, but today, all she wanted to do was work. "Nothing happened. I got a friggin' haircut. What's the big deal? Since when did anyone give a shit about how I looked anyway?"

Stella saw Nina flinch. Her eyes narrowed, and she bared her teeth in a forced smile. "Just a little word of advice," Nina said, moving closer. She reached out and touched the ends of Stella's new hair. "People don't like you enough for you to get away with being such a total bitch. So you might want to tone it down a little." She left Stella's office with the same smile on her face.

Stella fought the urge to pick up her letter opener and throw it into Nina's back, ninja-style. There was that rage again; she shook her head. She didn't actually want to kill

Nina, not with the jail time to consider and all. Maybe just hurt her a little. Wipe that smug smile off her face. She looked over at her computer screen, the cursor on the blank page blinked in an even rhythm. It was so hypnotic, she forgot all about Nina. The words just came to her: *equinox, tempest, earth, sky.* She lined them up and let them pour through her fingers. Writing had never come so easily for her.

When her stomach growled for attention, Stella looked up at the clock. 1:00 p.m. She had worked for four hours without stopping. The article was all but done, so that left the rest of the afternoon to answer letters. People from all over the country wrote in to ask Stella's advice on down-home remedies for common problems. She published the most interesting letters alongside of her daily article. Her column was syndicated in many small-town papers; it had taken Stella a dozen years and about a thousand phone calls to make that happen. But she was at a point now where new papers were actually coming to her.

She had to eat something, though, before she could get to the letters. She needed fuel. The afternoon outside had the season written all over it. The sky was baby blue, the trees beginning to leaf out, giving depth and perspective to the downtown. Stella walked two blocks up to Pleiades, a small sandwich shop. The proprietor, Nelson Friday, had been a city boy chef, cooking at five-star restaurants. He had come across Avening while traveling with an old friend and decided to stay.

Secretly—well, probably not secretly—Stella had a crush on Nelson. He was in his late forties, tall and dark with brown hair and eyes and a rarely clean-shaven face. Even though his last name was Friday, Stella guessed he was part Latin. His accent, though obviously American, often had a lilt of something else, a pause between words. Although he was kind, he never flirted, and as far as Stella knew (and she knew, she had done her research) Nelson did not have a woman in his life. Stella thought he was probably gay, not that she had ever seen any evidence to support it; it was just her self-destructive style to like a man who wouldn't be interested in her.

But today, for some reason, she wasn't interested in the truth about Nelson Friday's sexual preferences. She was interested in a tuna sandwich so she could get back to her desk. She ordered briskly and whipped out a five-dollar bill.

Nelson looked at her curiously, stuck his large carving knife square in the center of the wooden cutting board, and crossed his arms.

"What?" Stella asked, half smiling. "Have you gone on strike or something?"

"Hmmm. You're different today."

"I changed my hair. Does that disqualify me from having lunch?"

"The hair is different, yes, but it's something else. Not just your clothes, either."

"It's nothing," Stella answered stiffly.

"I don't like it," Nelson said with one eyebrow raised.

"Don't like what? Jeez." Stella tossed her newly platinum-blonde head. "This is ridiculous. What makes you think you have a right to give me your opinion? I didn't ask for it." An alarm bell went off in Stella's head and rang down to the pit of her stomach. She had been rude. She took a deep breath and said calmly, "I just decided it was time for a change. I have things to do with my life. I needed . . . focus. Is that okay? Do I get a sandwich now?"

Nelson quietly made her order while Stella rapped on the stainless steel counter with her nails. When he was done, she took the bag, and threw a "thank you" in his general direction.

Stella went back to her office to eat her sandwich. She didn't want to deal with any more people. She knew she had needled people into spending time with her in the past, had pushed herself into people's lives. She had hated that about herself, but she had never wanted to be alone. It had been so easy to pretend that her acquaintances genuinely liked and wanted her around when she was with them. But it had been a lie, and she had always known it. And now, when she finally didn't care whether people liked her, when she was prepared to keep to herself, suddenly, everyone was making a fuss over her. She didn't get it.

That night, Stella dreamed bright and colorful dreams in quick succession, her closed lids flooding with images of both her younger and older self. In one dream, Pearl was the Olympian god Zeus hurling lightning bolts at her from the mountain—even her sleeping self figured out the significance of that one. In another, she was eating her entire house, taking slow and steady mouthfuls of her furniture and floorboards. When she got to her phone, it began to ring. She tried to answer it, but instead began to chew on the cord. The phone rang and rang until she woke with a start, realizing that someone was really trying to call her. She quickly rolled to the other side of the bed to answer it. Late-night phone calls never meant good news.

"Hello?"

"Oh Stella, thank God. I've been trying to reach you forever."

"Dottie?"

"Yeah. Listen. It's Jack, he's taken a turn for the worse." Dottie sounded frantic. "I don't think he's emergency room sick, but he has a fever and he's coughing something horrible. Do you think you could bring some stuff over and work some magic? Really, even if you just look at him maybe you could tell me if I need to get him to a doctor."

"Give me five minutes or so. Just calm down, Dottie, and go up and sit with him. Do you have a humidifier?"

"Uh, yes."

"Go and get it and set it up in Jack's room. I'll be there in a flash." Stella hung up and quickly dressed, and then threw everything she would need in an old leather valise and headed out the door.

Stella let herself into Dottie's house without knocking. From upstairs she heard the sound of Jack's coughing. It was deep and thick, a cough you would expect from an old man. No wonder Dottie was so concerned. Stella took the steps two at a time, her bag scraping against the faded wallpaper. She got to Jack's room, softly stepping through the door. "Hello?" Stella whispered, knocking lightly at the door.

"That was quick. Thanks so much for coming, Stella," Dottie said.

At that, Jack began another fit of coughing. He politely

covered his mouth, but she could tell that he was having difficulty catching his breath.

"You hear that? He sounds awful. I don't think he's ever been this sick."

"Oh, I've heard worse, believe me. It's nothing we can't fix, right, Jack?" Jack shrugged and dropped back down on the bed. "Okay, first things first." Stella opened her bag and took out a small bottle and several candles. "This is eucalyptus oil, Dottie. I need you to put about a quarter of this bottle into the water of the humidifier. After you've done that, I'm going to need you to light these candles. They have eucalyptus in them as well, which should help to break up the congestion."

Dottie got up and took the things from Stella's hands. Stella sat on the bed. "Jack, honey, can you sit up a minute? I promise nothing I'm going to do will hurt, all right?"

Jack sat up and Stella laid her hands on his small, bare chest. These were the moments that Stella had been born for. Whenever she dealt with someone ill, she felt a sense of purpose and connection to the universe, a feeling that she was fulfilling a kind of promise. It made her feel big and small all at once. Usually when she laid hands on someone sick, she knew immediately what the problem was. Her palms warmed and guided her to the place on the body that had broken down. The energy vibrated a silent hum that filled her bones and emptied her head of every thought so she could read the other person better.

But when she touched Jack, she felt nothing. Stella closed her eyes and concentrated harder, but nothing came: no images, no pictures, no guide. She simply could not connect. Could she have forgotten? Could she be out of practice? Stella doubted it. She had a feeling she knew exactly what was going on, though she didn't want to admit it.

Shaken by her inability, Stella made herself focus. She could not ease Jack's condition through energy alone, but luckily, she knew what to do homeopathically. As Dottie lit the candles, Stella asked if she could use her kitchen.

She tried to stay focused on Jack as she tromped back down the steps and through the hall plastered with pictures in simple black frames. She was thrown off, and pissed off. A gift, something she had taken for granted all her life, something that came as naturally to her as breathing, had suddenly disappeared. It seemed odd to her that she had not noticed it before. Even when she wasn't tapping into the energy, it was always there, in the corners, bleeding through her everyday life, touching her at odd moments. She supposed she had been too wrapped up after Equinox, too busy changing.

In an old iron pan, Stella fried onions and garlic. The smell jolted her back to the task at hand. She would deal with the other problem later, but for now, Jack had to be a priority. She spread the cooked ingredients into the middle of a poultice wrap she had sewn from an old flannel shirt. Then she added mustard powder and mustard seed and a few more pinches of various other herbs for good measure, and quickly went back upstairs. The boy's room, now dim with candlelight, smelled of the eucalyptus.

"Okay, Jack, I'm going to put this on your chest. It smells something awful, but it should help you break up some of that stuff in your lungs. First though, I want you to drink this whole glass of water. The more fluid we can get into your body, the faster the sickness will run its course."

Jack was reluctant to drink. Stella could see by the heavy pulling of his lids that he was tired and probably wanted nothing more than to sleep. But he drank the water, stopping once to cough. "Dottie, you gave him some Tylenol earlier, right?"

"Yes, is that okay?"

"Sure it is. He has a fever, and the Tylenol should bring that down. But we should take his temperature now so we can keep track of it. Don't worry, Dottie, he's going to be fine. Okay, Jack, arms up." Stella placed a couple of clean flannels on his chest and then put the poultice on, tying the flannel straps around his back. She laid him down again, but this time on his side, propping pillows up against his back. "I know it's not very comfortable, Jack, but you're going to have to sleep this way tonight. Lying flat on your back will only make the coughing worse." Jack mumbled something, and Stella realized he was already asleep.

Dottie hovered anxiously over the bed, her hands flapping as though she was restraining herself from touching her grandson. "Thank you so much, Stella," she stage-whispered. "You get so worried, you know? You feel so helpless when they get sick and you just wish more than anything that you could trade places." Stella nodded. She didn't know, but she could imagine. "I think we'll be okay now," Dottie said. "I'll take Jack into Dr. Balboa's office first thing tomorrow. Why don't you go home now and get some rest."

"Oh no, I think I'll stay if that's all right with you. I can just camp out on the floor if you have a sleeping bag."

"Stella, I can't ask that of you. It's too much. And you have work tomorrow."

"No, I think I'm gonna play hooky. Besides, I'll have to take the poultice off, maybe make a new one with different ingredients in it. Really, I don't mind at all. I love Jack, and I want to make sure he's okay. It's no trouble; I would tell you if it was."

"Okay, but I'm going to get the cot out and you can sleep on that. Sleeping bag . . . Christ!"

Stella tended to Jack all through the night, checking his temperature, making another poultice, giving him water. She may have drifted off for a few brief moments, but her dreaming was dark and rapid, the feeling of falling jolting her back awake. When daylight came, she gathered up her supplies, made the bed, and said a quiet goodbye to Dottie, who promised to phone when they returned from the pediatrician's office.

Even though Stella felt good that she'd been able to help Jack, she was nervous and upset that she hadn't been able to use her gift. She had to admit, since she had drunk from the bottle, she had been totally self-absorbed, rude, and out of tune. Not herself. It had all been a mistake. She had paid too high a price to become this new person. Stella pored through Pearl's book, looking for some way to reverse the spell, but she was not surprised when she found none.

It was true she liked her newfound sense of determination, her indifference about what others thought of her, and the ability now to see things for how they truly were. Stella's truth was that she was a healer, mountain or no mountain. Of course, the irony of it was that the very same incident that allowed Stella to have this personal revelation of her purpose in life caused her to lose her ability to see it through. The lightning burned it out of her, cooked the gift right through.

Stella stared out the window, swaying without noticing, back and forth like the trees outside in the breeze. She was out of her depth, way out. She knew there was only one person in town who could possibly help her. But somehow, the thought of telling Autumn Avening what she had done made her stomach tighten. She had the distinct feeling Autumn would not approve of her methods. But there was nothing for it. She had to go.

Demeter's Grove was cool and quiet the afternoon of March 23. Stella used to hate Autumn's shop, with its walls of books and chintz couches, its displays of antiques, body products, clothing, and crafts. For Stella, it touched on something too close and raw, made her feel unsafe. But today she felt different. Clearly, she was in the right place. But she suddenly felt drunk, or high, or something. She held onto a chair to steady herself.

"Hello, Stella," Autumn said softly, coming out from her kitchen. There were other customers in the shop, but it wasn't overly busy.

Stella looked up at Autumn, wanting to say something, but her senses were muddled. She felt like she might faint.

"Come into the kitchen, dear. I have something for you to drink." Stella followed her without meaning to. She felt her body pulled along by Autumn's voice. "There are certain 'precautions' I take in my home, Stella, and these precautions are now making you feel as unbalanced as you do. Though truthfully, after what you've been through, you should be much worse off, so that's interesting in and of itself. If you drink this tea you should feel better in a moment or two."

Stella sat at the kitchen table, too dazed to ask how Autumn had known she'd be dropping by, and drank as she was told. Sure enough, she began to come around. She felt her body trying to light the fire inside her, but it was like a car that wouldn't turn over. She thought she was angry at Autumn, but she didn't feel angry.

"What have you done, Stella?" Autumn asked softly. She looked at Stella kindly, but she kept her distance. Stella was glad of it. "Tell me the truth. I felt something on the Equinox. I had no idea you knew how to . . . " Autumn cut herself off and shook her head. "Just level with me, and if there's a problem we'll work it out."

Stella read the concern on her face. The real truth of it was, she wanted to talk, and she felt like Autumn might be the only person in town, heck, in the whole world, who could come close to understanding. So Stella told her about everything, about the mountain, about herself and about the storm and the lightning that had burned up her gift. Autumn's look of concern was replaced with a look of surprise.

"So you corralled the storm? In a circle? Created a potion which is basically the equivalent of drinking liquid fire . . . ?" Stella nodded. "And you learned the basics from your grandmother's journal, but you pretty much made it up as you went?" When Stella nodded again, Autumn leaned back in her chair. She failed to hide the amazement on her face. Stella began to get the feeling she'd had no idea how dangerous her little experiment had been.

"Stella," Autumn began, and then she paused. "I am so very impressed with what you have accomplished. Truly. Your grandmother would have been so proud of you, I'm sure of that. But the balance of things in the universe is much more fragile than you might imagine. A person may be able to physically drive a car, but controlling it is a different thing altogether."

Stella didn't feel like she was being scolded; quite the opposite. She felt a connection to Autumn, and Autumn must have, too, because she leaned in closer, as if what she was about to say was a secret. "I'm not surprised your gift is gone, Stella. I'm sorry. But it's about that balance. You take something from the universe without asking, and more often than not, the universe will take something in its place."

"So . . . I'm like this forever?" Stella felt her eyes begin to well.

"Maybe, maybe not. But making peace with your choice, and accepting the consequence, will go a long way."

"A long way towards what? What am I supposed to do?" Stella clenched her fists on her lap in a mix of helplessness and fury. "I'm dangerous. I scare myself. I feel like I could do something, bad."

"I cannot undo this for you."

"But you could try, right? I mean, maybe together we could figure it out."

For a moment, Autumn looked as though she were about to concede to something, but then her face returned to its sympathetic grimace and she shook her head. "Some-where, deep inside, you know the answer. You might not know it now. But you have a sense of it, the idea of it. There's a trail your magic left, and now you have to follow it back round again. I can almost guarantee that if I get involved, you won't get the result you want. So go home and have a good think about all of this."

"Anything else you can tell me?" Stella said, hearing her own sarcasm.

"Pray," Autumn responded flatly.

Someone was praying, even if it wasn't Stella.

Autumn was pleasantly surprised by the letter she found under her door later that day. There was no stamp on the envelope, only the word "Autumn" in loopy blue ink. The sender must have walked it over while Stella was in Autumn's shop, when Autumn had been too distracted to notice.

Dear Autumn,

Just to be clear, I'm writing this letter to be considered for your contest. But before I talk about your contest, I want to be clear about something else, too. It's this: I really do like and respect you a great deal. We've had our little tiffs in the past, and I have said some very strong things to you about who you are and what you do. It took me a long time to understand that maybe what you do isn't black magic, that just because you are a witch doesn't necessarily mean you're evil, and that you are really a very spiritual woman. I know you don't like that word, "witch," anyway. But I don't really have a better word to describe you. So that will have to do.

To tell the truth, I have to admit I've thought you were a good person for a long time. You're so wise in the way of things, and I've seen you help so many people. I know God wouldn't have given you that wisdom and power if you weren't one of His creatures. But I've had trouble juggling what I understand of my faith, which as you and everyone else knows is faith in Jesus Christ, with the things I've always been taught are against the way of my Lord.

I knew about your contest from my good young friend Stella. When I heard she was entering, I was torn, because on the one hand I know Stella herself has some special gift of God's. I've seen her use it on my own grandson, and on other people. But I wasn't sure I liked the idea that she wanted something called a Book of Shadows. You have to admit, when you call it that, a person can't help but think black magic kinds of thoughts. So I prayed for a long time about this, trying to understand my own feelings, and the funniest thing happened. In a moment of clarity, I remembered that there is no power on this good earth except that of the Lord our God's, and that any power you or your book might have must actually be God's power. On the one hand, it seems a little twisted. On the other, nothing else makes sense.

Autumn, I've spent my life trying to get closer to God. I've spent my life studying and worshipping. And I know my way of seeing God must be a little different from yours, but maybe you'll agree with what I've just discovered, that they can't be that different. If you decide that this old lady is your contest winner, you know that I will own your book and whatever is inside it respectfully.

Yours truly,

Dottie Davis

Autumn was very pleased to have this letter. Until she read it, she'd had no idea why Dottie Davis had been on her list.

Through the end of March and into April, Stella did what Autumn had suggested, and prayed for a reversal of the spell. She forced herself to be patient, to clear her mind and keep trying to connect with the earth, even when nothing came to her. She rose in the morning to pray before work, cleared her head and meditated every lunch hour, and cleared her mind every evening before sleep, trying to feel the pulse of the earth in her heart and stomach again. It was gone.

Stella willfully refused to give up, and reminded herself of the silver lining here. Not being able to summon healing energy meant she was forced to use all the homeopathic training Granny Pearl had drilled into her, and she loved reminding herself of home cures. Her columns for the *Circle* became even richer, and she started following other homeopathic journalists at other town and city papers, which widened her own knowledge. She had lost weight, and looked more like the person she'd always imagined she'd wanted to be. But to Stella, none of this was worth having given up her gift. She had to fight her temper and impatience every day, to struggle against the lightning in her belly that so wanted to dominate her personality. It was hard not to let it win.

When she prayed, Stella remembered her true nature: a person who wanted to help and heal others, who wanted to serve her community. She worked hard to keep doing these things, but they were no longer natural. She prayed to turn her brain off, and relied on a nightly mix of herbal tea and Klonopin just to be able to sleep six or seven hours. When it got really bad, she replaced tea with wine, or pot, or both. She paced her tiny house, trying to throw out the frenetic energy that had collected beneath her skin.

No amount of research turned her onto a cure; the fact that she couldn't find one was so overwhelming she thought panic alone might give her a heart attack. She knew, without a doubt, that she could not go on like this forever. She had to reverse what she had done. The question was, how? How to undo such a thing?

Then, one evening at the end of April, while Stella was praying quietly in her kitchen, the answer hit her like, well, like a bolt of lightning. Sure, lightning was dangerous, fascinating, and powerful—but there was one thing that diffused it, that took away that power. Earth. The earth grounds and absorbs the phenomenon as if it were nothing. Such a simple and obvious answer, but it had taken her all this time to figure it out.

Stella went out to her garden, and almost without thinking unleashed her garden hose on the small space that once was the circle she had thrown to call the lightning. She wasn't sure how long she stood there, but it was long enough to turn the hard-packed soil into a small field of mud. She walked into the middle, bending down to feel the mud between her fingers. It was smooth and silty. Then she stripped down naked, indifferent to the crispness in the April air, or to the fact that anyone might see her small, round body.

Stella centered her breathing, trying to calm herself by telling herself if it didn't work she could try again, although she knew that wasn't true. She outlined a circle with her foot and then stood in the middle again to call down the elements. She could not pin down the energy, though, not like before. Instead, she felt it race through her and over her, slipping around her thoughts. Stella was frustrated, but let it go. She had to stop fighting with herself; she had to empty herself of thoughts and plans and fears.

Stella felt herself fall to her knees, compelled by some greater force. The next thing she knew, she grabbed a handful of mud, closed her eyes, and stuffed it into her mouth. The taste of iron shocked her. The aware part of her certainly hadn't intended to eat mud, but there she was, unable to stop herself. She had to concentrate on the earth, on grounding herself, on being restored by the greatest healer of them all. She pleaded and begged and choked out a cry for help, covering the length of her body with mud, rolling around in it and working it into her hair. She kept on eating it and then, remembering Autumn's words, began praying to someone, anyone, for the return of her gift.

It could have been five minutes or thirty-five minutes. Time did not move normally inside the circle, and once again she relied on her instincts to tell her when to stop. Her body hummed. Stella got to her knees, feeling heavy and slow, and then she threw up. Her stomach heaved and heaved until it felt like it had turned itself inside out. She didn't really want to look, but she had to. Here and there in the mess of vomit, gold flecks caught the sun. She was sure of it. Stella, giddy with gratitude, banished the circle and pulled herself into fetal position under a giant fir that stood in the farthest corner of her yard.

More lost time. More black and brown and deep purple instead of dreaming. Stella opened her eyes. She had passed out, sort of, her face pressed into the earth at the roots of her garden fir tree.

The first thing she felt was worn out and hollow, but then she immediately realized she was hungry; that was a good sign. The mud had dried on her skin, leaving a tight and unmovable case. She let herself into the house and went directly to her bathroom to run the shower. Under the deliciously warm spray she tried not to think of anything at all, concentrating instead on watching the mud rolling down her legs and ringing the drain, which carried it away in a red-brown swirl.

When she was finished she wrapped herself in a towel. In her bedroom, she let the towel slip to the floor and examined herself in the full-length mirror. Her hair fell in damp clumps around her face and she saw that some of the old softness in it had returned. She felt calm, so unlike the anger she had felt toward herself in the last few weeks. Why had she had so much contempt for herself, for her life? Stella drew her arms up to her chest in a gesture of forgiveness. Everything she had done, every choice that she had made had led her to this exact moment. She was right where she was supposed to be.

She felt her gift come back, the slight tingles under her skin, the awareness of something making her hands want to reach out to connect. It had worked; the lightning was gone. But so were her feelings of being inconsequential. She had kept the new ability to see through her past, through her pain, and recognize that there was so much more to her, more for her, than she had allowed herself to believe. And in that split second, she felt it: happiness. Then she let it go, let it back out into the universe where every other perfect moment lives, stretched out across the stars, hovering, just there.

Autumn was relieved to feel it all coming to an end. She could have undone the spell in two seconds, but she didn't experience much regret about having lied to Stella about that. She had known Stella was powerful enough to pull off a reversal of the spell herself. She wanted to see how Stella handled crisis. She wanted to check her problem-solving abilities. And she had to admit Stella had done a pretty good job. There was no way on this earth (or any other) she was eliminating Stella Darling from her list.

May 1:
Beltane

ANA BECKWITH LAY UNMOVING ON THE FARTHEST
reaches of her bed. Turned to one side, she
watched the numbers climb on the clock
beside her. All through the night she had felt a fist push
through her chest, squeezing her from the inside until her
breath fell out of her mouth, quick and strained. Ana listened to the steady rhythm of Jacob's sleeping, wanting
nothing more than to escape to the couch downstairs. That
would only have added to his suspicions that something was
not quite right with her, though, and today of all days she
needed to assure him that despite her moodiness as of late,
she was fine.

When the first birds began to call outside her window,
something inside her softened. The morning had finally
come. She turned over and watched her husband's profile as
it emerged dimly through the shadows. Guilt and excitement
surged through her, strong enough to make Ana flex her toes.
She closed her eyes and tried to imagine how to get through
the day, only able to visualize her actions in the most basic of
verbs. She would find a way to charm the hours left, to own

them, before the moment when she would give up everything entirely, including time itself.

❧

A couple of blocks from where Ana lay with her thoughts spinning, Finn Emmerling slept in the narrow confines of his daughter's bed. Janey had cried out in the night, often enough to make Finn wonder if she knew somehow his own frenzied mind. She was comforted by his presence beside her, and he found himself able to sleep in a way he never could have if he had shared his wife's bed.

Janey began her morning dialogue, a hybrid of singing and talking that pulled Finn slowly away from his dreams. With the one eye he had open, he saw her calmly sitting up, conversing with the air. Maybe she did see someone, or something.

"Morning, Janey girl," Finn said, running a hand over her hair.

"Hi, Daddy."

"You hungry? Want some breakfast?" Finn heaved himself out of the bed and picked up his small daughter.

"Yeah."

"Okay, then."

❧

"Mom!! There's nothing but gross grown-up cereal left," Ana's son whined. "I thought you said you were going to the grocery store. Mom? Hello? Can you hear me? I said—"

"I heard you, Russ. I'm sorry, I didn't get a chance to go

to the store yesterday, but somehow I think you'll live," said Ana, feeling the sleepless night weigh heavily on her limbs.

"What am I supposed to eat for breakfast?"

"Suck it up, Russ. A little bran won't hurt you." Ana pulled the cereal box from the cupboard, poured some in a bowl, then plunked the milk down in front of him. He was very particular about how much milk he liked in his cereal, and needed to pour it himself each morning.

The look on Russ's face worried Ana. She knew she wasn't being very nice, and the added guilt was enough to make her want to bury her face in her hands. "I'm sorry, honey, I didn't mean to be so crabby. I just didn't sleep well, that's all. You can go to the store with your dad today and get whatever you like, okay?"

"Okay," Russ said with a shrug.

"So you know I'm going to be gone today, right?"

"Dad says you're going to Autumn's to do girly stuff."

"That's true. I don't think it would be anything you'd be interested in."

"Naw," said Russ, his mouth full of cereal.

Jacob walked in the kitchen wearing an old pair of jeans and an even older sweatshirt. "Morning, guys," he said. He pulled a mug from the cupboard and poured himself a cup of coffee. "Jeez, Annie, you don't look so good. Guess it's a good day to 'nurture the woman within,' huh?"

Ana smiled. Her husband always made her laugh. She had told him the truth, mostly. Autumn was sponsoring a woman's Beltane Day. For the most part, it was a morning of meditation and discussions, and an afternoon of total pampering. The women would be indulging in facials, massages, and manicures, a complete day of taking care of the mind, body, and spirit. Ana was going to be spending the night at Autumn's, that much was true. She had not, of course, divulged just who she was going to be spending the night there with.

"Maybe you two could go down to the maypole at Brigid's Square, what do you think?" asked Ana.

"Great minds, my love. I was just thinking the same thing. What time are you going to head out?" Jacob sat at the table beside her.

"Actually, things are about to start over there," Ana said, standing and stretching. "I'm gonna go throw some stuff in a bag and get moving."

"Okay," said Jacob, who had begun to read the paper.

Ana looked at her son and husband. The guilt was visceral and exhausting, a different kind of tired than lack of sleep. It almost immobilized her, but she knew that this was something that she had to do. In fact, she felt in some way that she was doing it for her family, because the crazy way she felt was beginning to eat away at the very core of who she was. Before this option had been presented to her, she had been ready to run away and leave them both behind.

Ana shook her head and went up the stairs to her room. She pulled the Lone Star quilt up over her bed hastily and kicked the clothes on the floor to one corner. She threw things into her overnight bag without thinking. She couldn't name one single possession that could prepare her for what was about to happen.

As she changed clothes, Ana took a long look at her

naked reflection. She wasn't old, not nearly, and she had had Russ so young that her body held little evidence she had ever been pregnant. She wasn't a tall woman, but she never felt short. Ana was a natural beauty, looking her best when she wasn't trying to at all. Her chestnut hair framed her face in a long bob. Her brown eyes had flecks of other less common colors, and her freckles made her look much younger than she actually was. She was happy with the way she looked. In fact, she thought she looked better even than when she was in her twenties. But maybe that was because she simply liked herself more, knew herself better. That made all the difference. She dressed simply in a pair of wheat-colored linen pants and a white T-shirt and slipped on a pair of flip-flops. In the living room, Jacob was still reading the paper on the couch and Russ was watching TV.

"Okay, guys, I'm out of here. I'll see you tomorrow, 'kay?" Ana leaned over and kissed Jacob's head.

"Bye, honey. Have fun. And don't worry about us, we'll be fine. Won't we, Russ?"

"Yep," said Russ, engrossed in his program.

"I'll miss you tonight. Can I have a hug?"

Russell made one of his notoriously horrified faces but got up and gave his mother a hug anyway. "Bye, sweetie. And not too much TV, okay? I mean it. Thank you, Jacob, for taking over. I'll see you both tomorrow!"

"Yeah, and please, try not to let missing us too much get in the way of enjoying your massage, all right?"

"Tough one, but I'll try." Ana smiled and walked out the door. She climbed in her car and started the engine.

There is no such thing as spontaneity when a two-year-old is involved. Ginny Emmerling, Finn's wife, had prepared as much as possible in the days leading up to the trip to her parents' house. She had made a list, but she still had to gather and pack everything on it. Ginny raced around the house with Janey in one arm, muttering things to herself. Ginny always got very stressed out when she was going to visit her parents. Her anxiety baffled Finn. He couldn't imagine that after all these years, after all the time they spent treating her with such complete indifference, Ginny still cared about keeping up appearances. Whenever he tried to say this to his wife, though, she simply rolled her eyes.

"Gin, why don't you at least give Janey to me? Are you trying to make things harder for yourself?" She stopped momentarily and swung around to glare at him. "What? I'm only saying that this would be a lot easier if you'd just let me help you."

Ginny spared him one pitiful moment in her neck-breaking flurry. "You know how there are those couples who just instinctively know what the other half of that couple needs? The ones who finish each other's sentences, read each other's minds?"

"I guess," Finn said, noncommittally. But he did know, he knew exactly what she was talking about.

"Well, you and I aren't like that. By the time I finish explaining what needs to be done, I might as well have done it myself."

"Fine," said Finn, throwing his hands up to the air. "But

seriously, give me Janey. I'll entertain her until it's time for you to go."

Ginny gave him a look, then dumped their daughter in his arms. Why she was trying to start an argument, he had no idea, but he did know he wasn't about to buy into it. Not today.

He took Janey up to her room and read some stories to her. Then she made him dress her Barbie in at least a dozen different outfits. He tried to stay focused on his daughter; after all, he wasn't going to be seeing her for the next five days. But his mind wandered despite his efforts.

Finn wasn't at all sure he liked the idea of what was going to happen tonight. But he knew that he wasn't ready to leave Ginny, not yet, no matter how much he wanted to. She depended on him too much. Her fragility was tangible, something she wore. He felt responsible for her, and no matter how unhealthy that was, he could see no way to change it.

"Look, Daddy! The sun!" Janey said, pointing to a picture in one of her books, bringing him back from his daydreaming. He would figure it out in time, because, after all, Finn Emmerling was a patient man.

When Ginny was ready, Finn helped his wife bring two suitcases down the stairs and out to the car. It seemed like a lot to bring for such a short trip, but he knew most of what was inside was diapers, books, and toys for Janey. The bags were heavy enough that Finn was a little short of breath when he finally got them into the car. Ginny, meanwhile, settled Janey into her car seat. He heard the buckle snap and the familiar tug on the belts as his wife double-checked that she was strapped in safely.

"Okay, well, I'm off. You have the numbers if you need to reach us, and I'll be on the cell if you need me before we get there," Ginny said, still somewhat frazzled from her hectic morning. "Oh, and don't forget, the painters are coming tomorrow afternoon to give us an estimate on the kitchen cabinets. I'm sure I'm forgetting something . . . Oh well, it must not be that important."

"I can send anything you may have forgotten if you really need it."

"Right. Well, bye," Ginny said, giving him a restrained hug.

Finn hugged her back and kissed her on the cheek. "Bye, Gin. Have a safe drive. Make sure you call when you get there." She smiled at him briefly, as though she wanted to say something more. Instead, she quickly got into the car. She turned the ignition and backed up slowly out of the drive, leaving Finn alone on the pavement to watch the car make a slow and steady progress southwards.

Ana did not turn on the radio, but she did roll the windows down, letting the cross breeze ruffle her hair. Finn was stuck on her tongue, in her mouth; she whispered his name to herself. Ever since Ana had met Finn Emmerling, when he was picking up his two-year-old from day care at her school, time itself seemed to slip sideways and the air around her was sucked into some kind of cosmic vacuum, leaving her little oxygen to breathe. She was sure everyone in the room must have caught it: at thirty-three years old, after a happy if not eventful marriage, a solid career, years of raising a young son, a life, full and steady; after all of this, after Ana was sure she understood the path her choices so far had made for her, she had met her soul mate.

There was awkwardness in those first few moments, but as soon as she began to talk to Finn, all the awkwardness disappeared. It was as if she had always known him, like they were picking up a conversation they had just been having. He certainly was handsome: a wild mass of Byronic hair; skin that held onto a bit of long-lost Mediterranean heritage with a tinge of olive even after a full stretch of winter; tall, but not overly so, broad and muscled, which Ana soon discovered was a product of his constant physical labor at the nursery. But it was more than that, it went deeper than his skin. If she had to describe it, she would have had to say that from the moment she laid eyes on Finn, a thread of her very being, strung from the core of who she was, escaped from her belly and connected itself to Finn's chest. From that time on, she always had a sense of him, where he was and what he was feeling. Eventually she would learn that Finn, too, had experienced something similar.

Those first few days, she tried to convince herself it was nothing more than mere flirtation, a crush, harmless enough in and of itself. In believing this, she allowed herself to pursue it, pursue him, mentally. She lived in a state of perpetual daydreams, surprising herself with the scope of these fantasies and the excuses her mind invented to bring the possibility of being with him that much closer. Ana had to see him, even if he didn't see her. She had to give her eyes another image to wrap her dreams around.

Ana had never been much of a gardener. She had meant to become one, really had wanted to, when they first bought the house years ago, but she had just never made it a priority. She occasionally bought potted plants from the grocery store or the local hardware store, but it never went further than that, for the same reason they never had pets: it was too much of a commitment for their already busy lives. But now she was thinking of starting a small kitchen garden. Ana loved to cook, and it would be really nice to have some fresh vegetables and herbs available right outside her back door. She even managed to convince herself that really it had very little to do with Finn, that seeing him at the nursery was just a bonus. Her mind, like anyone else's on the precipice of morality, was a marvel at justifying.

On Ana's next day off after she made this decision she paid a visit to Bellaverde Nursery. It had taken her too long to decide what to wear. Of course she wanted to look good, but she absolutely could not look like she had tried to look good. And she could hardly explain to Jacob wearing stiletto boots to the nursery. Subtlety was the key. Jeans, white tank, silk scarf—French style—and a pair of ballet flats.

Surprisingly, Jacob had shown a lot of enthusiasm towards her idea about the garden. He even wanted to go with her, a suggestion that made Ana's mouth grow dry and her stomach roll over. She held him off on the pretense that she needed some alone time, which, she supposed, was not far from the truth.

On the way there she calmed herself by slipping a Lori Carson CD in the player. She leaned back into the headrest and centered her breathing. Bellaverde was on Caradoc

Road, not quite out of the center of town. There were other businesses there, like Silvermoon, Ana's favorite clothing boutique. Unlike other commercial areas of Avening, the lots along Caradoc were much bigger, and the houses that sat on it were some of the oldest and most impressive in Avening. They were mostly rambling Queen Annes in a wide array of dazzling colors.

Ana pulled her car through the tall fence around the parking area just in front of the entrance. There were a few other cars there, which momentarily caught her off guard. In her fantasies, of course, she and Finn would somehow find themselves alone. She made one final check of her appearance in the rearview mirror, an action even she thought silly, and got out of the car.

She walked slowly through the graveled entrance, marveling at the arched trellis and the blooming, fragrant flowers that wound their way around almost every inch of it. She wished she knew more about plants, and hoped she wouldn't say something stupid. But she knew she would, somehow, screw everything up. She had never mastered the art of being demure or casual. Whenever she tried to be, she came across as ridiculous and she knew it, knew by the awkwardness that settled around her and made others smile at her in a "bless her heart" kind of way. She would just have to try to be herself, her best, most cool self.

The arch opened up to a vast area of table upon table of potted flowers and plants. Finn kept it all very organized and labeled, and soon Ana began to realize the displays were divided into sections of trees, shrubs, annuals, and perennials. There was also a good selection of pots, tools, and architectural elements. From somewhere in the distance, Ana heard the flow of water, and over that, from speakers set in hidden locations, Alison Krauss was playing. Ana, who had never in her life stepped into a nursery, felt strangely at home.

She looked at the various customers and wondered where Finn might be. It suddenly dawned on her that he might not be around at all. But something told her he was here, and close. She walked over to a table on which sat a plant with gorgeous purple flowers. She moved her face in towards it and delicately lifted the petals to her nose, taking a deep breath in.

"Viola odorata. It smells wonderful, doesn't it?" Suddenly Finn stood there before her, in old jeans and a thin gray T-shirt. Ana could hardly believe it, but he looked even more handsome than he had when she first met him. He was the kind of man that looked better a little dirty. He had the beginnings of a beard, which suited him completely.

Ana wondered what she should do with her hands, so they moved in a variety of awkward positions before one settled on her hip and one on her bag. "Finn, hi! You startled me. I . . . umm . . . yes, it does smell wonderful."

"What brings you here, Ana? I thought you said the whole plant thing wasn't for you?" Finn was smiling.

Ana panicked: had she said that? She supposed so, but why on earth would she have? "It isn't."

Finn raised his eyebrows and with that there was no pretense, no excuses as to why she was there. They looked into each other's eyes in silence. This is a dangerous game, thought Ana. She broke out into a wide grin. "Well," she said finally. "Jacob and I were thinking of starting a little kitchen garden. I don't know how successful we'll be, but we thought it would be really nice to have fresh vegetables just outside the door."

"Really." Finn crossed his arms. He wasn't buying it for a minute. "Well, then come over here. We have a section I think you'll be interested in."

Ana followed him through a maze of plants to six tables off to the side. The sign above read The Kitchen Garden.

"I don't believe it!" exclaimed Ana.

"Oh yeah, I had a feeling you were coming, so I set up this little area just for you."

Ana knew he was joking. Wasn't he? "Well then, thank you, I'm flattered."

Finn smiled broadly and ran his hand through his hair. It was kind of a girly thing to do, but the way he did it seemed rugged and nonchalant.

"Seriously, though, around this time of year a lot of people get the very same idea as you. It's hard for most people to grow things from seeds, so we started these plants weeks ago. Is there anything you want in particular?"

Ana could think of about a million things she wanted in particular from Finn, but she restrained herself. "Listen, Finn, just give me the run-of-the-mill, first-time-out package. Really, I trust you," she said, looking straight into his eyes. At that Finn looked away. Her heart began to pound. Had she been too forward? Had she put him off?

She thought he might have said something else, but he began to pull various plants from the tables. "Hey Vic!" he yelled to a young man spraying some plants. "Grab the dolly, will you?" Ana stood by silently and watched him work, her skin tingling with irresistible anxiety.

A couple of minutes later, Vic returned and Finn began loading plants onto the cart. "So, here you've got basil, cilantro, rosemary, dill, chamomile," he said to her over his shoulder. "Those are your herbs. Here are tomatoes, squash, beans, lettuce, peppers, onions . . . That should be a start. Vic, put those by the front. I'll ring it up later." Vic, cheerfully obedient, disappeared with the loaded cart, leaving Finn and Ana alone again. "Would you like some coffee or tea? We could have some out back. We could talk about taking care of all of this stuff."

Ana, hugely relieved by the invitation, smiled and realized that she was actually batting her eyes, which she stopped. Immediately. "I'd love that."

"Great, follow me." Finn led her to a green door and opened it. Inside was a small office with a desk and a computer, and a counter with a sink. Finn flicked the electric kettle on and pulled two mugs from a shelf above. "Hope peppermint is all right with you, Ana."

"Yeah, sounds good."

"Why don't you go out here?" Finn said, opening another door off to the right of the room. It led out to a small patio, completely shaded by a white canvas awning, under which was a round wooden table and two wicker chairs. "Let me make the tea. Just make yourself comfortable and I'll be out in a minute."

"Are you sure, Finn? I don't mind waiting with you. I'd feel weird just sitting there while you do all the work."

"Please, Ana, go outside and enjoy the weather."

"All right." Ana settled herself on one of the chairs and began flicking through a magazine he had on the table. When she looked up, she could see him through the window, opening his huge filing cabinets to pull out leaflets, lining up mugs and spoons on a tray. Was it her imagination, or were his hands shaking as he poured? Ana looked quickly back down at the magazine as the patio door opened again.

"Here we go," Finn said as he set the tray down on the table.

"Let me get those." Ana offered, and she stood behind him, placing one hand on the small of his back while with the other grabbing the papers from his arm. It seemed a natural thing to do, though she knew as soon as she touched him that it wasn't.

"So . . ." Finn said.

"So . . ." Ana responded. They looked at each other in silence. There were words, thousands of them, that Ana wanted to give him. The words had lined up inside her mouth since the day she had met him, but she did not know how to let them go, so she looked at him and said nothing.

"Right. Well, here are the instructions I was telling you about, and there's even a little diagram there that will tell you where the best place is to plant each thing. We could talk more about the garden, you know, if you have any questions . . . "

"No. I mean, if I do, I'll just call you." Ana squeezed honey onto a spoon, which she then submerged in her cup. And then, without thinking, she took the spoon out and stuck it in her mouth, sucking the remaining bit of honey onto her tongue. Finn's breathing shifted.

"Ana . . ."

"Yes?"

"Can I ask you a question?"

"Sure."

Finn smiled, but Ana wasn't sure if it was to himself or to her. "How much of you being here has to do with starting a garden, and how much of it has to do with seeing me?"

"My, my, Finn. That's a bold question." Dammit, thought Ana. She must be horribly obvious.

"Really, let's cut the bullshit here. Life is too short to dance around."

Ana felt suddenly, weirdly, confident. "Why would I do that, Finn? Why would I lay all my cards out on the table like that without being able to gauge where you're at yourself? That's not fair."

Finn's hands shot up in a conciliatory gesture. "No, I suppose it isn't. Okay . . . I'll say it. I can't stop thinking about you." He dragged his hand through his hair again; it was clearly a nervous tic of his. "Ever since I met you, I walk around feeling like I've forgotten to do something, like I'm missing something. And now that you're here in front of me, I realize it's you." She didn't think he meant to say so much, but she got the distinct impression that he couldn't help himself. "This is crazy: I'm married, you're married, and I don't even know you really, but being around you, it's . . ."

"Like striking the head of a match." Ana finished. Wow, where did that come from? Good one, Ana. She wondered where he got the courage to make such an admission. It was like watching an avalanche.

"Exactly."

The two of them looked at each other. Ana's stomach seemed to drop to the floor. Surely there was more to it than that? She didn't know anything about cheating and she barely remembered courting. She figured they would have danced around it for a while. But Finn was right: now that the two of them were together, it was obvious. She wanted to grab him and kiss him — hard. But her body wouldn't let her. She was nervous. He was nervous. So they both did nothing, other than sit and look at each other for a while.

"Finn, I love my husband. We've been together a long time. We're a team, we're a good team." Ana wanted Finn to know how much she cared about Jacob. She wanted him to know she wasn't a slut. "A long time ago, we were . . . you know, hot for each other or whatever. But it was nothing like this. This is pretty crazy, this attraction, right? Pretty off the charts?"

Finn looked like he was grasping for the right words too. She was sure he didn't want to come off as a slimy guy who cheats on his wife all the time. "Ana, I promise you that this not normal. I almost feel like I've been drugged. I haven't been, have I?"

"Finn, if I could bottle this, I would be just about the most powerful woman on earth, I think."

Finn laughed affectionately, and then there was more silence. Ana knew it was because they had to be so very careful with their words. The quiet wasn't awkward, just hopeful and maybe a little sad. Finn spoke again, and there was a seriousness to his voice that Ana wasn't sure she was ready for.

"You do realize, Ana, that now that we've actually said it, now that we've let it out into the world, there's just no way we can shove it back inside. But Ginny and I have been together since we were sixteen years old, and Janey isn't even three yet. I don't know what to do about this. I suppose the honorable thing is to just stay away from each other, but . . . "

"I don't want to do that, Finn."

"Neither do I."

Ana smiled, reached across and gently laid her hand on his.

After that, the lying began. A situation turns itself inside out, and the mind excuses the body. Ana left the nursery that day more confused and excited than she had ever been. Infatuation consumes, but it doesn't settle. Not the way Finn wrapped around her, making her feel both lit and secure all at once. She wanted to tell someone, wanted to tell everyone. She found herself pressing her hands into her chest, as if to close an opening that her feelings for Finn had created, but there was no stopping it. It poured out of her and into every action she did and every word she said.

They did not kiss that day; they did not even touch apart from when Ana touched the small of his back, and when she reached out her hand to his on the table. But they did agree to meet for lunch the following day.

Ana remembered going home with her plants, remembered feeling nervous as she opened the door, afraid that what had happened would be written all over her. But when she saw Jacob, she felt oddly relaxed. It was so easy to conceal. That was the moment when she felt herself break in two. There was her life with her husband, her son, her job, her home, and then there was this other self, the part of her that belonged to Finn. She felt no one had a right to that part; it was strictly her own.

From that point on, Ana became more tolerant, nicer to be around. But if she ever felt anyone coming close to intruding on that other self, she was all at once guarded and defensive. Jacob had known his wife well enough and long enough to understand something had shifted inside of her, but she became so angry when he tried to approach her about it that he let it drop, intuiting that there were some things people had to figure out on their own.

They began the kitchen garden that day, and Jacob marveled at Ana's vigilance. He had no way of knowing that Ana felt close to Finn when she dug into the earth, when she watered the plants he had given her, that to Ana, the garden was Finn.

Ana and Finn met the following day outside Avalon, a restaurant both of them liked on Mabon Road. They played their parts to the hilt for the lunchtime crowd bustling inside.

"Ana? What are you doing here?" Finn said. He was glowing. Ana didn't think she'd ever seen anyone who was so happy to see her.

"Oh, Finn, hello! I was just doing some shopping and I realized that I was about to faint with hunger. I haven't eaten all day. What are you doing here? Are you with Ginny?" said Ana, her voice catching slightly on his wife's name.

"No, she's at home. I had a consulting job close by this morning and I was just going to grab a quick bite before I headed back. Would you like to join me?"

"Yes, that would be lovely. I just hate eating alone." Both of them understood the need for the big show, or at least they thought they did. They figured that to look at them was to conclude they were lovers. It never occurred to them that they had tucked themselves so deeply, so neatly into their own little world that no one else really noticed them at all.

They put their names in with the hostess and after five minutes or so were shown to a perfect table far away from the window and set back almost in the corner. Avalon was not the fanciest restaurant in town, but it was one of the quaintest. As the name suggested, it had a somewhat medieval theme, reinforced by the one-hundred-year-old house it used to be. Even the cutlery looked somewhat primitive. But there was cutlery, proof positive that Avalon did not go overboard with its theme.

Ana and Finn sat down in a surge of nervous energy. Call it whatever: they were on a date. Ana lifted up her napkin, shook it out and placed it on her lap. Finn strummed his fingers lightly on the table.

"So . . . " Ana said.

"So . . . " repeated Finn.

"You know, I think we should eliminate that word from our vocabulary."

"I agree," Finn said, smiling.

Ana lowered her voice a little, aware of the people sitting close by. "God, I feel like I'm back in high school. Like I'm breaking curfew and I'm afraid my parents might catch me."

"Me too. Come to think of it, where did you go to high school?" Finn asked.

"Right here, Avening High. Obviously, you didn't, though. Where are you from originally, Finn?" Ana wondered if Finn was a man who disclosed easily.

"San Francisco." Finn looked up like he was remembering. Ana liked that look, filled with longing and nostalgia. He obviously wasn't bitter about his childhood. At least they wouldn't have that baggage to carry around.

"We moved to Avening about six years ago. I had an aunt who lived here, and I always loved it when my family visited her. We were pretty close; she was married but didn't have any children. When she died, she left everything to me, including her house, which was in pretty bad shape." He shrugged sadly. "She went a little crazy after my uncle died. I remember it used to be such a beautiful place, but it would have cost us so much money to renovate. I ended up tearing it down and building Bellaverde there instead. I'm sure she would have approved."

"I was wondering where you got that lot from! And now I know. So . . . Ginny's from Frisco, too?"

Ana saw him stiffen, just a little. "Oh God, are we really going to do this, Ana? Talk about them?"

She knew she probably shouldn't ask, but she was greedy for him. Greedy for any bit of anything that she could learn and take with her to think on later. "Well, I want to know you. I want to know everything about you. You've been with Ginny since you were a kid, which means that she's been involved in most of your life. I'm not trying to be morbid or anything. I just have to know why . . . why you chose her, and why you stay with her."

"Okay, but let's make a pact: let's talk about this now,

and then let's never mention them again. This has nothing to do with Ginny or Jacob." Ana watched him purse his mouth, searching for words. "I know it's crazy. But . . . for some reason, I don't feel like my feelings for you are betraying my wife. I mean, you can't control the way you feel about someone. But to talk about her . . . I guess I feel like that is betraying her in some way. I know she would hate it." Finn was uncomfortable, and it made Ana feel secure. He was not a naturally disloyal man, even as he was betraying the one person he promised not to.

"Good point. I agree," said Ana, nodding.

"Okay, well." So Finn began to tell Ana about Ginny, how they had started dating in high school, when Finn was only sixteen. She'd had a hard life, a bad childhood, and there was something about her that made him want to protect her. When he was around her, he'd felt like a man. They'd graduated and went to SFU together, where Ginny, being her practical self, had majored in accounting. He'd loved her, but in a day-to-day way, not a soul-searching one. "I mean, if you had asked me back then if we would still be together now, I would have said no way," he told Ana. "But it just became easier to stay together than be apart. We grew used to each other." When they had moved to Avening and started the nursery, it was Ginny's genius with numbers and good head for business that got the place off the ground. It was still Ginny who kept Finn from accidentally running them into the ground; she kept the books perfectly balanced, knew exactly how much money they could afford to risk on new plant buys each season based on their net profit from the season before, and found creative solutions for discounting or donating their unsold stock.

"There is a side of Ginny that no one has ever seen except me," he said. "I mean, I know people don't get her. They think she's cold and . . . awkward, I guess. But the truth is she has too much love to give. She never got to really give it to her parents, so she gives it all to me. Well, to Janey, too. I stay with her because I'm afraid of what would happen if I left. She's a fragile woman, Ana, and the mother of my daughter. I owe her a lot. I love her, I do, really, but it's a hard thing to be responsible for another person's happiness." A look of sadness settled on Finn's features.

Ana was torn: she felt sorry for Ginny, who had obviously had a tough life, but she was angry as well, furious that her weakness hung around Finn's conscience like dead weight. He deserved so much more out of life than a relationship more about duty and obligation than love and freedom. Afraid that her opinion would insult him, she said nothing.

"So what about Jacob, Ana? You guys seem, well, pretty happy with each other."

Ana thought for a moment about how to frame her answer. She was happy, on some level. Though now that she thought about it, contented might be a more appropriate word. She wished for a moment that she actually was miserable. That Jacob were a drunk or that he hit her so she would have some kind of a justification as to why she was sitting at that restaurant with a man who was not her husband.

"Oh, we are happy in a way. I mean, I love Jacob, but I'm not sure I ever really was in love with him. But we're good together. What was it that Gibran said in *The Prophet*? 'Let there be spaces in your togetherness,' I think. There are a lot of spaces in our togetherness. We married young, but we grew in the same direction. There's a lot of freedom in our relationship, to be our own people, to do our own thing. I think that's why I married him. I knew he would never try to control me."

"Do you think he's ever cheated on you?"

"He might have, but if he has, I don't want to know about it, and I know it hasn't affected our marriage in any way that I can tell."

"Have you ever cheated on him?"

Here it was, the subject that was woven around every word they had said so far, an invisible thread that both of them knew had to be pulled out and examined. "No, I haven't. What about you, Finn?"

Finn looked down at his hands. By his energy alone, Ana knew the answer.

"Yes, I have. I'm not proud of it but . . . I needed to connect with someone normal, you know? Ginny might go for days without really communicating with me. Some days she's just plain old mean, she puts me down, tries to make me feel bad about myself. I used to wonder why. I think it's because she hopes I'll think I'm not good enough for anyone else. Then there are some days, the good ones, when I think she realizes what a total bitch she's been and she absolutely smothers me with love. But it doesn't feel right, it feels forced, like she's playing the role of a good wife."

Ana sat back in her chair. Finn was making it very easy to dislike this woman, maybe too easy. But he had clearly given it a lot of thought, which was important to Ana. He was involved in his dysfunction, trying to sort it out as opposed to letting it happen all around him. The cheating made her nervous, but she kind of understood it.

"So you've seen other women," Ana said. It wasn't a question, just an open-ended statement, implying she needed more.

"I needed to feel intimate with someone without a past, you know?" He was looking down at his hands unhappily. "It's happened more than once, but certainly isn't something I do with any kind of frequency. I got glimpses of normal, and that has helped me gauge where I'm at in my marriage. It's messed up, I know, but . . . I'll tell you, Ana, if what's between you and me were just about sex, I would have been all over you yesterday at the nursery. Or at least given it my best shot. It's more than that, more complicated. I'm not sure I could just sleep with you. I'm afraid I'd want more."

Luckily, there was a lull in the conversation then as the waitress came and took their orders. Ana realized this was not the right venue for this particular conversation. But what could they do?

"Finn, sex is sex," Ana said after the waitress walked away, "but there are a thousand ways to betray. I have already cheated on Jacob mentally, and sitting right here, right now, sharing my life and my past with you, that's a betrayal, too. I don't know what to do, either. As much as I want you, I'm not sure it's the wisest thing to jump into right now. Maybe we should take it slow, see if this is just an infatuation or something more. Something that could really change our lives."

There was a tenderness in the way Finn looked at her, but there was a hint of skepticism too. Ana knew there was no "right way" to proceed. She allowed for the idea that she was misguided in the whole thing.

"I guess you're right," he said softly, "but in the same sense, you're talking about beginning a relationship, Ana, and that's a lot more duplicitous, in my eyes, at least, than having a quickie in some motel. Are you ready for that . . . that kind of lying?"

Was anybody ever ready for such a thing? She wasn't ready. But she was willing. She leaned in a fraction of an inch closer to him. "I am if you are. Because I know that if I were to walk away from you right now, I would regret it later on, I'm sure of it. I don't want that. I think we have to see this through to its natural conclusion." She nodded to punctuate herself. "Maybe we'll discover that it is really about companionship, maybe we'll figure out that it's all about sex, maybe it will be more . . . I don't know, but we have to find out."

"Okay, then," Finn said, almost angrily. He let a long breath escape.

Over the next few weeks, Ana and Finn saw each other as much as their lives would allow. It was hard to get away, hard to keep track of their excuses. They never talked on the phone, never sent e-mails or letters. They arranged each meeting at the rendezvous before. If one of them didn't make it, there was never anything more than disappointment. They would find a way to bump into each other and set a date for another time.

They rarely touched, using their words to reach out to each other instead, letting their stories penetrate in a way that sex simply could not. They soon found themselves bound to each other, but still unable to put a title or name to their relationship. And then there was one afternoon when everything changed, when Ana became instantly dissatisfied with their platonic arrangement, a day that set in motion everything that was to follow.

A parent of one of her students had given her a gift of an orchid, one she suspected was very rare. As soon as she set eyes on it, she knew she had to give it to Finn. He would appreciate it more than she ever could, and there was much less of a chance of it dying prematurely in his care. On a lunch break from school, she raced over to Bellaverde to give it to him.

Ana made sure he saw her as she entered the nursery. He was helping a customer and she casually walked past him, the orchid wrapped in tissue paper in her arms, and let herself into his office when she was sure no one was looking. A few minutes later the door opened, and Ana felt that now familiar tug in her chest at the sight of him.

"Well, this is a nice surprise! Aren't you supposed to be at work?" Finn said, moving closer to her.

"Lunch break. I don't have a lot of time, but I thought I'd stop by and give you this little present."

"A present? For me? What for?"

"Because you deserve it." She couldn't stop herself from smiling at him. "Because I can't stop thinking about you, and I'll take any excuse in the book just to see you. Go ahead, open it."

Finn took the package from her hands and gently kissed her forehead. He carefully opened the paper. "Oh my God, it's beautiful! It's a type of Vanda, isn't it? A tricolor. Where on earth did you get it?"

"One of my kid's parents. She's been growing a whole crop of them for ages, apparently. She got the seeds from some kind of orchid enthusiast club. Do you like it?"

"I love it. Thank you." Finn put the pot down and placed his hand on Ana's cheek. She closed her eyes. "I'll make sure to put it in a place where I can see it every day to remind me of you."

His touch hot on her cheek, Ana couldn't stand it anymore. "Finn, I . . . don't laugh, but I . . . I just want to smell you. Is that okay?"

Finn said nothing, but he stepped back from her and raised his eyebrows. Ana drew her hand up to the collar of his shirt, an old flannel that he was wearing over a tee. She slid two fingers inside at the neck and pulled the material away from his skin, then took two steps so that she was right up against him. She put her nose in his collarbone and inhaled. Keeping her two fingers where they were, she walked behind him and smelled the back of his neck and the small hairs that ended where his skin began. She noticed Finn's breathing become heavier.

Ana walked around to face him once again, giving him a half-smile. She turned around so that her back was up against his chest. Finn tried to return the caress, but Ana pulled away. She wasn't done. She grabbed his right arm and let it rest flat against her hip. Tenderly, she rolled up his cuff, making perfect folds until it sat neatly at his elbow. Then she picked up his hand with both of hers and smelled the length of his forearm. She stopped at his wrist and let her nose and her lips settle there to breathe him in. Then, without even thinking about the consequences, she pushed her tongue through her teeth and licked the exposed skin in one straight line. At his wrist, where his veins looked like a winter tree, she circled her tongue slowly two or three times. Finn moaned and spun Ana around.

Ana's eyes opened and her breathing concentrated in her chest, making it heave up and down in a rhythm that was much faster than normal. Slowly Finn kissed her, kissed her eyes and her nose and the side of her neck. When he finally moved to her lips, she felt almost faint. The feel of his mouth against her own sent a jolt that made her momentarily stiffen and then melt into the shape of his body. The kiss, which started out gentle and soft, swiftly moved into something hot and restless. Finn slid his hand down to her buttocks and picked her up, carrying her over to the desk. Her legs wrapped around him, her fingers wound around his hair. The need she felt was so intense that she momentarily forgot where she was. Something in the back of her mind, however, made her open her eyes, and the sight of Finn's small office brought her back to reality.

"Finn, honey, stop . . . please."

Finn stopped and looked at her. "Ana, for Chrissakes, don't ask me to stop now."

"Finn!" Ana spun out of his arms. "I'm not going to do this here. It's too dangerous, and we deserve more than fifteen minutes on a desk. Come on, I want you all to myself for hours and hours. I can't go back and teach a class after something like this."

"Ana, I love you. I mean it."

"You misunderstand me, Finn. The timing is what's wrong, that's all."

"Well when is it going to be right?" Finn was visibly in distress. "Ana, I want to be with you so badly it's killing me. If not here, then where? Where are these hours that you talk about magically going to appear?"

"I thought we agreed that we weren't going to take this next step until we figured out what we were going to do about what happens afterwards." She looked him in the eye. "Are you going to leave Ginny, Finn? I've already given my heart and soul to you; the only thing I have left is my body. If I give that to you too, where does that leave me? How am I supposed to function in a marriage when I have absolutely nothing of myself left to give my husband? If we do this, then I'm afraid it means that we do . . . the whole thing. Stop lying, stop denying, and really be together. Are you ready for that, Finn?"

He had distanced himself from her, looking away from her, past her. "I don't know, Ana."

"No, and neither do I, but . . . I . . . " Ana stopped, though she knew she had to say the dark and horrible thing that had been really bothering her lately. The thing that hadn't been clear in the beginning, but was coming more and more into focus each day. She put her fingers up to the skin around her eyes, unconsciously trying to smooth out the fine, almost invisible lines. "What if we're doomed, Finn? I mean, what we've done is so wrong. Falling in love, that's not wrong. But the lying, the betrayal: those are wrong on every level. We know now how big this thing is between us. But every day, every day we go home to our families with this secret. Every night we get into bed with different people. And it would kill them if they knew that as we lie there, we are wishing they were someone else. Can the universe really repay this kind of behavior with a 'happily ever after'? Do we even deserve one?"

There was silence between them. Ana's words were ugly, like a jinx. Maybe Finn had been thinking something similar, but he never would have said it. Why had she had to say it?

"So what, Ana? What should we do then?" Finn spat out angrily.

"I don't know." Tears welled in her eyes. "I don't know, but I know I love you, and I can't continue to function like this. It isn't healthy. We have to do something."

"Yeah. But what?"

Ana could no longer speak. All she could do was shake her head and walk out the door.

Getting through the rest of her afternoon was nearly impossible. Teaching twenty nine-year-olds was challenging at the best of times. But that day, after the final bell rang and her kids had left, she literally sank in her chair and put her head on the big oak desk in front of her. Retail therapy suddenly seemed like an excellent idea.

Ana parked her car across the street from Justy Bluehorn's at exactly 2:45 p.m. She knew spending a small fortune on a pair of shoes probably wouldn't go very far in terms of alleviating her guilt. But she also knew that on some level it would make her feel good, pretty, even optimistic. Ana put one feeling aside so she could experience the other.

In the rounded Dutch door of Justy's shop, Ana closed her eyes and allowed herself one full moment to breathe that perfect smell of leather and dye and something else, something exotic that she couldn't name. Being this close to so many beautiful shoes did something to her spiritually.

"Hey there, Ana."

Ana's eyes flew open, and she threw Justy a coy smile. "Hey yourself there, Mister. How are you?"

"Not as good as you, apparently. You look like you might just sprout wings and float. Life must be good." Justy examined her a little.

Ana knew Justy well enough to believe it was unwise to let him look for too long or too close. His instincts were uncanny. "Life is good," she said. "But . . . complicated."

"Well, maybe that's why it's so good, then."

Ana just smiled. There was no way he was going to bait her into saying anything. She chided herself momentarily for even mentioning complications. But Justy did that, made you say things that weren't even on your mind.

"So, what can I help you with today? What do you need?" he asked innocently.

"Oh, I don't *need* anything," Ana replied. "But I *want* a pair of your shoes. Something sexy and totally impractical. And for God's sake, please don't ask me why. Shoes are about all the therapy I can handle right now."

Justy stood back. "Ana, I've known you since you were a girl."

"I'm well aware, Justy."

"You are wearing this thing, missy. I won't make you tell me what it is, but I want you to know that I know."

Ana stopped herself from huffing. The arrogance! "Well of course you do, Justy," she said, deferring to his arrogance. "Not much gets by you, but at the end of the day, you are nothing if not discreet. So what you got?" She sat and slipped out of her shoes.

"Now, if I were a responsible man, I would give you a pair of these chocolate driving moccasins," he said as he held up a gorgeous pair of shoes. Then he put them down again. "But seeing as I am a cobbler in this day and age, you already know responsible isn't exactly my thing. So how about these?" Like a magician, he seemed to pull the single shoe out of nowhere. It was a black, stiletto snakeskin, with just a hint of a platform and a peekaboo toe.

"Oh, you glorious beautiful thing, you." Ana slipped it onto her foot. Of course it fit. Justy never had to ask what someone's size was. You never tried on more than one shoe in Justy's store unless you were going to buy more than one pair. "Where's the other one?"

"You sure now, Ana? These shoes are serious business," Justy said, his face as straight as a stretch of road.

"Just give me the other one, Justy."

The old man rolled his eyes and scooped up the twin from a bottom shelf.

"I'll take them, please." They made her feel like the kind of woman who walked down the street and was stared at and fantasized about. Like the kind of woman who had a lot of sex, and all of it good. Finn made her feel the same way. She couldn't walk down the street with Finn on her arm, but she could walk down the street with these shoes on her feet.

"Okay, Ana." Justy softened. "Everyone deserves at least one pair of bad girl shoes."

Ana fished her credit card out of her wallet and handed it over. She didn't even bother asking the price. It would probably nauseate her. She closed her eyes, thinking about the things she had to juggle into her day—Russ, Jacob, Finn, work, grading papers. She realized she had forgotten all her stress for these blessed moments in the shop, and it all came rushing back to her.

Justy returned the credit card slip for her to sign on an old-fashioned service tray. "What is it?"

She sighed. "Nothing. I just have a lot to do. And sometimes I feel like, I don't know, like . . . time just screws with me. I have so much to do and like five minutes to do it in. You know what I'm saying?"

"Sure I do, honey." Justy helped her stand and put a reassuring arm around her waist, as if he were about to lead her out onto the dance floor. "But you just bought these shoes here. And the owner of these shoes isn't a slave to time. That's far too gauche for her. So relax and take all the time you need."

Ana laughed and gave him a kiss on the cheek. The door tinkled and chimed behind her as she closed it. She got in her car and rested her head against the seat. Ana looked at her watch, and then tapped its face. It said 2:46; according to her watch, she had only been in Justy's store for one minute. Ana groaned as she mentally added the repair shop to her list. Then she looked at the clock on her dash. 2:46. She shook her head. She was probably just losing her mind.

The situation was past the point of being something she

could simply figure out on her own. She needed an unbiased opinion. When Ana finally made up her mind to tell someone, she felt a pressure lift from the place between her shoulders. She did need help, and she knew exactly where to go to get it.

Ana told her son that he would have to stay at school in the day care program for a couple of hours. He seemed neither pleased nor displeased, reacting with a resolved indifference more suited to an old man than a boy of just under ten. This was her fault entirely, her feelings for Finn having made her de-prioritize Russ in her life. He, in turn, had begun to extract himself little by little from her. She was losing him because of her distraction. Before she left, she gave Russ a huge hug, smothering him in her arms and kissing the side of his face. She had told him she loved him, and he responded, instinctively knowing her desperation, by letting her run through the emotional good-bye without trying to squirm himself away.

ℒ

Autumn Avening's store was not far from the school. She stopped the car in the nearby parking lot and ran her thumb and forefinger along her closed eyes. She knew she was doing the right thing, but once she told another person about what was happening between her and Finn, it would become that much more real, that much less magical. Although Ana was sure her relationship with Finn was nothing close to ordinary, she was terribly afraid that for some reason Autumn would see it that way.

It was a day for confidences, the clouds covering the sky

in a gray vigilance that made the night feel close at hand. Ana climbed the four steps to Demeter's Grove. When she opened the door, a flurry of bells announced her arrival. There was something about being here that made her muscles relax, and she noticed that she had unknowingly been clenching her jaw.

Ana found her friend organizing a bookshelf, her cat, Willow, weaving between her legs.

"Finally, Ana!" Autumn called, her back still to the door. "My goodness, it took you long enough. I put the kettle on. It should be boiling, so why don't you go to the kitchen and make some tea."

"Miss Psychic Show-off," Ana told Autumn fondly, her affection for her old friend momentarily overcoming her anxiety. She dipped into a rounded hallway and into the familiar kitchen, which immediately engulfed her in its cloud of eucalyptus and cloves. Ana knew her way around; she had been coming here regularly since she was a teenager. She pulled a tray from the cupboard and set the tea service. When she emerged, she found Autumn in her favorite green velvet chair. Ana placed the tray on the small table in front of it and sat down.

Like every other resident of Avening, Ana had no idea how old Autumn was. It was the stuff of legend. She didn't look old, and she didn't look young: she was suspended somewhere between the two. Autumn claimed that she was mostly a Celt, but for a Dutch grandfather and a Native American grandmother, a combination that gave her somewhat exotic looks. Her blue-black hair was cut in a pixie style, her eyes were green, and her cheekbones were high and defined. Today, she wore a black turtleneck and straight-legged pants, Audrey Hepburn-style.

Autumn gave Ana a long, unblinking look. "Really, Ana, why have you waited so long to come and see me?"

"Autumn, don't start. I was just hoping that I could figure this one thing out on my own. But clearly . . ."

"Relax, I'm not giving you a hard time. I just wish you understood better about how things are supposed to be. We are women: if we have a problem, we get together; we solve it together. That's what we do. We aren't men, holding everything inside. You're going against your nature, making things harder on yourself. Just admit it. You love another man. It's written all over you."

Ana paused before answering, only because it seemed so obvious. Why hadn't she told Autumn? Maybe, she thought to herself, the secret was part of why it felt so good and bad all at once. Either way, it was time to talk.

"Okay, I'm in love with him, but I . . . it wasn't on purpose. And I thought there was a chance it was just a crush, or even lust, something that, in the grand scheme of things, was harmless."

"That's horseshit, Ana. You knew exactly the way you felt from the moment you set eyes on Finn Emmerling, and I must say, I'm not surprised." Autumn took a sip of tea.

"You're not?" Ana was past the point with Autumn of asking how she knew she was in love, how she knew it was Finn. Ana wanted to believe in the extraordinary, and she saw it aplenty with Autumn.

"Goodness no," Autumn replied. "Don't get me wrong, I like Jacob. He's a good man, and he's good for you, but I knew from the beginning that he wasn't your soul mate. I really do detest saying that—it's a silly sounding sort of word—but still, it fits. I also knew that one day you would draw that person, that soul mate, to you. You are a very powerful woman, Ana."

Ana balked. "I don't feel very powerful right now. I feel quite the opposite, actually."

"Oh, Ana," Autumn said tenderly, "this is an awfully difficult thing for you to deal with on your own. How are you managing?"

Ana felt tears pool in the corners of her eyes. She felt like she deserved a lecture on her behavior, and Autumn's kindness and empathy were overwhelming in a way she had not been prepared for.

"Take a moment, Ana. Really, it's all right. You can't choose who you fall in love with, let alone when it happens. This too is part of the journey. You're a good person, or else you wouldn't be here asking for my help. I know your marriage is pretty good; how is his?"

Ana considered everything Finn had told her before answering. "I feel bad saying this, but I don't think it's very good at all, and I don't think it has that much to do with me." She shook her head. "Autumn, I am so confused. I'm perfectly happy in my life, you know, with Jacob and Russ. I love them. They're my family. And at the same time I'm desperate to run away with Finn." She knit her fingers together, trying to sort through her own feelings. "Finn and I are not, you know . . . intimate. But it's getting to the point where we have to be. I know this sounds ridiculous, but it hurts, physically, not to be able to be with him, like I'm burning up from the inside out. But if we take that step, there's no turning back. It's not right to Jacob, or to Ginny. They both deserve more." Ana looked away from Autumn. There was so much more than those few words, but she suddenly lacked the strength to find them. She could only hope that Autumn would understand, from experience or intuition, and be able to guide her in the right direction.

"Well," said Autumn. "More than anything it sounds like a question of bad timing. Listen, my dear, let me absolve you. You have done nothing wrong . . . so far. Love is a gift from the gods, and you have been granted it twice, which makes you very lucky indeed. But there are as many different kinds of love as there are people in the world. The love you have for Jacob is a steady, solid thing. But the love you have for Finn? That is the truest, purest love we can be blessed with. And of course it hurts. Nothing that feels that good could ever be ignorant of its darker twin."

Ana looked at her old friend, already feeling better. Her mind was clearing, allowing the probable outcomes to take shape inside her head.

"Let's talk about time, shall we, dear?" Autumn put her cup of tea down on the table.

"Time? But—"

"Time is the greatest obstacle you and Finn face right now. There are two kinds of time: the one that man makes, and the one that makes man. We arrange our days according to the former, and think we're clever to have created a system the entire world can move to. So we race about to keep up with time, never feeling like there are enough hours in the day."

"But Autumn, what's that have to do with me? And Finn?"

Autumn ignored the question and kept talking. "But the latter is where the magic lives, in our own bodies. It's part of the wheel, the biological clock that ticks away, telling us when to sleep, when to eat, when to reproduce and so forth. If we keep these clocks in tune with the rest of the natural world, they also tell us when to plant, when to sow, when to harvest, when to gather and store. This is where your love for Finn lives: in time without numbers or divisions. Your life with Jacob is wrapped up in the man-made structure. So how do you reconcile the two?"

"I don't know. That's why I'm here, talking to you."

"Ana, sweetheart, you know I can't tell you how to reconcile them. Only you and Finn are capable of doing such a thing. But I will tell you this: no true happiness can ride on the back of someone else's pain."

There it was, exactly what Ana had feared. What was the point of causing so much pain and so much destruction if they wouldn't be together in the end? It seemed suddenly pointless, or hopeless, or both. Ana's longing turned, in a split second, to anger. The whole situation felt suddenly so unfair that she clenched her fists unknowingly.

"So that's it? The 'gods' have seen fit to give me a gift that I can never open? That's cruel, Autumn." Ana felt her anger rising, uncontrollable. "I mean, I go back to living my life, he goes back to living his, neither of us ever truly happy? And meanwhile, we're distracted, and resentful, and end up taking it out on our children and spouses, and letting our unhappiness turn us into mean, unloving people?" Ana shook her head furiously. "I'm a good person, Autumn, but not that good. I'm not going to live out the rest of my days with a grocery list of regrets so that Ginny Emmerling can be happy with my man."

Autumn set her lips. "Ana, stop thinking in the realm of time as you know it. We are given just the right amount of time to get done what we are supposed to in life."

"What are you saying? That I have to wait for my next life to be with Finn? I don't think so."

"Maybe, maybe not." Autumn shrugged. "I'm not completely sold on the whole reincarnation thing, to be honest with you. If you're supposed to be together in this life, though, your natural clocks and the universe will clear the way—something that, as of yet, hasn't happened."

"Autumn, I love him. I can't just turn that off like a tap. I think about him about a million times a day. Now that we know each other, we can't just go back."

Autumn leaned in to her friend, looking her straight in the eye. "Let me ask you something, Ana. What's the most important thing in your life?"

"My son," said Ana, without hesitation.

"Right, and my wager is that Finn would say the same thing about his daughter. So those two people come first. There has been a significant amount of betrayal, not just to your spouses but to your children. I'm not busting you. Clearly, you were too close to see it. But this is where you went wrong. The sneaking around and the lying have done a fair bit of damage, I'm afraid. 'Polluted everything' would be the right phrase." Ana knew it was true already, but hearing Autumn spell it out brought instant tears to her eyes. Autumn went on, "But the damage is done. Now we just have to find a way to deal with this. I think I have a way to help you, but I had to give you the hard truth first, as your friend, though I know it hurts to hear."

"No. I mean, yes, it's hard to hear. But I know you're doing it out of love." Ana had to force herself to swallow her own desperate optimism. "You have a way to help, though? Really, Autumn?"

Autumn obviously hesitated. "Well. I want you to arrange a time when both you and Finn can come and see me. I need to tell both of you together how it will work, since I don't want anything lost in translation, okay?"

Ana was giddy with excitement. She trusted Autumn enough to know that anything she suggested would indeed be the best solution for everyone involved.

"So give me a couple days," Autumn continued, "and then, well . . . We'll see. Now go and pick up your son. I've got lots of work to do."

They both stood, and Autumn followed Ana to the door. Before she left, Ana turned to face her friend. "Autumn, whatever happens, whether this idea of yours will work, I want you to know that you've helped me already. You are a good soul and a good friend, and I can't tell you how much your words today have meant to me."

"I know, I know," said Autumn, pulling Ana into a long embrace. Ana felt a piece of herself break open in her friend's arms, and she walked out the door that much closer to finding her way.

ℒ

Autumn let the door slide closed with a soft click. She must have been mad to promise such a thing to Ana, but what could she do? Ana was on the list. She couldn't have her directing all her magical energy to a miserable domestic situation.

This whole thing was getting unexpectedly messy. Autumn had put her own needs first, selfishly, before those of her friend. But on the other hand, perhaps her selfish behavior would work out for the best; she could kill several birds with one stone — save two marriages, make six people happier, and test Ana's true ability. She felt guilty about it, but she knew that all of this was for the greater good. She just wished it actually felt good getting to the greater good.

ℒ

The next day, Ana did something she had never done: she called Finn at Bellaverde. Luckily, he was the one who answered the phone.

"Bellaverde." There was something in his voice, something sad and caught that made Ana's heart lurch.

"Hi. It's me."

There was a momentary pause. The seconds seemed like minutes. "Hi, me," he answered at last. Ana could tell he was smiling.

"Do you have a minute? I need to talk to you."

"Yeah, I'm just in the office going over the deliveries from this morning. What's going on?"

Ana felt her pulse race, and her mouth go dry. Why

was she so scared? She was a grown woman, and she certainly didn't need Finn's approval for anything. "Well, first of all, you're probably not going to like what I'm about to tell you, but I had to do something. Yesterday was so . . . difficult, and it made me realize that I needed some help."

"You told someone, didn't you?" The silence that followed was a good enough yes. "Jesus, Ana, why the hell did you do that?" Finn's voice was angry in the earpiece. "Who was it?"

"I'm not going to argue with you, Finn," Ana said breathlessly. "All you need to know is that I did what was best for me. For us, actually. I needed someone else's opinion to get some clarity. I told Autumn Avening. She's my oldest friend, not to mention my wisest. I trust her completely, and she says she may have a way to help us."

In Finn's silence, Ana could hear him mulling this over. Everyone knew Autumn, and everyone knew her reputation as the de facto village wisewoman. Ana hoped he would come to the conclusion that consulting Autumn was akin to consulting a priest or a rabbi or any other kind of spiritual adviser.

"What kind of help, exactly?" he said at last.

"She didn't say. She wants to tell us both in person, which is why I'm calling. Is there any way that you could make some time tomorrow to go and see her? I have the day off, so . . . "

"Yeah, I could probably get away around lunchtime, say twelve-thirty?"

Ana was surprised Finn was being so accommodating;

she thought she was going to have to do a lot of convincing. And then the conversation was over, not because they didn't have anything left to say, but because they simply had too much.

The next day, Finn sat in a back room at Demeter's Grove and looked anxiously from Autumn to her colorful store. It was complex and diverse, exemplifying everything he had learned so far about women. He was smart enough to understand, however, that no matter how long or how carefully he observed, no matter how diligently he listened, the darker and more mythical aspects of women would remain as hidden from him as a new moon. It made him uncomfortable, made him feel like an outsider. He crossed and uncrossed his legs.

"There's no need to be nervous, dear," said Autumn with a smile. "You won't find any cauldrons or Shakespearian crones about. Our approach to the spiritual is thoroughly painless, I promise you."

Finn managed a little laugh. Autumn made him both anxious and calm all at once, a feeling he hadn't ever experienced before, and one he wasn't sure he liked.

"I won't torture you two any longer. I think you've done enough self-torturing to last a lifetime. I have a plan to help you out of your problem. But be warned, when I say out, I mean out."

Now Finn was alarmed. "What? Like dying or something?"

"Finn, I told you Mr. Shakespeare is not in residence; no melodrama here. So relax." Autumn gave him a smile Finn thought looked suspiciously patronizing. "No, no. Oh my, how shall I begin? I've said before that the main problem both you and Ana face is a question of time. Of timing, to be more precise. Would you agree?"

"Absolutely," said Finn, nodding.

"Well, I have to ask you now to forget everything about time as you know it. Time is not a solid, linear thing, no matter how much man tries to pretend it is. Time has humored us, much like a parent does a child, bending this way and that, to make us think we have the upper hand, but make no mistakes: we do not. There are levels and dimensions of time, unimaginable twists and nooks that our puny brains cannot even begin to understand."

Finn struggled to wrap his mind around her implications. "Are you saying . . . you can stop time?"

"Why yes, Finn, I believe I can."

Autumn said it so casually that at first Finn thought she must be joking. But then he saw the serious expressions on her face, and on Ana's. "No way. Not even you can do anything like that."

"I asked you to throw everything you think you know about time out the window. I can stop time, or at least a part of it. I can make a few hours live outside of the normal context of time as you understand it."

Finn looked over at Ana; she seemed thoroughly credulous, but he wasn't sure he even understood what he was being told. "You can . . . create hours that don't exist? For . . . for us to be together? Is that it?"

Autumn gave him one sharp nod. "The memories of such time will exist, just not in any part of your mind that you will be able to access."

"Let me get this straight," Ana said. "We can do whatever we want, but it won't count, because according to the clocks around us, it will never have happened?"

"Something like that, yes."

"And then . . . we won't remember it?" There was some struggle on Ana's face; she wasn't sure if she hated that idea or loved it.

"That's right," Autumn said.

"But what's the point?" countered Finn. "That will just bring us back to where we are right now."

"No, because that's only part of it. In order for this to work, it has to be done on Beltane, a very magical and fertile night. Whatever you two do will be planting a seed."

"Wait, what do you mean, a seed?" Finn broke in nervously. Ana was fingering her blouse around her stomach; she was clearly thinking the same thing.

"Not a physical seed, Finn," Autumn said. "Don't worry; I wouldn't trick you two into getting pregnant. That would be horrible for you both right now." She smiled kindly. "I mean more like a seed of the future, a metaphysical seed of what might be. The seed will grow, or not grow, depending on you, and not because of what each of you want, but rather what each of you need. It will give each of you the time to figure out what must be done, according to your own clocks, at a much more lenient pace than the emotional roller coaster of love at first sight. Think of it like having a past life experience. But . . ."

"There's always a but," Ana said sadly. "What is it, Autumn?"

"Nothing comes without sacrifice. The spell will work at the expense of your feelings, and your memories of each other so far."

There was a moment of dead silence. "Wait a minute," Finn said finally. "What you're saying is that after we get these few 'non-hours,' we won't remember any . . . anything that's happened between us up 'til now? We won't have any recollection of the feelings we have for each other?" Finn shook his head. "I'm not sure I like this at all. That's like mind control or something."

Autumn leaned forward, her voice gentle but direct. "Finn, I asked Ana to tell me what she thought was the most important thing in her life, and she said that without question it was Russ. It would be the same for you and your daughter, am I right?"

"Yes . . ."

"She also hinted that her feelings for you were alienating her from her son. Not to mention the karmic payback that you both may have coming to you based on how you have managed this situation. So, the two of you can go on the way you have been, hurting everyone you care most about. Or you can do it this way, which ultimately may or may not hurt those same people, but at least it won't devastate them. It's your decision; believe me, I'm not going to force this on anyone."

"I don't need to think about it," Ana said with conviction. "I want to do it, Autumn."

"But what if this seed takes fifty years or something?"

Finn asked. "What if, by the time we find our way to each other again, we are too old to enjoy it?"

Autumn blinked her long green eyes at him patiently. "Again, I would ask you to stop thinking about time as a tangible thing, a line that stretches from point A to point B. Your inner self will be your guide. The deepest, truest self connects with a greater power and has no sense of increments of time, only of the journey itself, and what you learn on the way. Your intuitive self will know when the time is right to clear the path for you to be together, if that is indeed your destiny. The seed you plant on Beltane night will sprout and grow, make itself known to you at that time. You should know better than anyone, Finn, that a garden will flourish when it's good and ready."

Somewhere in the back of Finn's mind, there was a small voice encouraging him to say yes. Over the years he had learned to trust this voice. He looked at Ana, this woman he loved more than anything, and realized that she was worth waiting for, worth waiting his whole life for if necessary, and other lives too. He placed his hand on her knee, which fit snugly, perfectly, and nodded.

"There is one thing I would ask of you," Autumn said. "I want each of you to write the other a letter. If you two find a way to be together again, then I will find a way to get these letters to you. I don't like dishonesty. I especially don't like the fact that I will have to keep such a thing from you, Ana. One day, I will want you, both of you, to know what has happened here. Knowing the sacrifices each of you made for your families will make your love story that much greater. Do you agree to this?"

They both agreed, and walked out of Autumn's store in

a kind of daze, each to their separate cars on the busy street, like two strangers.

Dear Ana,

I suppose if you are reading this, then we have found a way in the course of our lives to be together. I hope I am not a doddering old man, I hope I am still young enough to hold you, to bend and move inside you in the magnificent way our love deserves. From the moment I saw you, I knew my life had changed its course. I understood momentarily the nature of all things and maybe, just maybe, why it is that I was born. Six weeks can be a lifetime, as it is for some creatures. This was only the first chapter of our love, and like so many beautiful things, it was fleeting and miraculous, only living long enough to float just under the heavens without being touched by everything ugly and tainted in the world. Despite what Autumn says, I cannot, will not believe I will forget every-thing so far. I believe there will be something that lingers, something my senses will cling to. I will find a way to remember my way back to you, my love, and know that somewhere, somehow, you were always close.

With all of my love,
Finn

At 4:45 on Beltane evening, after a luxuriating afternoon of group spiritual cleansing and self-indulgent pampering with other Avening women, Ana sat on an old loveseat in one of the many nooks of Demeter's Grove. Both her fingernails and toenails were wet, which meant that she couldn't really do anything but stare, watching the goings-on inside the shop and grabbing snippets of the conversations that drifted within earshot.

In a chair across the room sat Piper Shigeru. Ana wouldn't exactly have said that she and Piper were friends; acquaintances would have been a better description. Ana had been Piper's daughter's teacher a couple of years ago, and of course Ana had read all of Piper's books; every mother, father, and teacher in Avening (and most other places) had. But looking at Piper now, so still and small in the great overstuffed chair, Ana wished she had tried harder to befriend her. Autumn had told Ana that Piper was sick, but until this moment Ana had no idea how ill she truly was.

Ana looked down at her pale pink fingers and breathed a deep sigh. If she was any kind of woman at all, she would go over there and talk to Piper, but she couldn't force her body to move. Truth be told, Ana didn't even want to look at Piper, let alone talk to her. Her suffering was too close, too painful, too real.

Instead, she closed her eyes and thought, not without a pang of guilt, about the better parts of the day. The two lectures, one on graceful passages through the maiden-mother-crone stages of life and the other on creating sacred spaces in your home, were both informative and entertaining. The massage and the mani/pedi had gone a long way toward soothing her frayed nerves. She could now even sit somewhat harmoniously in her surroundings, as ready as she could be for what was about to happen.

When she opened her eyes, she looked to where Piper Shigeru had been sitting, only to discover the seat empty. Instead, Autumn was there talking to someone familiar. The woman was older but small, petite and elfin, her hair was short and silver. She was the type of woman who could have gotten away with being mistaken for someone much younger if she'd done away with the gray. It was Eve Pruitt, another good friend of Autumn's, whom Ana couldn't help but like. Eve was Avening's trained pharmacist; the only time she'd left the island was to go to a top pharmacy program on the mainland, many, many years ago, back when it was still unusual for women to earn that kind of degree. She owned and operated Eve's Apothecary on Brigid's Way. She also had a reputation for concocting non-chemical herbal supplements, of course. No one would expect less of a close friend of Autumn's.

Ana remembered the first time she came to Eve on her own. She'd been fifteen and desperate, in love with Monty Sherman. She stood there in front of the wood counter and stammered and begged for a love potion. Eve returned with a small paper bag.

"Is this it?" Ana asked.

"No, honey," Eve said kindly. "You wouldn't want to be with anyone you had to trick into feeling strongly about you. It would be a lie." Eve pushed the bag into Ana's shaking hand. "You drink this instead. Directions are on the bag."

"So . . . What is it then?"

Eve answered a little sadly, like she knew exactly how Ana felt. "It's tea to ease a broken heart." Which is, after all, sometimes all you need when you're a fifteen-year-old girl. That wasn't the last time Ana went back for that particular set of herbs, and others, over the years. Now, she walked over to the two women who were deep in conversation, their heads bowed.

Ana wasn't uncomfortable interrupting. "Hi, Eve. How are you?"

"Oh, Ana," Eve answered, letting go of an audible breath. "Hello, dear. I'm fine. Really well. I was just talking to Autumn about our Piper."

"I didn't know she was so sick," Ana said, lowering her voice. "I heard, but it's different when you see it."

Eve's eyes were wet with her trademark compassion. "I've tried every trick up my sleeve, and so has Autumn, with no luck."

"Did you both think . . . that you could cure her, or something?" Ana didn't really know what they thought they could do, or how far their expertise went.

"No," Autumn said, shaking her head ever so slightly. "I think we're past that now. We were both just trying to ease the pain somewhat, and the fear." Eve looked down, and Autumn glanced at her. "I was just trying to explain to Eve that Piper is on her own path now. Her body is determined, and maybe she is too.

"Yes, and I was just saying that I find your fatalism truly annoying, Autumn," Eve said with a sharp chuckle. "But how are you, Ana? Everything okay?" Eve raised her eyebrows ever so slightly. Ana wondered what she had written on her face.

"I'm fine," Ana answered, trying to keep her voice level. "I'm good."

Eve nodded and smiled broadly. "Well, you come by and see me if you need anything, even if it's just a chat, okay?" She was so earnest that it made Ana tired. She couldn't do much but give Eve a quick hug and return to the couch, where she had a full view of Autumn's antique grandfather clock. Ana watched the hands crawl around on its ornate face, and waited.

Autumn stayed next to Ana as she said good-bye to her guests. As twilight descended, she took Ana's hand and led her out the back, through the wild patches of a well-tended English garden to the small guesthouse that sat at the farthest reaches of her yard. Ana was aware of the sounds of birds and insects, of her feet moving lightly along the gravel path that led to the door. But she felt, at the same time, oddly disconnected, as if her body instinctively knew it had to let go.

Autumn had lit dozens of candles in the cottage, each one giving off a smell of warm spices. Fresh flowers sat on the bedside tables, the desk and the dresser, and the windows were open, letting a slight breeze ruffle the thin cotton curtains.

"Are you ready, Ana?"

"Yes, I am." Ana sat on the bed, but took her friend's hand. "I won't get a chance to thank you for this, for everything you've done for Finn and me. I will be blissfully ignorant, but you will have to carry this around for God knows how long. Words are just not enough, but . . . thank you, Autumn. You are changing my life."

Autumn gave her a beatific smile. "I believe I am help-ing you. And, well, that's part of my job, part of my journey. I know you're scared, but I have a feeling this will all work out for the best. Now we need to make some preparations. Take your robe off, please."

Ana slid off the Japanese kimono she had donned before leaving the store, completely comfortable with her own nakedness in front of Autumn. Beside the bed was a small brush and glass jar of paint, which Autumn picked up. "I'm going to have to paint some symbols on you, but don't worry, they will wash off." Ana nodded and closed her eyes.

Delicately, Autumn began to move the brush across Ana's skin. The pleasant sensation centered Ana and seemed to bring her closer to the power of the mystical Beltane night. When Autumn was done, Ana looked down and saw small characters painted in various locations on her body: her fore-arms, thighs, stomach and forehead all decorated with sym-bols she did not recognize.

"I'll have to do this for Finn as well. Actually, he should be here any moment, so I'm going to go inside the store and wait for him. Are you all right? Anything you need?"

"No, I'm fine. You go and wait for Finn."

Autumn smiled and slipped out the door, leaving Ana, who had put her robe carefully back on, alone on the big white bed. She did not know how long she sat there; already, her mind seemed to be sliding away from the boundaries of time. She heard them walk quietly in before she actually saw them. At the sight of Finn, covered in the same symbols and in a thin white robe, Ana had to brace herself, her fingers clenching the sheets beneath her.

"Go ahead and sit down beside Ana, Finn." When Finn did as he was instructed, Autumn went over to a tray that she had brought with her. She poured two steaming cups from a small brown teapot. "I want you to drink this, please."

"What is it?" asked Ana.

"Something that will help . . . with the process."

"Is it some kind of drug or something?" asked Finn, a look of suspicion on his face.

Autumn laughed kindly. "It's something, but don't worry, you won't hallucinate or anything like that."

"Wait a minute . . . How are we supposed to know that what is about to happen is really magic and not some kind of drug-induced amnesia?"

Autumn shrugged. "Faith, I suppose. Regardless, you must drink this in order for tonight to work."

Ana needed no more than that and drank her cup down in a matter of seconds. Finn looked at Ana with great concentration, then seemed to make a decision and drank.

"Good." Autumn took the cups from their hands and placed them back on the tray. "Well, that's it. I'll be back in a few hours. I know this is . . . difficult for both of you, but please, try to enjoy it. Open up and let the experience become part of you." Autumn smiled briefly, and left the room.

Upstairs in her study, Autumn stood calmly and went through her Initiate Lessons. They were as natural to her now as breathing. They centered and steadied her so she could access the kind of magic she needed to. The elements sat close, and threw off their own kind of steady hum, an energy like a song. She opened her arms, and spoke the words to the spell in an ancient, now forgotten language known only to the Jaen. She could sense Finn and Ana both, but mostly Ana, who had no idea how much her own magic and not Autumn's was making this all happen.

Autumn wondered if Ana knew the amount of power gathered in her genes. It would be such a waste . . . Autumn shook her head and concentrated. Now was not the time to think about it. She centered her thoughts instead on Finn and Ana's love and desire for each other, and their auras burning into a deep berry red. She pictured another circle around the two, a rainbow of brilliant lights enveloping them. Then she steadied herself and opened a doorway across time.

℮

Finn was cautious, at first, to touch her. His fingers reached out gently to slip the robe from her shoulders. When she was naked, he moved in to her neck, to the place where her hair and skin gathered, to get a true sense of what she smelled like, copying those same movements that had so undone him days before. Her scent invaded his nose and shot through his bloodstream.

Ana closed her eyes and let out a sigh. She wanted to float away, she wanted both of them to leave behind their bodies and connect someplace entirely other. But then she knew that it was her senses that truly needed this first experience and she wanted to drench them, every single one of them, in Finn. Ana opened her eyes and roughly pulled his robe away. The sight of his naked body made her breath catch in her throat.

With both hands she pulled his face to hers, giving him a long, deep kiss. She then climbed on top of him, wrapping her legs around the small of his back. It was the urgency of the first time, the need to feel him inside her, that made Ana realize they had already had six weeks of foreplay. When he entered her, she cried out and then lost her place.

It didn't take Finn long. He had known it wouldn't, not after waiting and fantasizing about this very moment for so long. The climax wasn't really a climax, though, because he was far from done. At that moment he knew she was indeed his soul mate. There was none of that usual awkwardness or fumbling; their bodies knew exactly how to move against each other. And he felt somehow complete, finished and understood, in a way he had never felt before.

He then lay Ana down on the bed and began to touch her. He touched every single inch of her, turning her gently this way and that until his fingers knew her. When he was done, he did the same with his tongue, so that sense, too, could be satiated.

Tears sprung from Ana's eyes. She felt like she had never let anyone so close, that Finn had truly seen her, every single thing, both beautiful and horrible, about her. She also knew he accepted these things, had taken them into himself so that he could, in some way, become her. It was more than sex, it was something alive. It was living.

In the end, when they knew their time was growing

short, the animal inside each of them crept away, full and drowsy, on instinct alone. Finn lay on top of Ana, inside her, aroused, but somehow not sexually. They had not spoken a word yet, but now it was time. He kissed her face.

"I love you, Ana, always, always . . . "

"And I love you." She pulled him as close as he could get. She whispered in his ear. "We are blessed." And then came the quiet knock on the door.

Autumn had each of them bathe quickly but separately. Neither one talked: the spell was beginning to work and their individual minds were caught up in hiding those secret hours. They said good-bye with a long embrace, then Autumn led Finn to his car, laying her hands on his face to make sure he would get home safely. Then, as Ana rocked back and forth in a rocking chair, Autumn changed the sheets. When she was done, she put Ana in a cotton shift and led her to the bed. She tucked her in as if she was a child, blew out the candles. Ana was asleep before Autumn even closed the door behind her.

Finn awoke at 8 a.m., much later than usual. Not even the strong shafts of sunlight through the window had managed to rouse him. He rubbed his eyes and reached across the bed, remembering suddenly that Ginny was at her parents'. He had slept well and deeply, not remembering the last time he had slept a full night so soundly and without interruption. He remembered he had dreamt something, something wonderful and exhilarating, but the dream eluded him. He got up and went down the stairs to the kitchen. He drank his morning coffee to the sounds of the birds outside and the clock above the stove ticking away. He was alone. With a pang of guilt, he realized he liked it.

"I'm home!!" Ana called out as she walked through the door. She had a sudden feeling of déjà vu, as Jacob and Russ were almost in the same exact places she had left them the day before.

"Hi!" they answered in unison.

"So how was it? Did you go to the maypole?"

"Yeah, it was so cool, Mom. People were dressed up in, like, clothes from the olden days, and there was music and hotdogs and I got my face painted."

"Sounds like fun. I'm almost sorry I missed it."

"What about you, honey? Do a lot of female bonding?" Jacob asked.

"Loads and loads. I'm all estrogened out, as a matter of fact. Thanks, though, for giving me the day off."

"No problem. I'm glad you had fun."

"I'm going to take my stuff upstairs. I'll be down in a sec." Ana climbed up the short flight of stairs and into her bedroom. She looked through her bag, and then looked again. She had a feeling she had forgotten something at Autumn's, but she shrugged it off, knowing her friend would tell her about anything she found. She looked at her alarm clock. 9:09. She checked herself briefly in the mirror. "Hmmm," she thought. Hmmm, and hmmm, and hmmmm.

My dearest Finn,

What an adventure . . . It seems fitting that this first part of our story will end in a kind of miracle, because everything so far between us has brought me that much closer to God. I am not a writer, I am not a natural observer of things. I tend to let life happen all around me, and take those happenings as a given. But since the day I met you, I started thinking and wondering and questioning; you have done that, you have made me break through the surface, push my hands through it and pick through the things on the other side.

We have work to do, you and I, we have the threads of many lives to reweave. I have faith, so very much faith, that we can do this. When the web is rewoven, we'll find those strands that we thought were too fragile and incomplete, and they will lead us on a clear and steady path to each other.

Already I have made a space for you inside. I imagine a wild summer garden. Lilacs and honeysuckle and great bushels of lavender line intervals of stones to a willowed trellis. You stand there, like a sentry, watching for the first sign of my arrival. I will come to you, I will find you again. You are the love of my life and when you read this, you will know I was waiting for you all along . . .

Three days after Beltane, Autumn pulled her mail from the mailbox and was nearly astonished by a plain white envelope that fell from the usual packet of catalogs and flyers. It was a security envelope, the thick white ones used for business transactions, and the unfamiliar handwriting had marked no return address. Autumn didn't open it until she was in the privacy of her study.

Dear Ms. Avening,

You could hardly be expecting this letter of interest from me; we've barely had anything to do with each other over the last eight years. This is mostly my fault. I've never made an effort to reach out to you, although you surely would have helped me assimilate better into this town. That's part of the reason I'm writing now, applying for the position as your protégé, I guess. I am not from Avening, but I've always loved it, and I always wanted—this will sound weird—for it to love me back. I realize now that will take some work on my part. So I want to be more involved; I'm ready to surrender, I guess, to Avening.

My marriage is failing. That's my secret. I know you would never say anything. But sometimes I'm sure it must obvious to anyone who sees me in the street how unhappy and trapped I feel. My life is my husband's: my job is ancillary to his, since I just do the books on what's really his dream. He shares every worthwhile moment of my personal history. Even my child, the actual product of my body, is his. I have nothing of my own—and there's the other reason I'm writing to you. I desperately want something of my own. I don't know much about magic, but I do believe you do it. I hope that's not offensive to you. Your book, your ideas—however unlike me they might seem, they're something Finn just couldn't touch. They'd be all mine, something I could give myself to.

Reading over what I've written, I sound pretty angry to myself. I guess I am a little angry, but maybe writing this letter is the first step to breaking out of whatever poisonous life patterns I've gotten stuck in. Even if you don't pick me—I can't imagine you will; the choice seems unlikely, even to me—I hope maybe you'll have some advice for me about making myself matter in Avening.

Sincerely,
Ginny Emmerling

Well, Autumn thought, drumming her fingers on her desk. Now things were getting very interesting.

August 1: Lughnasadh

To Piper Shigeru, midnight hardly mattered. It could be one o'clock or two or four. There wouldn't be any real sleep for her. She longed for it, ached to fall into the black of temporary unconsciousness. Instead, she stared at the black ceiling, lying in the bed she had shared with her husband for more years than she had fingers to count. There were many lifetimes woven into a single life, and she had passed a happy one inside that house.

Piper shifted, moving slowly, pulling the covers away from her thin form. She glanced down at the wreck that had once been a body she was proud of. She looked like a prisoner of war, and she supposed that in the strictest sense of the words, she was. It was her own body she was fighting, and losing to.

Before the treatments began, her denial had been enough to push her through the days. Like homecoming, like a first kiss, she thought back on that time with a nostalgic fondness now. She was sick then, but she hadn't felt sick, so she could pretend and forget and be stoic. But after the doctors, the hospital, and the poison, a mirror had become her cancer's greatest weapon. She hadn't been smart enough to banish mirrors—she was afraid that she would come across as vain, of all things—so now she saw in them, with a kind of fascinated helplessness, that she was truly wasting away.

After Piper's hair retreated, the psychological warfare ended and the physical battle began in earnest. To be sick, to be ill: Piper was offended at the vocabulary. There were no words invented yet in the English language to convey the kind of suffering she endured. Perhaps this proved something about the hopefulness of the human condition. If we could not name it, then maybe we would be spared it. But Piper knew better.

The fact is no one is ready to die, even those with the greatest faith that they are being taken on a journey to a better place. To lose your body is one thing; to lose your mind is quite another. Every time she had one bout licked, the cancer regrouped and found another place to attack until, finally, it had amassed itself inside her brain. There were no more lies, no more hope. When she saw her children looking at her with both revulsion and desperation, Piper was filled with violent, biblical anger. No mother can tolerate seeing her children hurting. To know that she was the cause of their suffering was the worst part, far worse than the pain, and she hated herself for it.

The bonus to being sick, she supposed, was that she could look back on her history without pride or ego. Piper saw herself now for what she truly was. She was born and raised in Avening to middle class parents. She was never just an average person, though in fairness few who call Avening their home ever are. She excelled in school, both socially and academically. Things came easy for her, maybe too easy. Piper had always felt like a cheater, like she didn't work hard enough to deserve all of her achievements.

She tried not to take these things for granted: the popularity, the awards, the praise. She tried to look at all of them as blessings, to remember their value. She knew with karmic clarity that somewhere, somehow, down the line she would have to pay a price.

Piper went to Yale. She would have liked to have gone to a more liberal college, a smaller, more artistic, less expensive one, but she just couldn't pass up the opportunity to go to an Ivy League school. She had a gift for both words and illustration, and although her professors tried to lure her into academia, Piper wanted nothing more than to write children's books. She imagined she could create stories that would endure, characters that would last generations.

Unlike most of her peers, Piper looked at Yale more as an experience than a competition. Sure, she applied herself, but not in the same crazy way she saw other students did, as if good grades were the Holy Grail, the ticket to happiness and immortality. It was college, four years of her life, and probably the most fun and irresponsible ones.

Who plans to fall in love? Certainly not Piper, who thought planning for love could easily be called distasteful. She had dated here and there, but found the boys she met and kissed, and sometimes even went to bed with, were either too immature or too serious. But at one of those obnoxiously loud fraternity parties, the ones where she thought everyone was trying just a little to hard to have a good time, Piper met Will and everything changed. He was sexy, charming, witty, and approachable, somehow without being the slightest bit pretentious or obvious. Will, whose parents were both Japanese, was a thoroughly Canadian boy who had cultivated an ironic Asian mystique for himself. Even though he had grown up on a different coast (in Ottawa), their joint nationality seemed like more than mere coincidence to her.

He had looked at her across the room from under his glossy black hair and winked at her like a dorky rock star. Piper was captivated. All that night they circled each other, a look here, a smile there. Piper had been talking to someone, a girl from one of her classes. When the girl (whose name for the life of her Piper could not recall later) left to get another drink, Will made his move. One minute she was alone, and the next he was right beside her.

Piper flushed to think back on those years. Such passion, such abandon. She loved him desperately. She truly did, and she knew there were moments when she simply lost herself in him, as if he had devoured her whole. For a while, she was content to live inside of him without really caring about the direction her own life was going. Will hated those times, when she no longer resembled the strong, fiercely independent woman he fell in love with. He would pull away, and then, shamed and contrite, Piper would get her sense of self back. They would begin again, but from a different place.

He was unique, amazing, beautiful, and naturally gifted at anything he tried. In the beginning she was just so afraid she would lose him somehow that she held on too tightly, she loved him too much, giving him little space to give his own love in return. But when the novelty wore off, when they found that they sometimes were too tired and slept instead of making love, as happens with every other couple, Piper found her footing. She expected to marry him, expected to stay with him forever. She called it Scout Love: she was prepared for anything, and knew that whatever happened, it would not destroy her.

Will, for his part, was more practical about it. He had seen her, wanted her, gotten her, fallen in love with her, and was willing to wait out the dizzying passion to see what kind of companions they would make. But somehow he had always known Piper was the woman for him. Will graduated a year ahead of Piper and went on to law school in British Columbia. Piper finished her degree, flying across the continent to see Will on vacations. She was glad, in a way, of the year they spent apart, as she sensed that after it was over she would begin life in the plural. When she graduated, she moved into Will's cramped studio apartment. After she started working, managing a children's section in a small bookstore, they moved to a one bedroom in the same building. They were small steps, leading to inevitability.

Each night, Piper retired to their bedroom, to an ancient drafting board she had picked up in a used furniture store. She began the slow process of working through her first book. Will, up to his ears in torts and trademarks, sat at a desk in the living room writing papers on an electric typewriter that would hum and purr under his fingers. It was comfortable, predictable even. But at night, their bodies would find each other on the soft sheets donated from various family members, smooth and worn in from years of use. Sometimes he would move on top of her with a kind of gentle precision that made her eyes pull to the back of her head. Other times, they would simply sleep, but always touching, hands on shoulders, feet on feet.

On Piper's birthday, a year before Will was due to finish law school, he took her camping an hour north of town. They set up camp and devoured a dinner cooked over the open fire and then they walked on a westward trail, following the sun's descent. At an open clearing, with a spectacular view of the river running below them, Will dropped to one knee and proposed. It had been coming for years, so Piper had envisioned the moment to be tempered with relief more than anything else. But she was overcome, and she had that same feeling that she had had back at the party where they first met. She felt special; maybe she wasn't the only woman in the world, but surely the only one chosen.

It was an autumn wedding, held outside under the changing leaves of a hundred-year-old maple. When Piper looked at the pictures later, she saw them both as young and untouched, fragile. She felt for them, those two ghosts, when she looked at herself. They had had no idea. She was ashamed, as if they could see her from beyond the paper, see what had become of her and what the future really did hold, so unlike the fairy tale they believed in.

There had been no question about moving back to Avening. Piper insisted, but she didn't even need to insist; Will was enchanted by the eccentric town. When he passed the bar, they packed up their small apartment and headed home. It only took him a couple of months to satisfy the regional requirements and start his own small law firm, at which point Will and Piper both knew he had, in a sense, taken on another wife. Piper was prepared to let him go, knowing that he wanted to be his own boss and build a career on his own terms. Piper was lonely, but she used that opportunity to flush out the other man in her life: Dexter Sagebrush.

Dexter came to her suddenly, without warning, like Will. One day he was just there. He wrote himself into her life, an eccentric wizard offering magical cures to common childhood behavioral problems. *Sagebrush Moves In*, her first book, was outlandish, imaginative, and humorous, sentimental without being cheesy. It surprised her how easy it was to get published. She had heard the stories of scores of suffering unpublished writers, but in this as with other things in Piper's charmed life the stars aligned and there it was. The book was an instant success and Piper, having conquered the world of children's literature, decided it was time to tackle having a child of her own.

To Piper, being pregnant was like doing hard time. She disliked every minute of it. She would wake up in the middle of the night, huge and heavy, to paddle down the hallway to empty her ever-shrinking bladder. She would look in the mirror and wonder who the person was staring back at her. She was a woman taken over, no longer given the opportunity to choose when she slept, when she ate, or how to handle her pendulum-like mood swings. During those months, she rarely socialized, not only because she did not have the tolerance to deal with her female friends, who annoyingly went on about how great it was to be pregnant, but also because she knew that soon she would not ever be alone again. Her solitude became a sacred thing, and she would spend hours in the garden, lying still in a hammock stretched between two oaks, imagining what it would be like to become secondary in her own life.

Sylvie was born on a Tuesday morning, the day before Halloween. For all the hours that Piper had spent contemplating what it would be like to be a mother, the reality was nothing like her assumptions. She had loved her parents, her husband, her friends, but that love had come from outside, had been delivered to her from someplace else. The love she had for Sylvie welled up from the very same place that her daughter had begun in. It was organic, running through every cell, every tissue, every single pore of her being. It began inside, and she kept it close.

Piper wasn't sure if she was a "natural" mother, because she found motherhood itself to be a difficult task. It wasn't just the emotional toll (the paranoia, the worry, the anxiousness) but the physical toll as well. She was constantly running after her daughter, who took life at full speed. Sylvie was a firecracker. Piper loved her daughter's exuberance, her happy and joyous nature; she even admired her defiance, which she knew mirrored her own.

As Sylvie grew into a young girl, it became obvious that she took after her mother. Sylvie could pass for almost anything: Asian, Latin, Eastern European. Like Autumn Avening, she looked like she could be from anywhere and everywhere. Piper didn't think that she herself was truly beautiful, yet even though she saw her own features on her daughter, Sylvie was the most striking child she had ever seen.

They waited five years, and then started again. But after Siobhan was born, Piper fixed it so that she would never have to endure another pregnancy. Siobhan, her baby, her angel, seemed to sense that Sylvie belonged to Piper, and as she grew, there could be no doubt that she had found her place as Daddy's girl. She looked far more like Will, and acted like him too. She was quieter, more unaffected, but had that same aura of coolness, the same magnetism. She too was a beautiful child, and Piper thought once again: This is too easy, too good. There have been too many blessings, this luck can't go on forever. And she was right.

It began with exhaustion. The kind of tired that Piper hadn't felt since being pregnant. She tried homeopathy, she tried changing her diet, she tried sleeping more, but nothing helped. Then they found the first tumor in her right breast. She and Will only called it what it was in hushed whispers, never right out loud. She believed she would get better, and after treatment and surgery she did for a while. Then it spread to her lymphatic system, but she eventually went into remission again after a difficult round of therapy.

She knew instinctively, though, that she was buying time. She knew her suffering was an offering to the disease, an offering she made so that she could be a mother and wife just a little longer. Somewhere inside her she knew from the beginning that it would take her. The tumor in her brain was its last call. It was inoperable and inescapable. She had maybe six months.

Though her children were her life and her immortality, in her darkest hours she wished they had never been born. It was a selfish thought, one as ugly as the disease itself, but it would have just been so much easier on her if she hadn't had to prepare herself for leaving them. She supposed if she had lived an empty, meaningless life, maybe she wouldn't have minded giving it up. But her girls were so good, so happy, and so remarkable; the thought of dying, of leaving them to face the world motherless, was a burden that she did not feel she could bear.

It was the small things that took her breath away. When Sylvie laid her head on Piper's almost fleshless shoulder while watching TV, or when Siobhan brought juice to her in the morning. It wasn't simply that she cried; her body broke apart in a thousand tiny fragments, and then reassembled, but never wholly. Each time this happened, she moved further and further away from who she was before.

Piper had to blame someone, had to have a place to throw her anger. At first it was at herself. She despised her own body, hated the yellowing softness of her skin. She had a total loathing for her organs, her immune system, her inefficient constitution. But when she looked at her daughters, who were, after all, half her, she realized that she could not blame or hate herself. She wasn't overly weak; she was simply human. Humans die. So she turned on God, with vicious intensity. Why her? She had been a basically decent person, if an overly blessed one. Why not give such an evil disease to someone who deserved it, like a child molester or a serial killer? She knew everything happened for a reason, but that excuse became just that, an excuse.

Then one day, as she was sitting outside, she looked all around her. She noticed one season overtaking the next. She saw the flowers budding, the plants stretching to move closer to the sun, the birds flying wing-to-wing below the sculpted clouds. Everything seemed to exist at once in perfect balance, and she suddenly realized that what was happening to her wasn't God's fault, or even part of God's plan. It just was. She didn't have to accept it, or look forward to it, or be brave about it. Just as her body knew instinctively how to push her girls into the world, it would know in the same way how to die. She didn't have to do anything but hold on as long as she could.

The cancer moved brilliantly, like a dictator or false prophet, manipulating the cells around it into submission. For the longest time, Piper had no awareness of it other than the pain and the nausea from the medication. But gradually, she began to forget little things. What day it was, what month it was, who that actress was on the TV. Piper knew where it was headed, that it would take everything from her. Just when she needed her memories the most, needed to recall the times when all was good and right, they would not be there.

She spent hours thinking, understanding that time was now a wild thing, untamable, and that soon her mind would be gone. She lacked the physical strength to really do anything remarkable. She would never climb Everest or build schools in Africa. Not that she really would have anyway, even if she hadn't been sick, but still.

Now all she could really do was think and write. She had been keeping a series of journals and sketches for almost twenty years; they would be her legacy to the girls. She tried to write down every lesson she had learned through her years as a woman, a wife, a mother, a writer, an artist, and a citizen, not only of Avening, but of the world. Piper knew that they would not listen, that they had to make their own mistakes, but at least there would be proof that they could recover from every bad decision.

After one particularly long session of self-examination, she sat down at the kitchen table and saw that Will was preparing dinner.

"You know . . ." Piper began.

"What?" Will said as he put a pot of water on to boil.

"I'm not going to die here."

Will sighed loudly and sat down to face her at the table. Piper knew that Will loved her. She knew that he would probably never stop loving her. But her illness had created a divide, as illness does so often. She moved ever closer to the edge of the cliff, and he was miles away where it was safe. He felt guilty about that, the fact was he could not control what was happening, though she told him it was silly and useless and to knock it off. The truth, that he could not save her, had changed him. He was a very unhappy man. Piper tried not to think too hard about that. The list was too long already of things her body had to atone for.

Will looked at her stonily. "I thought you said that you

didn't want to be in a hospital. Remember, honey? This is your turf, your territory. You thought it would be harder for death to get you here. Why make it easy for him, right?" Will wasn't exactly trying to make a joke, just trying to diffuse the situation a little.

"That's true. But this is your home, too. I don't think it will be easy for you all to continue living here if I die here," Piper said as she looked out the window above the sink.

"So you want to go to the hospital when it's time?"

"Nope."

"No games, Piper, all right? This is hard enough."

Piper picked invisible lint off her sweater. She hated this conversation, and Will was so stubborn, she wondered why she was trying at all. But still she had to try, to explain. She took a deep breath and looked at him steadily. "What I'm trying to say is that one day, I'll just be gone. I'll find a way to get to the water and I'll let it take me."

"That's ridiculous, Piper. You know as well as I do that when it gets that close to the end you won't be able to move, let alone . . ." Will sighed. "Let's be realistic, for the girls, okay? While you're . . . you know, still yourself, you have to try and be practical for the girls' sake."

"I am being practical, Will," Piper said stubbornly. "I don't want them to see what the end of this is like. They're terrified enough as it is." Piper crossed and uncrossed her arms, looking at her husband defiantly. "I might not have any say over my body right now, but I do have a right to die with dignity." She wasn't sure if she wanted him to beg her not to do it or help her with a plan.

Will put his hands over Piper's own. "So you're . . . going to kill yourself?" he whispered.

"Technically, I'm already killing myself, Will." She was trying to sound light but she heard her voice catch. "I'm talking about choice, about choosing, about for once being in control of this fucking thing."

Will let go of her hand. He looked at her as if to argue, but then rose from his chair. "I don't even know what to say to that," he said. He backed out of the door into the living room, leaving Piper alone in her kitchen. Her dream kitchen, which they had redone three years earlier. The hard lines of the stainless steel glinted in the sun. Three years ago this space had been so important to her; now it was just another room. Piper sighed as she pulled herself to her feet. She missed loving the kitchen, but she was glad in a way that she had detached herself. It was one less thing to miss when it was time to go.

From some lost corridor of strength in the maze of her body, Piper had committed to ending her own life. This took far more courage than she ever thought would be necessary. She had thought that in general people who committed suicide were cowardly. Now she understood that they were very brave indeed. The revelation didn't stop her from being angry at those healthy men and women who offered up their lives when people like her would have done anything to trade places with them. It was a grudging respect, she supposed.

A plan began to form in her mind, but she no longer really trusted her own mind. She needed advice, and of all her friends, there was only one person to ask who she thought had the right perspective to give it.

Piper no longer used her car. Luckily, Demeter's Grove was only a few blocks from her house. If she walked slowly, and rested frequently, she could make it without asking Will or Sylvie to drive her. After half an hour, she slowly climbed the steps to Autumn's shop.

Autumn steeled herself when Piper walked in. Piper, so strong and indomitable, threw off her own kind of energy. At this point, her energy was mostly despair, with a drop of false hope.

This too was part of Autumn's job, facilitating the passage of Transcending. Her faith was so strong that Autumn actually felt good, or at least useful, about helping people die. It sounded strange, even to her, but true nonetheless. But Piper Shigeru was different. It felt all wrong, from the inside out. She had tried (without Piper's knowledge) to do some mending. It was no use. For some reason known only to God, Piper's body was desperate to let go. Autumn could do nothing but wait and help and talk and soothe.

"Hello, Piper dear," Autumn called as the doorbells jangled. "Listen, it's very busy in here today. Why don't you go outside to the back porch? There is a lovely big comfy chair out there and I'll make some tea and we can have a chat, all right?"

Piper nodded, looking relieved. The people, the looks, the staring, would clearly tax her; she could do without. Autumn led her to the door, sat her down, and left her to make the tea. •

𝒞

Piper leaned back, falling into the softness of the chair. The day was so beautiful, very warm, but not hot at all for July. Autumn's English garden was like a storybook painting. Piper closed her eyes, listening to summer's long-bodied insects call out to one another and the birds drifting from branch to branch like kids playing tag. She took a deep breath in. Suddenly she felt as if something had shifted. It was a little like being dizzy, but not quite, and there was a new smell, rich and earthy.

Piper's eyes flew open. She was no longer in Autumn's yard; she was in the middle of a forest. Not just in a clearing, but deep in the heart of a thick and vast forest. Her mouth grew dry and she opened it, although why, she didn't know. Possibly to speak, but it seemed more likely that it was so she'd remember to breathe. And then just like that, the scenery turned itself over, like a stadium full of people who hold up cards to create a word or a picture, a change that shuttered over her. The forest was gone and she was back on Autumn's porch.

Piper gripped the seat. What had happened? But she knew. She knew. She was losing it. Her friggin' mind wouldn't even stay in the same place as she was. That was unexpected. Her first instinct was to let out a string of curse words. But then she stopped and noticed her body. She didn't feel any pain, she didn't feel tired. In fact, she felt strong. Like she could jump up out of that chair and actually do something.

𝒞

Autumn startled Piper when she came back out to the deck. "Sorry about that, took a little longer than I expected.

Seems like everyone wants to talk today . . . Piper? What happened?" Autumn noticed the change in the air, a crackling of energy, like the opening of a gate. She thought for a brief moment one of her Sisters had been there, a Mend Sister, perhaps. But no, that wasn't it. Piper's energy shimmered, like little golden stars cascading around her. A gate had been opened, but not by any of Autumn's lot.

"How long have I been out here?" Piper asked excitedly.

"Fifteen, twenty minutes." Autumn sat down beside Piper, putting a warm cup of tea in her hands. "Why? Did it feel longer or shorter than that?"

"Shorter, much shorter . . . I went somewhere. A forest? I swear to God, it felt like I was somewhere else, really. It sounds crazy. I dunno," Piper babbled happily. "Maybe it's a symptom, but it didn't feel like that, it felt so real."

"Piper, I believe you." Autumn said calmly. Something significant had happened. Something so strange and unexpected Autumn thought it might have been out of even her league. She racked her brain, trying to find the words to use, words that would help but not scare the pants off Piper. "I have to admit, hon, I'm not an expert on this. But there are places between places, or under or over them."

"It was green, and dark," Piper said. "The thickest forest I've ever . . . Autumn, it made me well. I'm—" She touched her cheek, and her face fell a little around the eyes and mouth at whatever she felt there. "Well, at least, I was better, for half a minute. Where did I go? How can I go back?"

Autumn shook her head, knowing she wasn't doing very well. "I don't know how to explain this. I'll probably muck it up. It's like this: to a bird, the idea of flying to the moon is impossible. Just the very concept of it would never occur to a bird. But you, in theory, could get to the moon. It has been done, if not necessarily easily, or by everyone." Autumn put her hands in Piper's, which were trembling ever so slightly. "Most people are like the bird. They don't think going to different worlds, or realms, or whatever those alternate places are, is even possible. It's make-believe stuff. For others, like you, like me, who have a broader perspective, we know that it is indeed possible, but . . . well, you know how few astronauts are around. Generally one needs quite a bit of training. It's a rather specialized field. However, I know of at least one person here in Avening that can do this kind of travel without the training."

Piper, in trying to process what Autumn had just said, could only shake her head. "Autumn, it's not just that I went there. Being there, it made me feel better. I mean, I don't think I'm cured or anything. But . . . I mean, it felt like I was." She laughed embarrassedly. "Do you think . . . Maybe, if I can visit this place every so often, I can get a boost. It will help me hang in there, for a little longer, you know?"

Autumn looked down, to try to diffuse the anger she felt welling up inside her. Piper did not deserve this, and the hope that had leapt onto Piper's features was heartbreaking. Autumn hated not being able to tell Piper more. Autumn didn't entirely understand what was going on, but she was going to find out.

"Piper, go home. And please, I know you came to talk about doing yourself in, but let's not go there, okay?" Piper looked shocked, and Autumn chided herself for bringing it up so unceremoniously and, really, unnecessarily, but decided to barrel on. "One thing at a time. And for now, it's this. As soon as I find out some answers, I'll be in touch."

Piper didn't bother to even wonder as to how Autumn knew her dark secret. Instead, she picked herself up, went out the door and walked home without stopping, not even once.

&

It began to happen a lot. Piper readjusted her head-space and reexamined her agenda to accommodate the change. She would rise from her bed, and her feet would touch grass instead of carpet. She would open a door and find herself on a rise, the forest behind her, a valley below. She was sure she saw the outline of buildings there, faint on the horizon, but she couldn't be sure. She was only ever given a matter of seconds in this other place.

The girls somehow intuited that something was going on with Piper. They thought all her brooding and fundamental disorientation meant she had given up all hope. The house had become somber. The girls were quieter, their steps softer, as if Piper would find their youth disturbing. As if being healthy and having their lives ahead of them was perhaps another cause of their mother's sadness (when in fact the opposite was true). They were old women, older even than Piper sometimes, though she did everything she could to encourage them to be themselves.

Sylvie and Siobhan dealt with their mother's illness in different ways. Sylvie, who was seventeen, hung on, shadowing Piper's every move around the house. She had no social life. The phone stopped ringing; friends no longer came by. Sylvie did not see it as a sacrifice; she knew that she had only a finite amount of time left with her mother. But Piper knew differently, she knew that these were magical years, where a girl could experience independence and discover her womanhood while still living within the safety of her family. The real world wasn't quite real yet, without deadlines or bills to worry about. She tried to explain this to Sylvie, but Sylvie would turn away, embarrassed that her mother loved her so much she was telling her to leave.

Siobhan, on the other hand, could not be in her mother's presence for more than an hour at a time. Piper understood why, but that did not make it any easier. She longed to take her baby girl into her arms, though at twelve she was hardly a baby anymore. Piper knew Siobhan was preparing to be motherless, and she was trying to prove that she did not need anyone in order to function. She could not quite look Piper in the eye; she fidgeted and scratched. There were times when Piper thought Siobhan wanted to reach out for her, but then would do something else with her hands, pull her hair behind her ears or pick at her nails.

At first Piper thought she was scared of having death so close, though Shiv knew she wasn't contagious. Then Piper began to understand that she wasn't scared at all, she was angry. She was thoroughly pissed off with her mother's sickness, mad that she could no longer do what normal kids did with their mothers, and most of all irate at the thought of being left behind.

Twelve was such a hard age. Piper could hardly blame Siobhan for being so self-absorbed, for making it all about her, like she was the victim, which wasn't entirely inaccurate. Pubescence called for selfishness, demanded it. Piper didn't

blame Shiv at all. More than anything it broke her heart. She
knew that years later, when Siobhan became a mother herself, she would look back on this time with great disappointment. She would feel guilty, she would wonder, Why didn't
I try harder to get to know her? Why did I make it so much
harder for her? Piper hoped that Shiv would forgive herself
without too much self-destruction in the process. It was hard,
though, to think about the future, hard to imagine how much
she would miss.

Piper would never have called herself a Christian. She
did not believe that things were as simplistic as heaven or
hell, and she certainly did not believe in angels. But she did
hope that there was a place where she could watch them,
guide them, even, and it was a hope that kept her going.
Sometimes, when she found herself in the green forest, that's
where she thought she was going, to that gathering place, for
watching and waiting.

While she brooded over the mystery of her traveling,
the going itself lent her energy. She tried, during those times
when she felt truly well, to be normal, even if the thing allowing her to be well was anything but normal. When she felt
good, the girls felt good too. Piper would walk out of the bath
and almost smack dab into a tree and then down to the dinner table in her dining room. The girls picked up on her vibe
during times like that, and were much more talkative and
animated. It was casual, as if it were any other meal that
would be like every other meal to come. Piper was determined to make the most of it.

"So, Shiv. *Jane Eyre* is the last book on your summer
reading list. What do you think of it so far?"

"It's okay. I've got like about a hundred pages to go," Siobhan answered.

"I never really knew what to think of Jane. She never seemed like the brightest girl. I used to think that I would have marched right on up to where those noises were coming from and done some investigating." Piper put her elbows on the table and leaned into it. "Of course, women weren't supposed to question these things back then. Aren't we lucky to have been born now instead?"

"Oh, I don't know, Mom," Sylvie countered. "It was such a romantic time, wasn't it? Men were chivalrous. At the end of the day, I think all women are genetically programmed to want to be saved at least once in their lives." Piper felt her eyebrows rising, but Sylvie was smiling a faraway kind of smile. "At least back then they could admit it without seeming weak or backwards." Piper wondered if Sylvie really wanted saving. From what? From whom? There was no point asking, illness or not. She didn't think she'd get a real answer anyhow.

"Wow, Sylvie, I am surprised," Piper said. "Do you really think it's genetic programming? Or maybe social programming?" Her voice rose with enthusiasm; she was looking forward to her daughter's answer. "Every form of media, even children's books, perpetuates that mythology."

"Here we go," said Siobhan, rolling her eyes.

"Basically," Sylvie went on, ignoring her sister. "I mean, we are animals, right? Look at animal behavior. Females don't flock to the weakest male, they're not attracted to the puny one who brings home the crappiest food supply. They want the alpha male, the strong one, the mate they know will keep them fed well and protect their offspring. So I think that females, all females, including us, factor this in when they're looking at a man's potential. We might not necessarily think we need to be saved, but we like to think that option is available if necessary." Sylvie leaned back in her chair with a rather smug look on her face.

"I won't argue with that, Sylvie, but that's just it. A hundred and fifty years ago, the general attitude was that women did need to be saved. We were inferior in every way. And I don't think it was nearly as romantic as it's made out to be. Now Shiv, what do you think of Jane?"

"Well," she began, putting down her knife and fork. "I think she was pretty brave. I don't know what I'd be like if both my parents died."

"Yes," said Piper sadly, looking at her daughter. She knew Siobhan was capable of surviving just about anything, but did not know herself well enough yet to think so. "I think you're right. She was very brave."

Autumn dropped by the Shigerus' for a chat a couple of weeks after Piper had visited her. She didn't bother with the usual small talk. "Now listen, Piper, I've been doing a little research about your phenomenon. I think I might have some ideas, but it's not totally clear to us quite yet."

"Us?" Piper raised an eyebrow, but Autumn hurried on.

"You've traveled again, right, Piper? At random? Since that first time?"

The leaving had felt so secret, so private, Piper had almost forgotten Autumn knew. "Yes. Quite a few times, but always, as you say, randomly." Piper shook her head. "It was so disorienting at first."

Autumn plonked down her oversized purse on a chair and turned to face Piper, her long skirt swishing over Piper's ankles. "Right." She was clearly excited. "The next time you go, try not to concentrate on what's happened but rather where you are and see if you can tell your body to remain there instead of jumping back home. Try to breathe into the place, imagine that your feet are roots and plant them there."

"Uh, yeah, well," Piper said noncommittally. She had wanted to know why she was going, and where, what the point of it was. She was hoping Autumn would tell her. But Autumn was as mercurial as she was mysterious. She would only ever give as much away as she wanted to, and if you pushed for more, she would give you even less, as if impatience itself meant that you weren't ready to hear the truth. But from a practical standpoint, Piper couldn't afford not to ask all her questions. She didn't have time. "What if I get stuck there? I don't know if I should even try something like that. I have no idea how I do this, and I wouldn't have the first idea of how to get myself home if I decide to try and take control."

"Piper, I promise you, you will not get stuck. If my theory is correct, you are meant to control this ability you have. It's a matter of will. Focus and concentrate on where you are and where you want to go." Autumn sounded sure; she was sure. Piper couldn't share her confidence.

"Okay, I'll try it. But . . . do you know why I can do this? Am I meant to do something with it? I just . . . don't understand." Piper regretted the words as soon as they left her mouth.

"Let's start with this experiment first, and then we'll go from there." It was the kind of vague answer she was expecting, and maybe even that she deserved. She was beginning to feel this was her mystery to solve anyhow, so she said goodbye to Autumn and watched her friend's progress across her lawn. As ever, Autumn moved with the grace and ease of a cat. Sometimes Piper wondered if her feet ever even touched the ground.

Piper's books had given her quite a bit of notoriety, although really it was more like cult status than actual fame, which suited her just fine. She had actually been surprised when the first book had done so incredibly well. There were nine books in all, and though Piper's publisher and agent begged her to try and finish another, to wrap everything up in a neat little package so the children reading would have some sense of closure, Piper declined. They had offered her a ridiculous sum of money to write a last installment, and she was tempted. Ultimately she decided against it for two reasons. The first was that she didn't want to spend her last few months working instead of being with the girls and Will. She also felt there was a lesson in leaving off without a definitive end. Endings in real life rarely come about with every question answered. People change, people leave, people get sick. Piper felt she was making a statement.

She almost never gave interviews, though she tried to answer fan mail whenever possible. She didn't want her own personality to affect how people interpreted her stories. But in June, a well-respected magazine contacted her about doing an interview and she surprised herself by accepting. Her ego had gotten the better of her.

A reporter would come round on August 24th to spend the day with her. She'd forgotten the date over the last several confused weeks, but when it came and she saw the note on her calendar—interview with Charlie from *The Review*—she found herself inexplicably excited, energized. She dressed in a pair of soft, black sweatpants and a long-sleeved orange shirt made from Indian cotton. She certainly wasn't looking her best, but at least she didn't look horrific, either. It was no secret that she was ill; in fact, that was the main reason this woman was there to begin with. But Piper didn't want to come across as pathetic; she didn't want to see her fragility in bold black print for the whole world to bear witness to.

At 9:00 a.m. sharp the doorbell rang. Piper was surprised at the woman on the other side of the door. She was so young and small-boned that she looked like she could have been a friend of Sylvie's. "Piper? Hi, I'm Charlie Solomon."

"Hi, Charlie. Come in, please," Piper said as she gestured the woman into her house. She had been hoping that whoever would be doing the interview would have a little more life experience. How could this young person possibly capture what Piper was going through?

Charlie caught her eye and must have interpreted the look on Piper's face. "I suppose you thought I'd be some fierce old bat, huh?" she said through a big grin. "I promise I'm older than I look. Good genes."

Piper lead the tiny woman down the hallway and toward her back porch, still not quite sure what to make of her interlocutor. "If you don't mind, just how old are you? Or is that rude? I'm sorry, it's just that this is very important to me."

"It's not rude at all. Let me just get some of my credentials out of the way; maybe it will make you feel a little better. I was a Rhodes Scholar, I got my journalism degree from Brown. I worked for the *New York Times* before I got this job, and I've traveled and reported from over seventeen different countries. I am also a mom. I have a one-year-old son. Does that help? I really want you to feel comfortable."

"It does, yes, and I'm sorry. I just . . ." She felt stupid now for questioning her, and looking at her more closely, she saw that Charlie carried herself with a grace and ease that only comes with years. "Please, sit down. Can I get you anything to drink? Coffee, tea?"

"No thanks, I'm fine for now. I stopped on my way over at this great little coffee shop." She tapped her fingers on the table, thinking. "Hallowed Grounds. That's what it was called." Charlie began to rifle through her bag as she spoke. "This is a remarkable town you have here. It seems so, well, it seems really familiar somehow." Charlie finally found what she was looking for, a small recording device that she placed lightly on the table. "And it's not because it's like every other small town. I don't mean it that way. But . . ."

Piper smiled. She knew this story already. "You don't have to explain it to me, Charlie. I've heard people say the same thing for years. It's a special place, but it's not for everyone." She felt unexpectedly at ease with Charlie; normally she didn't like journalists. But Charlie's whole demeanor was so open that it made Piper want to open up, too. "So where is your son now?"

"With my sister," Charlie said happily. "She's quite a bit younger than me, and she's my nanny this summer. I don't really like to travel without Jesse, I miss him too much."

Piper nodded her head. She understood that feeling all too well. "Does your husband mind? You two being gone so frequently?"

There was a small little beat, a silence just long enough for Piper to count two or three ticks from the clock on the wall. "Oh, I'm not married," said Charlie finally, casually, as she fiddled with the littler recorder. "I hope you don't mind if I use this. I just don't want to get anything wrong or out of context."

"No, not at all. I'm sorry I asked, I just assumed . . . You must think I'm terribly provincial."

"Not at all." Charlie shrugged and smiled that broad smile of hers again. "Please feel free to ask me anything you want. It's only fair, considering how much I'm going to be asking you today. I wanted a baby, but not a man, if I can be so blunt. It's an awful lot of hard work, to be honest, but worth it. You have two daughters, right? How old are they?"

"Twelve and seventeen. My oldest, Sylvie, is going to be a senior this year," Piper said, smiling as she thought of them.

"That must be great. I can't wait for Jesse to grow into himself more, you know? I can't wait for him to be able to communicate with me. You must be at the point where the girls are your friends. What's that like?" Charlie casually flipped a button on her recorder and set it down between them.

Before Piper could answer her, she felt that odd tilting, that shift telling her she was going to go. She looked at Charlie. It had never happened before when another person was present. Out of all the people in the world to do it in front of, a reporter! Piper opened her mouth to say something and took a step forward. But instead of walking towards her, she found she had walked into the forest.

Piper cleared her head. She would deal with Charlie later. For now she had to try to follow Autumn's instructions. She took a deep breath in, like her friend had said. She fought the sideways feeling of going back home. Stay, stay stay stay, she said to herself like a mantra. Sure enough, the disorientation she felt when she was about to move again left her. For the moment, she was there.

She didn't know quite what to do with herself. So without thinking she began to walk. Wherever she was, it wasn't Avening. The forest was greener somehow, lusher and louder than any forest she had ever been to. Some of the tree species she could have identified, but some she was sure didn't exist in her world. Leaves grew in the shape of stars, fat, blue flowers ringed trunks, fruit hung low and heavy off branches. The place felt right but unfamiliar. And then, out of nowhere, a little girl stepped from behind a tree so massive its trunk was wider than a car.

"Hello," the girl said happily.

"Hello," Piper said, trying not to show how startled she was.

"You're from home, right? That's so cool, I thought I was the only one who came here. I'm Maggie." The girl was smiling. "I'm not supposed to talk to strangers, but bad people aren't allowed here, so I know you're not going to kidnap me or anything."

"I'm Piper," she replied. Piper had found, over the

many years of writing children's books and meeting many of the kids who read them, that some children were just special. And this child was. "Maggie, can you tell me, how did you get here? Do you know?"

"Um, I dunno. I think there must be some kind of special door or something in my backyard. That's how it started. But now I just think about this place and I'm here. Is that what happened to you?"

She sure was a cute little thing, with blue-grey eyes and a blonde bob. She had the features of a girl who would soon be striking. She was maybe ten, or eleven? Probably ten, definitely younger than Shiv. Piper knew she needed not to stare, to keep it casual or Maggie might become guarded, so she smiled as brightly as she could before answering.

"Not quite. But wait. You said there were no bad people here. But there are . . . people?"

Maggie squinted one eye. "Sort of, yeah. Not like normal people. But they're really nice." She pushed some hair off her face with one hand. Piper noticed she was clutching a notebook in the other. "My best friend lives here. He's super cool, for a boy. We have a fort."

Piper surveyed the forest around them, turning her head slowly. On some level she was afraid of becoming nauseated if she moved too quickly. "And . . . Maggie, what . . . what do you do when you come here?"

"All kinds of things," Maggie told her. "I play with Dade. That's my friend. Or if he's busy, sometimes I play alone. Or do homework." She held up the notebook for Piper to see. "Today I'm writing a letter to Ms. Avening. She's having a contest, and the winner gets her magic book. Dade thinks I could win it, maybe, so I'm trying to write a really good letter."

"Wow," Piper said, having the presence of mind, even here, to smile encouragingly. "That sounds like a really cool project. Good luck on your letter."

"Thanks." Maggie smiled largely, revealing two missing molars. "Oh! I've got to go. Time moves different around here, you prob'ly know that, right? I've got to go in for lunch." Maggie smiled and walked forward and then disappeared before Piper's eyes.

Could it be that easy? Piper closed her own eyes and concentrated on home, on the exact place she was when she left. She wasn't really expecting anything to happen. She expected it to be more difficult. But it only took a moment or two, and when she opened her eyes again, she was back. Piper was shocked. It had worked.

Charlie stood there wide-eyed. Unsurprisingly to Piper, Autumn was there with her.

"Ah, there you are dear. See, Charlie? I told you she'd be back."

"Did you feel a disturbance in the Force or something, Autumn?" Piper said dryly. "It's pretty coincidental that you'd show up at this exact minute."

"Hardly. I was in the neighborhood and I decided to drop by. The Goddess does indeed work in mysterious ways." Autumn chuckled. "Lucky I came by. You've been gone more than an hour, and I've been having a lovely chat with Charlie." The older woman looked at the young reporter conspiratorially. "She's thinking of settling down in Avening, she's taken such a fancy to it. Haven't you, Charlie?"

Charlie opened her mouth, but looked a little too thunder-struck to reply.

"I was . . . I was missing for an hour?" Piper had never been observed in her going missing before; she hadn't been clear on how this worked. Somehow she had imagined the other world as a blip in time, something that happened mostly in her head and self, not something that coordinated with the real world. "So wait, my body wasn't here at all? For an hour?"

"Your body was definitely gone," Charlie piped up, her eyes still wide and round as if she was afraid of what she might miss if she blinked.

Piper looked at Charlie and swallowed. "So you saw me . . . you saw me evaporate and then reappear an hour later. That's what happened here, in my kitchen."

"Now don't look so worried," Autumn broke in. "Charlie has agreed that this will be our little secret. Not that she had much choice. It would be rather hard to get anyone to believe her story, I think." Autumn was quite animated; she was at least as excited as Piper or Charlie about what had happened. "It's most curious that Charlie was here though, isn't it? That's never happened before this. Yet another thing for me to look into. But it's all part of the puzzle." She all but clapped her hands with glee. "Now, I'll leave you two to fin-ish up, but Piper, when you get some free time, I'd like to come and talk to you. Give me a ring and I'll stop by. And you, Charlie, don't forget to enter my contest. I'm absolutely holding you to your promise!" Before either one of them could say a word, Autumn had escaped out the door, leaving Piper and Charlie alone in the kitchen.

Piper gave her youthful guest a sideways glance, not sure if she felt horrified or amused. "Well, it seems like Autumn Avening got her claws into you pretty quickly." She smiled tentatively. "She's really pushing that contest of hers, isn't she? You're the second person I've talked to today who's going to enter and—" Piper looked at the clock and laughed. "And it's only ten in the morning!"

"She's a persuasive lady," Charlie replied, her eyebrows waggling. "So, I guess I'm to take it that unusual things happen pretty frequently around here? Do you want to . . . tell me a little bit about whatever just happened when you disappeared?"

"Look," Piper said ruefully, "I'm not trying to be mysterious. But whatever your questions are going to be, I don't think I'll be able to answer them. The truth is, I don't know. I just don't know how I do it, and I don't know where I go." She heard what sounded like pleading in her own voice.

Apparently Charlie was going to make this easy for her; after a tiny pause, she simply changed the subject. "You know what? I think I really like Avening. I think I'd like to stay for a while. I feel like I'm supposed to be here. Is that weird?"

"You basically just watched me reappear out of thin air. I'm not sure that question really fits, given the circumstances," Piper said with a little grin.

"No, I guess not. So—shall we get on with it? Quick and painless, I promise."

"Absolutely." Piper should have felt odd or strange or at the very least embarrassed about what Charlie had seen. But Charlie made Piper feel like they were old friends. And so Piper began to speak, and as she did so, she realized that she was right. Charlie's questions were so right on that she couldn't help but feel she had made a friend. She knew without a doubt that Charlie would protect her, and she was right.

The next day, after sleeping for thirteen hours straight, Piper awoke with the girls. Shiv was going to band camp in the mornings and Sylvie was working at Totems bookstore three days a week. She was sorry to see them leave, but she knew they needed something else apart from Piper's illness to occupy them. She pulled out her latest journal, to write her daily entry in the garden. She took along some watercolors as well, wanting to reproduce an old photo of the girls taken at the Summer Solstice fair ten years previous.

She sat on a painted Adirondack chair and opened the book to the next blank page. The spine bent and creaked and Piper smoothed her hand over the white of the paper. She had called Autumn and told her to come over any time, and it seemed like a good thing to do while she waited. Yesterday had been busy and taxing; Piper felt exhausted and worn through. Even with the restorative effect of her visit to the forest, she was beginning to slow down.

She wrote quickly. Of course she had detailed the phenomenon of her traveling. It helped her deal with the craziness of it, and she did want the girls to know, eventually, about this breathtaking kind of magic. The painting she did more leisurely, taking her time in slow, even brushstrokes. When she was finished she left the book open to dry and closed her eyes.

She awoke with the pressure of Autumn's hand on her shoulder.

"Oh, Autumn, I'm sorry. I must have dozed off. Were you at the door long?" Piper tried to shake the sleep off her.

"Not at all. When you didn't answer I walked around back. How are you feeling today?"

"Tired. Tired of being sick and tired." Piper sat herself up in her chair, which took a disheartening amount of effort. "I meant to tell you, though, before you rushed off yesterday. I did what you said and managed to stay . . . there. In that place. I met a friend of yours. Maggie, right? She's lovely. I spoke to her, and then I got myself back home. So you were right."

"We thought so."

"We," Piper repeated. "There's that 'we' again."

"Yes. That's why I'm here." Autumn settled herself in the chair closest to Piper's. "You see, I have these friends. Well, they're more than friends, more like sisters, really. And some of my friends can do what you do. They've been where you've been, and other places too. It's quite an extraordinary gift. I told them about you, and they did some investigating, you see. They asked some of the folks that live in this place. It was quite a summit, I'm told. Very few people, or very few untrained adults, I should say, have done what you've been able to do." Piper was charmed to see Autumn quite caught up in her little inconvenience; Piper's strange habit was at least as exciting for her older friend as it was for Piper herself, and Piper had thought Autumn had seen everything. "The point is, Piper, I think you've been given this ability because . . . I think, we all think, actually, that you are meant to go there. I mean live there. And by live I mean live."

Piper felt her stomach drop. For the briefest moment she had forgotten her illness, but this was about her illness, after all. Autumn was waiting, watching Piper's mind churn as the possibilities started to occur to her. This was it. Her way out. What she had talked about so painfully with Will— only perhaps not as painful as she had thought.

Autumn must have seen the hope kindling in her eyes. "They can't cure you, not for this world," she warned. "You as you are. But we think you would live, there."

Suddenly Piper was fighting nausea. She wasn't sure why, whether it was confusion or feeling overwhelmed by her luck or just her illness rearing itself. She clamped her mouth shut and sucked on her tongue, swimming through Autumn's words.

"It's not straightforward," Autumn went on quickly. "You would have to change, if you lived there permanently. Change into what, I'm not sure. Not into a tree, or a glass of water, or anything like that. You would be a sentient being, just not entirely . . . altogether human." She let this sink in for a couple of seconds before going on. "The other thing I should say is that once you undergo this transformation, there is no guarantee that you would retain your ability to travel. More than likely you would not." Autumn finished talking and went quiet.

Piper stifled her imbalance and took a deep breath to calm her stomach. "Right. So I go to this place with no name, this nowhere place. I just walk away from my kids and my house and my husband. And I become . . . what? An ogre? A fairy? A tree frog?" Piper threw her hands around her rather wildly. "That's . . . I don't even know what that is. Ridiculous?"

Autumn stilled her with a stare that bored into Piper's sunken eyes. "You are going to die, Piper. Very soon and very painfully." Her voice was flat and not gentle now. "I'm sorry, but that's the truth of it. You are going to leave them anyways. I know changing, leaving, seems scary, but do you understand why it's not as scary as it could be?"

"I'm trying to understand," Piper said meekly. And she was. It was so much to wrap her head around.

"Think about it! Think about what an adventure this is." Autumn was pushing; it was most unlike her. "And let me tell you—those girls of yours. They are special too, just like you are. I'm sure at some point that we could find a way for the three of you to see each other."

That was it—the one thing she needed to hear. Her girls. Her lucky break. Yet another lucky break. "What about Will? Can I see him?"

"That . . . would be harder. Probably not, I'm afraid."

And like that, Piper's eyes filled with tears. Ten minutes ago she had been furiously resigned to abandoning her entire family; now, spoiled thing, she couldn't bear the thought of losing Will, being apart from him forever. "My Will," she choked, embarrassed at herself.

"Look," Autumn said, almost impatiently. "Stay here and die, or go there and . . . see. I feel in my heart that a great adventure awaits you there."

Piper was still on the verge of tears. "But why? I can't even begin to understand this. My mind is already starting to go. Maybe this is all happening inside my head. Could it be? Could I be imagining all of this?"

"You most certainly are not!" Autumn took Piper's hand and squeezed it hard. "I don't know why. If I had to guess, I would say the work that you do, the stories that you write, all that magic you spill from your fingertips when you press those letters into words, wove some kind of spell, one last gift after all the magic you've given to the world." She shrugged, and said firmly, "Sometimes we don't question things. Sometimes we just accept them. That's faith, Piper, and that's what's required here."

Piper said nothing; there was nothing to say. She wasn't sure there was enough faith in the entire universe to get her to knowingly walk away from her life in Avening. But whatever the state of her faith, even the vaguest hope of not having to totally abandon her children was more intoxicating than the morphine the doctors offered her. It alleviated a pain far worse than the physical.

She thought about it all the rest of the day and into the next, when the end of summer seemed to echo her despair. The usual blue sky was replaced with clouds, grey and melancholy, that rumbled and turned, setting one another momentarily on fire in quick flashes of light. Piper wanted to live.

She had always believed—in what she recognized as part of her denial—that even though thousands of people die of cancer each year, she was the exception, the mistake. And now she felt almost guilty at the chance to outwit death. That was the thing she couldn't get away from. She wanted to live—but was simply living enough, if it turned out she could never in fact see the girls again? Autumn had only told her it was a possibility—what if eternity in that strange time-skewed place was full of nothing but missing her family? She would not see Will; that much she had to accept. All spouses and lovers end up thinking about how they will survive should the day come when they are permanently separated from their beloved; it was searingly painful but not unnatural, not beyond the realm of getting through. Piper could live without Will, however difficult. But the girls? She wasn't so sure.

She had learned that motherhood was the greatest love affair of all; romantic love paled in comparison. How could she go on if she wasn't sure they were safe? How could she be happy not knowing if they were happy themselves? In death they would be beyond her grasp; in that other world they would be tantalizingly close, just on the other side but untouchable. She was at a loss. She had to talk to her family, let them in on her secret and let them help her decide.

The next morning, Piper insisted they all eat breakfast together on the old kitchen table that had belonged to her great-grandmother. Piper ate little, a piece of toast and a small glass of diluted juice. After everyone had finished, she sat straight on her chair and gently folded her hands into her lap.

"Everyone," she said. "I have something to discuss with you."

Will looked startled, but Sylvie perked up. "What is it, Mom?"

"Well, I have a decision to make, and since it involves you, I don't think I should decide alone." She saw sudden panic in Will's eyes—he thought he knew where this was going—and she quickly went on. "Now, what I am about to say will sound crazy. But I need you all to keep an open mind, which I know that you can do." She turned to her daughters. "Sylvie, Shiv, I want you to remember this moment. It's important. It calls for you to think like women, maybe for the first time in your lives."

Before she could go on, Will interrupted her nervously. "Piper, don't you think you should discuss this with me first, in private maybe? Then talk to the girls?"

Piper looked at him as if he had spoken some unintelligible language and continued. "Like I said, this will sound totally insane, I know. But Autumn Avening can back up every word I say. I would encourage you to go and talk to her. I think she can help clarify a lot of this." Piper took a deep breath in and exhaled loudly. "Whew. Okay. The thing is, I have recently started to travel to another . . . another place. Not travel, like on a bus. I mean, my body is suddenly in this . . . this other world, I guess. I mean . . . somehow I have managed to open up some kind of gate to a place . . . between places. I actually go there, physically." Piper's words were halting. But her face was so earnest that her girls knew she couldn't possibly be lying. Will looked daggers at her, which pissed her off in a way that made her want to go on.

"And Autumn . . . she talked to a bunch of her friends. You know . . . people that are like her. You know what I mean."

"You mean witches?" Siobhan said flatly.

Piper shot her a look—this was a conversation they'd had before, and which she'd quashed before, but now wasn't the time. And, now that she thought about it, she didn't know if she could honestly explain to Siobhan that she was wrong.

"Whatever they are. Other . . . spiritual people like Autumn. But they've all decided that instead of staying here, in this place, and dying, I should go permanently to that other place." Piper stopped. She wondered how she could say what she had to say next. I'm leaving you, she said to herself. I'm leaving you I'm leaving you . . . She was leaving, one way or another. But to say it? Out loud it made her feel like breaking apart. She concentrated on the facts and Autumn's words. She took a deep breath and continued.

"But . . . apparently being in that place would change me. I don't know how, exactly, but I'm pretty sure I would look different. To be honest with you, I don't really know much. Autumn says she thinks she can find a way to get you girls there at some point eventually. To visit, I mean. I know this all sounds too crazy. But I need to know your thoughts on this, to help me decide what to do."

"You should do it, Mom," Sylvie said immediately.

Piper looked at her eldest daughter, right into her beautiful green eyes. How was it that Sylvie needed no proof, didn't need to bombard her mother with questions about this impossible story? She must have had so much faith, the faith Autumn described. She was offering her mother a gift. A gesture of absolute solidarity in front of her father and her sister. She wanted them to know that she didn't care about the hows or whys. All she cared about was Piper and what Piper believed. "You should go," Sylvie said solidly after a moment's awkward silence. "Either way, we lose you. But at least I would know that you were alive . . . somewhere."

"Mom? I don't get it," Shiv said, clearly bewildered. "Where is it? Couldn't we all just go together?"

Piper bit her lip and fought back tears. How could she get through to her daughter? How could she explain when she didn't know herself? Piper didn't have words, only feelings, and she didn't know how to show them.

"Shiv, honey, you know I'm . . . sick. You know I don't have long. If the cancer gets me, you won't be able to come along . . . and—"

Will stood abruptly, kicking back his chair. "Enough!! Sylvie, Shiv, go upstairs . . . Now!" The girls, startled, got up and quickly left the room, not remembering a time when they had seen their father so angry. "I won't let you do this, Piper. I don't care how sick you are. I will not let you give these girls false hope like that. It's cruel."

"It's not false," Piper said desperately, "it's true. It's real. Like I said, Autumn can . . ."

"Autumn is crazy!" Will snarled. "She's a flaky new age weirdo who wants to believe in this just as much as you do. You have a tumor in your brain. You knew this was coming, you knew that you would see things . . ."

Piper closed her eyes and made herself be still. She thought she might actually shout at her husband, she was so angry. She could understand him not being able to believe her, but she could not understand how he would think her so insensitive that she would actually hurt the girls on purpose. She shook her head and tried to calm down.

"Will, stop. This is not my sickness. I know what's happening to me. And so do other people. This . . . going . . . it even happened in front of that reporter who came by. She saw me disappear and then reappear out of nowhere." She knew that anger wouldn't get her anywhere. She was speaking softly, like cooing almost. Just to get him to try and see, but he wasn't buying it. "I know, I really do, honey, that this is so hard for you to accept, but I promise. It's not my sickness. It's true."

Will's eyes narrowed and he stepped back from her with obvious disgust. "It doesn't matter now, because the damage is done already. They'll never really have closure. They'll never know if you are dead, or out there somewhere where they might be able to reach you. They're only kids, Piper, girls . . . our girls. Aren't they hurting enough?"

What had only been hinted at for months was now just out there, hovering. He blamed her for hurting the girls with her illness. She knew it at that moment as much as she knew that he hated himself for assigning that blame. But no more. No more guilt. She was going to do as she pleased, because it had been so damn long since she had any choice. Piper let the anger she was holding back fly at him.

"Is it hurting them to ask them to believe in the impossible? The miraculous? In magic? How can that hurt them? How can that do anything but open them up to the universe and an acceptance of everything that can't be explained except on faith? Tell me, Will. How is that damaging them?"

Will stepped back from her, and with each step, he became someone she no longer knew until he looked almost like a stranger. He was a closed door, and she realized that though he was the girls' father, in this, he was an outsider; he had no place.

"Will, you have lived in Avening long enough to have seen and experienced events that simply don't happen in other places in the world. So why now? Why refuse to accept it now?" she asked, though she felt kind of like she already knew the answer.

Will uncrossed his arms. His figure sagged under a hybrid of resignation and sorrow. "Piper, I moved here for you. I would have done anything to make you happy, and that includes saying whatever you wanted me to and trying to believe in things I thought were bullshit. You see what you want, in this town and in me." He sighed. "I thought . . . I don't know, that the magic you felt here would rub off somehow, but it didn't and it never will, Piper. It's all make-believe, all of it. Group think and mass hysteria and self-fulfilling prophecies. Let me take you to the doctor, honey, and we'll see where we're at, okay?"

Piper jumped up, faster than she had done in a long time, her anger and disappointment fueling her. "No. No more doctors, Will. This is my life, whatever's left of it. I know where you stand now. And as sad as I am, as much as it pains me to see that a huge part of the life we shared was based on you . . . you . . . humoring me, I am glad I know the truth." Saying it, she felt strangely calm. Almost like it was someone else having the conversation. "But you have to promise me, Will, that you will not push your beliefs onto the girls, especially Shiv. Let them make their own decisions about their spiritual path. Please do that for me. Let them see, or not see, for themselves."

"I'm sorry, Piper," Will said sadly. "I didn't mean to . . . I love you. Whatever else, I do love you."

"Yes," Piper said as she looked at him square in the face. She had flashes then of that party at Yale, and the blue jacket and their tiny first apartment and the look in his eyes when he held Sylvie that first time. He couldn't help how he was built and what he could see and what he couldn't see. But in her traveling she had moved past him. She might indeed change in that other place, but she already felt like she was someone else. Love changes course and flies away sometimes, that was all. It made her sad. She touched his face gently and walked out of the room.

And so it was that night Piper made up her mind to go. Will had fallen into an almost unnaturally deep sleep, and when she turned on the light beside her bed to pack a few things into her rucksack, he did not turn or wake.

Piper gathered many of her favorite pictures of the girls, a few letters and paintings they had made for her, a couple dresses of lightweight gauze (out of habit, she included clothes; she was going on a journey, after all), a first edition of *Sagebrush Moves In*, her box of watercolors, brushes, and pencils, and finally, Sylvie and Shiv's baby blankets, which still, miraculously, held that wonderful smell of talc and soap.

She went to Siobhan's room first, pushing the door open just wide enough to move through. The moon was full, illuminating the room so Piper could see her daughter's sleeping face. The grief froze her momentarily. This was too hard. How could she say good-bye? It was like giving up an arm or leg, a part of her. No, it was not good-bye, not forever. She had to have faith that this was not the end, that she would see them again. That would be how Piper got through this.

She sat quietly on the bed beside her daughter, gently

stroking her face until Siobhan's eyes slowly fluttered open.

"Mommy?" she said, still half asleep.

"Yes, it's me, angel. Go back to sleep."

Shiv looked at her mother, as if it were a dreaming conversation. "Love you, Mom," she said as she rolled over.

Piper squeezed her fingers into her palm hard enough to feel her nails making deep half-moon imprints. "I love you too, Shiv," she whispered as she bent down to kiss her daughter's temple, letting her lips linger for as long as she was able. Somehow, Piper pulled herself from the room and made her way to Sylvie's.

Piper opened the door quietly. Though the curtains were closed, the soft green glow from Sylvie's stereo let her see her daughter sprawled out on the bed. Piper kneeled beside her, but did not touch or speak to her. There were too many words, too many embraces for Piper to even begin. Sylvie was no longer a child; it was the long and perfect limbs of a woman that she saw sleeping before her. She watched Sylvie, thanking her creator for the years they did have together, years some mothers never got. It was a long time she sat and watched, but then she stood and made her way to the door.

"Good night, Mom," Sylvie whispered. It was better than good-bye; it was more than words of love. It was simply good night, for it was good, a beautiful summer night, with a swollen silver moon and the air keeping just the right amount of the day's sun. It was a perfect night to slip away, and Sylvie knew as she felt her mother watching her that Piper was brave and strong and exceptional. However hard it was for Sylvie to let her mother walk out the door, it was a thousand times harder for her mother.

"Good night, my love," Piper said in a clear voice as she left the room.

Down the stairs and out the door, Piper walked. She had more energy than she had in months. She could already feel her old life slipping away, her old self which was known and examined. It had been a good life, she had done good things. Looking back, she felt the same kind of pride she did when her own children accomplished something remarkable. She was now a mother to herself, waiting to give birth to the different creature she would become.

She didn't have to do anything, and for that she was grateful. Piper was so tired of preparing for things she didn't know about. Scary things, dark and menacing things. But now she was going, and the thought of it made her feel light and hopeful. She felt like Houdini with this Great Escape of hers. She would see her girls again. She knew it down to her bones. Piper closed her eyes and imagined the forest, the smell and sound of it. Something unlocked and clicked inside her. Her own world fell away and she stepped into the lush green of her new one with a smile on her face.

Autumn's doorbell rang at 4:30 in the morning, either an ungodly hour or the most godly of all hours, she wasn't sure which. She sighed, pulled off her duvet, and threw on a worn cotton dressing gown. She wasn't by nature an early morning person, but she understood the appeal. The sun would begin to rise in less than an hour, and the approaching twilight was still and deeply peaceful. It was so quiet in the kitchen she could hear the gears moving in her grandfather clock.

Mave Moreau, whom Autumn admitted to her kitchen and sat at her table, hadn't bothered to call. Autumn had been sleeping fitfully anyway, and decided she couldn't ignore a worried mother, even if she couldn't answer all her questions. But Autumn did what Autumn always did in difficult situations: brewed them all—herself, Mave, and Mave's eleven-year-old daughter, Maggie—cups of peppermint tea.

Mave, a marine biologist who worked at the tiny teaching aquarium in Avening, showed signs of not having slept well herself. Mave was fair skinned and blonde with saucerlike eyes. Her complexion was flawless, but unforgiving; her exhaustion sat, purply and obvious, beneath her bottom lids. Maggie seemed tired but almost bored. Too many grownups and grownup talk for her liking.

"I know you have explained, Autumn," Mave said, clearly frustrated, "that Maggie has a special gift. A gift for going places that others can't. I have begged and tried my damnedest to get you to tell me what it all means, to put my mind at ease about it. But you won't. You tell me I'm just supposed to be okay with my daughter disappearing from her bed for hours in the middle of the night!" Mave gripped her tea cup. "You tell me to wait. That everything will make sense soon. And I have waited, because I respect you and I trust Maggie. But enough is enough now." Mave's breath was becoming short. She was obviously trying not to cry.

"Try to calm down," Autumn said as gently as she could. She hoped she didn't sound patronizing. "I know it's difficult. I understand your anger and frustration. Now, just tell me everything that happened, and we'll see where we are."

"She left last night." Mave pointed to Maggie with a thumb jerk. "I checked her bed about midnight before I went to sleep. Gone. And she didn't come home until four o'clock in the morning. That's almost the whole friggin' night."

Maggie rolled her eyes. She was clearly frustrated, too.

"Maggie?" Autumn asked.

"I had to go," Maggie burst out, nearly shouting. "I had to go and meet that sick lady and take her through to the inner gate. They told me to. She was, like, practically already dead!" Autumn had the feeling Maggie had already been over this with her mother, to no avail. "What was I supposed to do? Say no? Autumn, tell her, please."

But before Autumn could get a word in, Mave cut in. "Tell me what? Look, I'm as open-minded as anyone in Avening," she said to Autumn, as if her daughter weren't there. "I get that she has a gift for something. I've always known she was special, always. But she's eleven years old. Who the hell is this 'they' she's talking about? Are they monsters? Fairies? Ghosts? And don't 'they' know they can't ask an eleven-year-old to stay out all night?" Mave took a swig of her tea and slammed the mug on the counter.

"Mave," Autumn said steadily, "I'm afraid I don't know exactly what 'they' are. They could be any number of things. But I know they would never, ever put Maggie in harm's way. Whoever they are, they honor her. And she was sorely needed last night."

"You realize how totally fucking insane you sound right now, right?" Mave was too emotional to censor herself in front of her daughter.

"Totally," Autumn answered honestly. "But nonetheless, there it is. It's just the truth. But in the future, she cannot leave her bed," Autumn said, turning to the girl sternly. "Ever. No sneaking out, Maggie. You can only go during normal play hours. Not during school, either. Right now you belong here, in this world. Got it?"

"This was really important," Maggie said defensively. "I've never snuck out before. And I can't ditch school. That would be, like, impossible. This isn't the fifties, you know."

Autumn laughed. "Tonight was important. But you have to let people here, especially your mom, know what's going on. You don't want to worry her to death, do you?" Maggie shook her head, and Autumn, sobered, turned to the girl's mother. "Mave, I think I've figured it out. It was Piper Shigeru. She got an exemption. That's who Maggie took through last night, right Maggie?" Maggie nodded, her eyes bright and full. "She wouldn't have known that world well enough yet to get through on her own."

Mave seemed to be processing this unwillingly. "Just so we're straight, Piper Shigeru, the terminally ill author, gets to live in this other world? But only because Maggie, my daughter, took her there?"

"Yes," Autumn said levelly.

"So that's it, then?" Mave stared evilly at Autumn." My daughter doesn't lead a normal life. She doesn't go to college. She just crosses back and forth into fairyland until she gets sick and tired of us and decides to stay there permanently?" Her words stuck in her throat.

"You never know what's coming." Autumn put her hand on top of Mave's. "I've been wondering for a long time why

Piper went through what she did. And I think I understand that her journey was about giving us all faith. Changing our perception of impossible." Maggie looked at her mother, her mother looked at Autumn. "You have been shown something extraordinary. You are blessed, so don't push against it."

Autumn had spoken with such conviction that Mave got caught up in her hopefulness. "Just faith, then? That will be enough to get me through?"

"Yes," Autumn answered. "It will be enough, and then some."

❧

That next morning in the Shigeru house, the family left behind sat around the table. They all knew that Piper was gone for good. The tears would come eventually, but in that moment they were too absorbed in the changing rhythm of the house, the silence of absence and the current of missing things.

Will cleared his throat finally. "I promised your mother that . . . She told you she had an ability to go . . . somewhere else. And maybe that happened." As much as Will tried to sound objective, his words fell flat and unconvincing. "But I feel I also must tell you that your mother did say to me, not too long ago, that she wanted to spare you the pain of seeing her in the end. The doctors did give us a glimpse of just how bad it would be. She didn't want that for you, and she told me . . . well, her exact words were that she would find a way to get to the water and let it take her."

"You think she killed herself, Dad?" Sylvie said angrily. "Is that what you think?"

"I think it might be a possibility, that's all. She felt so helpless, Sylvie." Will leaned over to take Sylvie's hand, but she moved it away. "She felt like she had no control over her own body. And maybe, well, maybe she wanted to take that power back and end things on her terms. If she did, I think it would have been a very brave thing to do."

Sylvie sat taller, looking so much older and wiser than she had done just the day before. She was different now, and her calm, level tone proved it. "Mom was not crazy. She never, ever lied to us, not even to make things better. If she said she could go from this place to another, even though that seems like bullshit, then I believe that's what happened. She never, ever lied to us," she repeated. "I also believe we can reach her, and I know she won't be the same, but I'm going to try."

"How, Sylvie?" Will asked with a mix of exasperation and sympathy. "How are you going to do that?"

"We could ask Autumn. She'd know," Siobhan said quietly. Will and Sylvie looked at her. They had both momentarily forgotten she was even there. Sylvie looked surprised at her sister's reaction.

Will, on the other hand, knew in that instant that on some level he had lost both his wife and his little girl in the same day. He had thought maybe, after Piper had died, they could all move somewhere else, start again fresh in a new place without memories. Now he understood that would never happen. They could never leave Avening.

Three people sat on hard wooden chairs, bound by blood and history. The thread that had connected them lay unraveled at their feet. New ties, made of things both harder and more solid, would have to be rewound. A new compass was needed, for they all knew in that moment they were lost without her. Each had their own ideas, their own theories about where Piper had gone, but they held them close, pushing them into the places inside that had begun to open and bleed in their grieving. Together, they were fundamentally alone. And Siobhan, unable to contain the great magnitude of her sorrow within the limits of her small frame, put her head against the battered wood of the old table and wept.

September 21:
Autumn Equinox

SYLVIE SHIGERU FELT AUTUMN COMING IN THE cool westerly breezes and the clear, russet-colored sunsets. It was still warm, but the humidity had released its heavy grip, and the days were lovely and still somewhat long.

As always, she thought of Piper when she stepped into the garden. This had been her mother's place, as much as her office had been. The stamp of Piper was everywhere—in the perfectly overgrown perennials, in the accommodating path, in the small but practical vegetable garden. Sylvie often came here, to swing in the hammock, to sit on the weather beaten Adirondack chairs and feel close to Piper. She spoke out loud, if she could be sure that no one would hear. She knew that technically her mother could not hear her, but pretending helped sort her head out. The house was still quiet with Will and Shiv both sleeping in their rooms. Unlike Sylvie, neither one of them were early risers or morning people.

With a steaming mug of peppermint tea in her hand, Sylvie sat down in her mother's chair. She tilted her head back and let the first soft rays of sun fall on her open face. The air was still permeated with the sweet smell of night blooming jasmine and she felt the excitement rolled up into a tight ball in the pit of her stomach.

"Well, Mom, today's the day," she whispered. "But let's face it, the chances of me actually getting to meet Callum West are slim to none, unless maybe you are hearing me somehow and can work some kind of mojo thing. But at least I'll be able to see him, I'll be close to him. And besides, I'm not so sure I would want to meet him. What if he's a complete asshole?"

"Who's an asshole?" said a voice from the open kitchen door. It was Siobhan. Sylvie found herself flushing; but at least it wasn't her father. "Who are you talking to?"

"Mom," Sylvie said, trying to sound casual.

"And Mom's an asshole?" Shiv smiled as she sat in the chair next to her sister.

"No, no one's an asshole. Well, this one guy might be; that's what I was saying."

"Oh, Callum West, right? Were you talking to Mom about the concert tonight?"

Sylvie shrugged and said nothing. There was no way her little sister would understand.

"You think Mom can hear you? I mean, when you talk out loud to her?"

"I don't know. Maybe. She might be able to sense that I'm thinking about her." She reached over to squeeze Siobhan's hand. She knew that Shiv was probably feeling a little left out. "Hey, listen. I've got a ton of things to get ready. I have to get all my clothes for the concert and for camping tonight, and I have to buy food and pack the cooler and stuff. I could really use your help today. Are you up for it?"

"I don't know." Siobhan picked a dandelion from the ground and began to peel off the small petals.

"If you help me, I'll take you to the video store before I leave and you can get any movie you want."

"Really?" Shiv's face lit up. "Even a rated-R one?"

"Only if it's rated R because of gratuitous sex and nudity . . . deal?" Sylvie winked and they both laughed now. "Why don't you call Lexy, see if she wants to spend the night, keep you company while I'm gone."

"Yeah, okay, but should I call her before or after I help you?"

"Before, I think. Give her some notice."

"Cool." She got up and started back towards the house, but stopped and turned back around. Her brow furrowed and she brought her finger to her mouth to bite the broken cuticle around her nail. "Thanks," she said after a moment.

Sylvie smiled. "No prob." She knew what Siobhan meant.

Piper had been gone almost two months. No body had been found, no signs or clues had been given as to her whereabouts. Like her sister had suggested, Sylvie had talked to Autumn Avening about the possibility of this "other world" her mother had described. Autumn told her that, yes, she had gone, but as of that moment, Autumn had no further information to give her. She promised to keep her posted. This thoroughly pissed Sylvie off; she knew Autumn knew more than she was letting on. But she wouldn't push. She couldn't have said she understood how Autumn operated, but she did understand well enough that there had to be a more than valid reason for the woman's reluctance to share. And so from somewhere she found patience, knowing nothing could be done until the time was right.

Sylvie knew she, too, would get through this. She looked in the mirror and saw herself, saw a separate future as an independent person, and still carried around all the hopes she had before she'd known she'd have to live that future without her mother. Sylvie was slight but curvy, a naturally beautiful woman. Sylvie knew this, knew that she took the best parts of her combined heritage, and was grateful for it, understanding that her good looks made her life that much easier. She was also pragmatic enough to know that a beautiful woman possessed that attribute only for a short amount of time. One day she would be old and gray and soft, and she wanted to be able to say that she accomplished more in her life than merely looking good. What exactly that was, she had no idea. She did not have her mother's gift for storytelling, but she had inherited her ability for illustration. She was thinking of going to art college and majoring in design. She had a few ideas, but nothing absolute. She found it impossible to think of the future without first getting past this one night.

Sylvie remembered the day when Piper plunked down all those tickets. She had bought them off the Internet, and had printed the tickets off the website. Dissatisfied with the flimsiness of the paper, with how ordinary it seemed, her mother, ever an artist, had painted and pasted two hand-made tickets. Sylvie kept the real ones tacked above her desk, but she framed the ones her mother had made and even now she stared at the purple and gold of the design, smiling as she always did at the color photos Piper had decoupaged on—Sylvie and Callum West, staring into each other's eyes. How her mother had managed to make it look so real, she had no idea.

Sylvie was fourteen the first time she heard the Callum West Band. She had been listening to the local college radio station as she always did, with a certain smugness. When Callum's voice traveled the frequency and slipped out of her stereo, Sylvie's stomach dropped and her heart raced. She was not silly enough to think he was singing directly to her, but it felt like that. His words sung their way deep into her brain and subconscious, where all her burgeoning adolescent fantasies resided.

Callum was Sylvie's first crush. Now, almost four years later, Sylvie had been involved with boys, flirted, dated, and even slept with a couple, but none of them came close to the way Callum made her feel when she heard his voice or saw him on TV. No one could deny that his face matched the sexy timbre of his voice; he was strikingly beautiful, with shaggy black hair and piercing eyes. A little bit of his mouth always remained open, even when his lips were closed in a tiny, perfect diamond shape.

He was two men: there was the one she saw in interviews—goofy, self-effacing, and gifted with the ability to make fun of himself and his profession, which put everyone at ease—and then there was the other Callum, the one on stage. Magnetic, dark, guarded, as if he was holding something back, as if it would simply be too much to give his purest and most authentic self to the audience.

She had never seen him in concert. There was no way she was going to go with her parents, and they had claimed she was too young to go on her own the last time he came close to Avening (and the closest he'd come to Avening was still a couple hours' drive away). So Sylvie waited patiently, all the while knowing that when it was right for her to see him in person, she would. And then last winter, her mother had given her those two precious tickets, for herself and a friend. Now, just mere hours before show time, Sylvie wished more than anything else it was her mother going with her.

Sylvie had planned everything down to the last detail. She had braided her wet hair the night before in dozens of plaits. When it was time to go, she would undo them and let her long, dark locks fall wildly down the sides of her face and past her shoulders. She was going to wear faded but tight-fitting jeans that rode low on her hips and a simple white tank. Her best friend, Molly Moralejo, would be there around three o'clock to pick her up. They would take the ferry to the mainland and then drive the sixty miles to the venue in her beat-up Volvo, and they would spend that night at the campground right off of the amphitheater. The day before, conscientious Sylvie had written out a checklist of everything they would need, and now she would have to get it all together.

All morning, Shiv held the list and read off items one by one till everything was collected and assembled on the front porch. Sylvie had set up the tent, hosed it down, and let it dry in the sun before repacking it in the small nylon bag. Sylvie taught her sister how to roll each piece of clothing to maximize space. The two sisters headed to Brigid's Way

Market, Avening's local grocery store, and then Zeus' Movie Depot so Shiv could pick out a movie. Siobhan browsed as her sister watched, stopping at foreign films, picking up boxes and pretending to look intrigued. Sylvie bit her upper lip to keep from breaking into hysterics. Finally she chose, as Sylvie had predicted, a silly high school film.

"It's for Lexy," Siobhan said, rolling her eyes. "I know she really wanted to see this one."

"What a good friend you are, Shiv. Above and beyond."

By the time they had returned home and finished packing gear and food, it was two, just an hour before Molly was due. Siobhan went upstairs to clean her room, a courtesy for Lexy that Sylvie had diplomatically suggested. With an hour to kill, Sylvie started an entry in her journal. It had been a gift from her mother.

Sylvie knew her entries were pedestrian compared to the kinds of things her mother had written in her journals, but that was okay with her. She would eventually look back and wonder what paths and choices had led her to the future, and her journal, however immature, would be a precious record of her perspective.

She did not hear her father come up behind her. In fact, as she thought about it, it was the first time she had seen him that whole day. Sylvie's body momentarily tensed.

She loved her dad. But she was extremely disappointed in him. She had little patience for what she considered was self-indulgent moroseness on her father's part. Personally, she found it irritating—but she was really angry on Siobhan's behalf. Shiv and her father had been so close, and instead of being that constant source of love and support that her sister needed, he had retreated into himself and into his work. It was like Shiv had in a way lost both her parents in one fell swoop, leaving Sylvie to deal with the brunt of it.

"So, you're all ready for tonight, huh?" Will asked.

"Yep, just waiting for Molly so we can get going. Lexy's coming over. You know that, right?"

"Shiv told me. As in told instead of asked. Oh, well," Will said with a tad of exasperation in his voice. He sat down on the couch beside her. "Sylvie, I know how important this concert is to you. I mean your mother, before she . . . well, she told me how much you like this Callum person. And I just want to say that I think it's really great, I'm happy when you're happy." Sylvie was shocked. She had expected some kind of a lecture from her father on safety and drinking. "So do you need any money or anything?"

"No, I'm fine, Dad. You put my allowance in the bank already this month."

"I know, but I thought you might need extra. For T-shirts or whatever."

Sylvie was torn. She knew this was her dad's way of reaching out, but she also wanted to prove her independence. "Dad, really, I appreciate the offer, but I've been saving up for tonight for a long time."

Her dad looked around uncertainly, and then hauled himself to his feet. "Okay. Well. I'm going to go upstairs and do some work. Have a good time. I'll see you tomorrow afternoon. And please . . . leave your cell on." Will bent down to kiss her forehead.

"I'll set it to vibrate and keep it in my pocket." She smiled at his back as he left. Maybe he was coming around.

Molly Moralejo appeared not long after. She didn't bother to knock; one minute, Sylvie was alone, and the next, Molly was sitting next to her. "Hey babe, ready to rock and roll?"

Molly was far too beautiful to ever really go unnoticed. She, like Sylvie, was of mixed heritages, something they had bonded over when they first met. Her father was a Venezuelan man who had tried for Molly and her mother to fit in in Avening's cold, trying climate and odd customs. He never stopped loving his family, but found it altogether too disorienting. His unhappiness was turning him into a sour man and a poor father, so he reluctantly returned home, knowing he wasn't doing his wife or daughter any good. Molly visited him sometimes and they kept in touch with emails and phone calls.

From her father she had inherited a beautiful olive complexion and defined angular features; from her Irish mother she got a mass of fiery copper curls that hung down to the middle of her back. The combination was almost outrageously unusual, and Sylvie was sure that half the male population of Avening was in love with her. Molly's looks were so loud that she herself spoke only when she needed to. But Sylvie and Molly had known each other for so long that often times they didn't say anything.

"I am soooo ready," Sylvie drawled. She was! "I thought you'd never get here. Come on, let's go load up the car." Sylvie yelled a good-bye to her father and sister, not really waiting to hear a response. With Callum's music blasting out of the car speakers, they sped from Hollygrove Road north on Brigid's Way until they hit the open road.

Neither one wanted to disturb the spell woven by Callum's music. Molly kept her eyes on the road, and Sylvie watched the season from her window. The leaves were just beginning to turn. Next month, by Halloween, they would be a remarkable sight. They caught the ferry on time and let the lull of the open ocean rock their thoughts back and forth. Sylvie felt drunk on anticipation.

The park was packed almost to capacity. Even though she knew Piper had booked it all in advance, Sylvie was scared that something had gone wrong, momentarily panicking as Molly gave the women at the check-in window her name. The woman smiled, handed a map to Molly and sent them off. Sylvie breathed a sigh of relief. They drove about half a mile until they found their site. They were old hats, having been camping together several times. Sylvie opened the cooler and pulled out some chicken breasts to roast on the grill over the fire. She had also brought veggies she had washed and precut at home, then packed in aluminum foil with oil and garlic.

"God that smells good, Sylvie. I'm friggin' starving." Molly settled into the black butterfly chair she always brought along when she camped.

"I know, right? Food tastes so much better out here. I guess it's probably because you have to work so hard for it, huh?" Sylvie poked the chicken to check its progress.

"Yeah, that and the fact that you cook like MacGyver. You could, like, make a feast out of two blades of grass and a mushroom, whereas I can barely manage to open a bottle."

Sylvie looked at her friend sideways, but said nothing to the contrary, they both knew the truth of it. "I haven't eaten yet today and I'm about to faint. I think instinctively my body knows I'll need my strength for tonight."

"Oh yeah? You got plans I don't know about?" Molly said jokingly.

"I plan on dancing my ass off," said Sylvie.

"Tell me please we brought a camera. We did, right?"

"Please. You know I'm half Asian, right? My Japanese ancestors would be horrified if I'd forgotten a camera." Molly exploded into laughter.

When they finished their dinner, they began to get dressed. Already from the amphitheater they could hear the opening act. The night outside had gotten cool, and each girl had a thick flannel on, knowing they could shed it within the heat and throng of the crowd. As they walked toward the theater, Sylvie began to feel a kind of mind-numbing terror, and an overwhelming part of her wanted to run back to the tent. She wasn't sure she could handle it.

Molly laid a hand on her arm. "Are you okay?"

"I don't know, Mol," she answered, wide-eyed.

"You're scared, aren't you?"

"Yes . . . No . . . I think I . . . " Sylvie was almost to the point of crying. She felt so stupid, like such a kid. Here she was, almost eighteen and afraid to go to a concert.

"Listen, it's okay to be scared. And you don't have to say why. I know why, believe me. But you're a total ass-kicker, you're, like, the bravest person I know. I'll be right there."

"Okay," Sylvie said, feeling the opposite of brave. But she borrowed some of her friend's strength and pushed her legs forward towards the heavy drone of amplified bass.

"I'm not going to waste your time with introductions,"

yelled the burly, bearded man on stage. "You all know who they are. Everybody, put your hands together, for the Callum West Band!" The stage went black, and from somewhere, the unmistakable keening of a single electric guitar. From those few short bars, the crowd knew the song, and the place went wild.

And so Sylvie heard him first, before she actually saw him, so close to her she thought the world had spun away, that she was left floating in the dark absolute of outer space with no way to get back. By the time the rest of the band kicked in, the crowd was on its feet, swaying back and forth, screaming his name. But Sylvie remained perfectly still, watching, opening and letting him fill her.

Sometimes Callum held the guitar like a newborn, cradling, delicate, other times it was a lover, rising and falling beneath his fingers. He knew how to read and work an audience. He knew when to be dark and somber, and when to be emotional and gregarious. He knew, somehow, the intentions of the people before him, he knew what they needed, and if he was able, he gave it to them. That night was pure magic.

Molly watched Sylvie watch Callum. She knew the way of it with true fans and their idols, but weirdly, she also felt the energy between them. Molly was a sensor of things, and there was something connecting them, something she couldn't put her finger on. And then she began to feel something else, a nagging that something was very wrong. The band finished their set and the crowd screamed and stomped for an encore. Her head began to buzz; she was afraid she might faint. She wasn't sure what exactly was going on, but it had happened to her before, and she had learned to listen to her instincts, because they were always right.

"Sylvie. Sylvie!" Molly shook her friend out of her daze, and Sylvie looked at her like she had just woken up from a dream. "We have to get out of here, right now."

"What? Why? They're going to come back for an encore, we can't leave."

"Sylvie, trust me, please, please. We have to go. Something's wrong. We can't be here."

Sylvie gave her a look of desperation. Molly knew asking her to leave now was like asking her to rip her fingernails out. But Sylvie had been through this before. Molly always had a sense of things to come; she just knew things. So she nodded her disappointed consent and let her friend lead her out of the crowd.

They walked in silence back to the tent. Molly wanted to say something to make Sylvie feel better about leaving early. About how great the band was, how tight and perfect. But she thought better of it. No words were going to find Sylvie, who was lost in him, full of him. Better to say nothing and simply hold her hand. They got to the site and undid the zipper of the tent, crawled on all fours inside and changed into sweats and sweaters.

"I'll go light the fire, okay?" Molly said.

"Okay," Sylvie whispered. She followed Molly to the chilly night outside.

As they were finishing their cups of tea, Molly looked up. She knew something had happened. She could hear the crowd behind them going crazy, as far away as they were. She opened her mouth, but closed it again. What could she say?

She didn't know what was going on. They sat in silence for a while until they heard the sirens and, from a distance, the rush of helicopter blades. It seemed such an alien sound in that quiet, reflective place.

Molly weighed her own worry about whatever unknown thing had happened at the amphitheater against the unhappiness she knew her best friend was feeling at having her precious evening cut short. "Sylvie. I have an idea." Sylvie looked up at her, her big eyes sad and dazed. "You could go to him. He's got to be staying at the Chester. It's the only decent hotel around here for miles."

"I couldn't, Molly; it would be wrong." Sylvie looked into the fire. "I've seen him, that's all I'm gonna get. I have to learn to be happy with that." She pulled her knees into her chest.

Their conversation was broken by the sound of running and loud voices. A young couple was crossing their path. "Hey!" Molly said loudly. The two turned and came closer. "What happened over there? What's with all the sirens?"

"It was fucking awful, man," the boy told her. "They were just finishing the encore when these drunk assholes in the front started a fight. And then it turned into some kind of free-for-all, and everyone started running. I think some people got seriously hurt. There was this one girl, she got air lifted out, she . . . fuck . . . it was bad." The girl beside him started to cry. "You guys might want to think about clearing out of here. I'm sorry, I've got to get her back to the tent. She's pretty upset."

"Thanks," Molly called as they walked away, the young man holding his girlfriend and speaking soothingly. Molly and Sylvie looked at each other. What could they say?

"Wow. Thank you," Sylvie said. Molly had no reply. They both knew one or both of them might have gotten hurt if they had stayed; they had been so near the stage. But Molly also knew Sylvie, however grateful she might be, was also convinced of a bubble of sorrow following her wherever she went, even here on this happiest of days, and there it was, hanging heavy and cumbersome in the air. They both sent texts to let their families know they were okay, but otherwise sat in stilted silence.

The bad energy made Molly want to crawl outside her skin. "I'm gonna go for a walk, all right?" she said after a couple of minutes. "I don't get any vibes like it's not safe."

"Vibes," Sylvie repeated, just barely audibly.

Molly ignored her this time. "You gonna be okay if I go?" Sylvie nodded. "Find him, Sylvie," Molly said before disappearing into the dark. "You'll feel better if you do."

℘

Alone in the tent, Sylvie listened to the sound of her own breathing. Being aware of one's breath was a skill that a lot of people couldn't master. Even Sylvie herself had had trouble in the beginning, but Autumn had helped her learn to do it.

Sylvie had been able to go outside her own body ever since she could remember. At first, she didn't realize it was unusual; when she did, she started keeping it to herself, or telling only Molly. For a long time, it was only random child's play. As she got older, she eventually worked up the courage to tell her mother's friend Autumn, who she correctly suspected would have useful advice for her.

With Autumn's direction, she learned to specify her destinations, to go to people and places that she had only ever dreamed about.

She had been to India, smelled the distinct smell of poverty and desperation, but also the woody amber of sacred water. She had seen the great cities of Europe, read newspaper headlines from balding men and bejeweled ladies refreshing themselves in the outdoor cafés. Sylvie had even spied on her fellow Aveningians, finding out secrets she herself had been too young to completely understand. When she had asked Autumn, quite innocently, why Mr. Atkins, who owned Thor's Hammer Hardware, looked so happy in his wife's cocktail dresses, she learned the hard way that people's private lives were private, and it was wrong to go somewhere she knew she wouldn't be wanted.

It was a novelty for Sylvie, but it soon wore off. Lately, she hardly had the energy for anything other than sleep. But even still, in that particular state, her spirit would demand its release from the pain, fly through the clouds, higher and higher until the sky itself gave her the peace that her life could not.

Molly and Sylvie had been friends since before either of them really had a concrete idea that they could do unusual things, and had fallen naturally into a gossipy, girlish way of sharing their strange discoveries: Sylvie the places she went when she left herself, Molly the things she saw before they happened. But as they got older, their abilities became a tacit secret, something they realized they couldn't share widely with everyone they knew, binding their friendship further in a kind of collusion.

Sylvie thought it out of character for Molly to suggest any kind of supernatural visit to Callum. However irresponsible her own behavior, Molly was a great proponent of karma and what was meant to be, and spirit-stalking a rock star in his private hotel room seemed unarguably out of karmic balance. It was wrong, and he would despise the intrusion. But Sylvie had a niggling suspicion Molly wouldn't have made the suggestion if she hadn't had some premonition about the outcome. And she just couldn't help herself.

Her breathing slowed and steadied until she felt that familiar click, of her brain releasing and sealing itself to guard what remained behind. She was light, lighter than air, lighter than thought. She saw herself straight and still beneath her. She rose, flying above the park, following the road out.

❧

Callum was not asleep. He lay curled in his thin hotel blanket, haunted by what had happened only hours earlier, the damage brought about by his concert. In a way, everything had been his fault. He was twenty-four, a grown-up, and had been performing for seven years now, but he'd never once been jarred this badly by the fallout of his music.

The moment she arrived, the hairs on his arms stood to attention and a warm breeze blew through the airless room. He was on his side, his back to her, but he found himself turning. The moment he saw the shimmering person by his window he knew it was her, the girl who had died tonight, trampled to death at his concert. This was her ghost, He was surprised by her beauty, her serenity and the kindness of her face. Tears sprung to his eyes and he got up so quickly that the girl flinched.

"You!" he couldn't help himself from shouting.

"You can see me?" she asked, sounding surprised.

Callum threw himself down on the ground in front of her. "I'm sorry, I'm sorry. It's my fault, all of it." He was weeping, and between his sobs, he kept on repeating his apology.

The girl reeled, her diaphanous arm reaching for the nightstand. "Most people can't see me," she said. "I didn't think you'd . . ."

The girl was clearly confused, not malicious. Callum began to calm down. "Just say you forgive me," Callum told her. "And then you'll be able to move on. That's what's keeping you here, right?"

"Forgive you for what?" Her puzzlement was heartbreaking. "Move on where?"

"Oh God. You don't even know, do you? You don't even know you're dead."

"Dead? Callum, I'm not dead! I'm—"

He cut her off before she could finish. "Can I know your name?"

"I'm Sylvie, but—"

"Sylvie." He digested her name, and bravely went toward her and sat on the bed. "Think back to the concert tonight. Think about what happened. There was a fight, people went crazy. You were crushed in the crowd."

"I had no idea someone died," she said softly. She looked horrified, almost embarrassed.

"Yes," he replied, the guilt welling up in him again. "Someone did."

"I have to go," she said, shaking her head. "This isn't what . . . I have to go, I'm sorry." And like that, she was gone.

The next morning was damp and cold. Molly and Sylvie woke at seemingly the same moment, sat up, and looked at each other.

"You have to go back, Sylvie," Molly told her matter-of-factly. "You have to apologize and tell him what really happened."

"Are you crazy? I can't go back!" Sylvie threw up her hands. "He'll hate me, he'll think I'm some kind of a stalker. No, no way."

"He knows your name. You told him. He's going to find out that you and that girl aren't the same person, and he's going to want to know just who the hell you were. He deserves to know the truth, don't you think?"

Sylvie flopped back down in her sleeping bag and closed her eyes. Of course Molly was right. But there had been a small part of her, a very small part, that had hoped somewhere down the line, when she was older, she would actually get to meet Callum and pursue some kind of relationship with him. Not necessarily romantic (although that would have been nice) but a friendship at least. If she went to him and admitted she had projected her way into his room, into his personal space, there would never be any kind of chance. She doubted she would even be able to fantasize about such a thing, and those fantasies had been part of her emotional landscape for years now.

They drove home in silence, the road bending around

their thoughts. Sylvie wished more than anything that her mother were there. She knew what her mother would have said; it just would have been so much easier to go through with it if she had Piper's approval.

As soon as they got to Brigid's Way, the girls exhaled deeply. Sylvie had to stop at Totems to pick up her pay-check, and Molly parked the Volvo around back so she could run in. It was early, the store would not be opening for another fifteen minutes, but Sylvie knew her boss, Michael River Dog, would be in already. She rang the serv-ice bell, and waited for him to answer the door. As always, when she saw him, her stomach did a little flip. Tall, long-haired, with beautiful tattoos on his biceps, he was undeni-ably gorgeous. There was an ongoing flirtation there, and Sylvie's favorite way of playful teasing was to hold up covers of various paperback romance novels and accuse him of modeling for their covers. Michael always laughed and shrugged and called her "Geisha Girl." It was harmless enough, but Sylvie wondered what would happen after she turned eighteen. She hoped he would ask her out, despite their eight-year age difference.

"Hey, Sylvie. Glad to see you." He gave her a quick hug. "The concert was all over the news last night. I was worried."

"It was? Good thing we texted our parents."

"Wow, so responsible. I guess you're here to pick up your check, huh? You shouldn't have spent all your money on drugs, Sylvie, seriously," Michael said, chuckling as he walked towards his office in the back. "Peer pressure. Just say no."

"Ha," Sylvie called to his back. "That is so funny. Make sure to tell that one to my dad, okay?" She looked around the bookstore as she waited. Michael had revamped it when he was promoted to store manager three years ago (the owners were an elderly couple who had all but retired). Michael said he wanted to give the community a book experience. He stocked a large selection of popular fiction, but also lesser known yet impressive work that usually didn't get any attention. But the best part of the "book experience" was Michael himself. Women of all ages came in and came often just to see him and talk to him.

"So, was it bad?" he asked, returning with her check.

"I don't know. Molly got one of her feelings and dragged me off before anything happened. But it was in the air, Mike, and it was horrible."

Michael grabbed her hand. "I'm sorry it wasn't what you wanted it to be. If anyone deserved a night off and deserved to have fun, it was you."

Sylvie smiled. "Thanks, Michael. I'll see you tomorrow." She stood up on her toes to give him a kiss on the cheek. She felt his cheeks warm beneath her lips.

Molly suggested they stop at Hallowed Grounds to pick up some coffee. They ordered their drinks from the ever-present Sean (did he ever go home?) and each got one of Rona's zucchini-walnut muffins. The morning was warm enough to sit outside, but cold enough so that a steaming latte felt good in their hands, and they watched the street come alive around them. They had missed the Mabon Harvest street fair, which had happened yesterday on Brigid's Way. In her life, Sylvie had never been absent from one, and she felt a bit sad that she had missed the craft booths, great food, and wandering bands.

At almost eighteen, she was just beginning to respect the importance of shared beliefs and values, how it made her feel like she belonged to something bigger than herself. She could never leave Avening. That wasn't strictly true; she could leave, she could go to college elsewhere, she could travel the world. But she would never live anywhere else. In and amongst the traditions of her community she felt the presence of the Great Mother whom Autumn had taught her so much about, and more than anywhere else, her real mother. She leaned into Molly, who was blowing at the frothy milk of her coffee. "Molls, I have a proposition for you."

"Oh yeah, what's that?"

"I'll go back tonight, to Callum. I'll tell him everything. But you have to do something for me in return."

"Wait a minute. You can't drag me into this." Molly put down her drink and folded her arms disapprovingly. "What's going on with you and Callum West has nothing to do with me."

"Not technically. But . . . It's something brave that I'm going to do. So you should do something brave, too."

"Eh?" said Molly, raising a skeptical eyebrow.

"You need to talk to someone about your gift. Think about all the good you could do for the world if you learned how to use it properly, if you learned how to actually ask for a premonition?"

Molly looked at her friend through narrowed eyes. There had been times over the years when Sylvie had asked her to do something similar, but Molly had always refused and sworn her to secrecy. Particularly in the last year, Molly had started to toy around with some really extraordinary skills—on St. Patrick's day, for example, Molly had dressed festively for school, including bright green hair. Sylvie had watched Molly comb the green into her hair while peering into her rearview mirror, the bouncy orange curls streaking shamrock green from root to tip behind the comb, and Sylvie was perhaps the only person who realized the result was neither a wig nor the product of a spray can.

Sylvie knew that that ability, to casually alter what nature had made without upsetting anything, was far from commonplace. Furthermore, Sylvie knew that on some level Molly was scared of the things she could do. She also wanted to be loved and successful for her accomplishments; she didn't want her gift to be the most interesting thing about her.

Molly still hadn't spoken, and was staring fiercely at Sylvie. Sylvie could tell she was thinking, processing. "Look. You and I both know you've reached some kind of turning point. Think how much easier it could be with help, or advice, at least."

"I still don't think it's right that you make this conditional. You have to go to Callum, it's the right thing to do. It would be downright mean if you didn't." Molly sighed. "But, unrelated, I will go and see whoever you want me to. It's time, I suppose."

"Excellent." Sylvie smiled broadly. "I'll call Autumn and set up a time for us to go to her together, all right?"

Molly nodded. They both knew she had the better deal by far. Molly wouldn't want to be in Sylvie's shoes for all the money in the world.

To distract herself all day, Sylvie cleaned the house from top to bottom, rigorously checked Siobhan's homework, and even tried to get through some homework of her own. She did laundry, she made muffins, she washed the floors. All through the day she had kept her anxiety in check with hard work.

When the house grew as quiet and dark as the night outside, Sylvie lit a candle that smelled like cranberries and pumpkins. She lay on her bed in a white, sheer nightgown and watched the flame throw shadows around the room. It took a long while to center herself, for her breathing to grow steady and deep. She had no idea where Callum might be. She knew his next show was south, somewhere in Oregon, so she focused on that particular element to guide her. Since the connection had been made, since she had already found him once, she knew she could do so again. She felt that familiar click of her body letting go and she went.

Sylvie found herself in another hotel room. This one was bigger and more lavish than the previous one. He was sleeping, half-naked. The sight of his bare skin, the defined muscles on his torso, took her breath away. She didn't want to talk to him at all, she wanted to climb underneath the sheet beside him, she wanted to touch every inch of his body and open herself up so he could fill her. But she couldn't, she was simply a projection. There was no substance to her form.

"Callum?" she said softly. There was no way that she could do this without scaring him senseless. She imagined what it would be like if she awoke to a figure at the foot of her bed; she would have been terrified. He opened up his eyes and turned. Instead of jumping up, like she thought he would do, he sat up slowly and rubbed his eyes.

"You're back."

"Yes, I am. Umm." She tried to fight her nerves, and at the same time stop gawking at his beautiful face, so close to her, again. "I'm, um, I'm pretty sure you're really pissed at me, and you have every right to be. I only came back because I owe you a huge apology and because I don't know any other way to reach you, and then I promise I'll go."

He got up from the bed. "I know you're not the girl who died. Her name was Lisa, Lisa Took. You're Sylvie, right?"

"Yes, Sylvie. Sylvie Shigeru." She shook her head, trying to keep her voice steady. "I didn't know last night that anyone had died. My friend and I left before it all happened."

"You left early? Why?"

She was prepared for anger, and even a degree of curiosity, but not the gentle tone of his voice. "My friend, she gets these feelings, premonitions, really. She dragged me off, but I didn't want to go. I had been waiting to hear you sing for years."

"So you're not a ghost, you're real?" He crossed his arms over his chest, like they were having an everyday conversation. "You're a real person who can . . . what? What is it exactly that you can do?"

"Well, technically, it's called astral projection," Sylvie said carefully. When was he going to realize she had essentially broken into his hotel room? When was he going to become irate or creeped out? "I can project my . . . I don't know, my spirit, I guess, out of my body and I can go places."

"Really? That's wild. I mean, I've read about it. But I

didn't think it was actually real. I'd love to be able to do that."

"You could, anyone can, you just have to be taught. I mean, for some people, like me, it's natural, but anyone is capable." She was getting sidetracked. She was really only there to apologize. "That's not why I'm here though. I'm not part of some wacky cult or anything, and I'm not a stalker, which all things considered, you probably don't believe. I just wanted to say I'm sorry, for invading your space. It was wrong of me, I never should have come, and it won't happen again."

He cocked his head. "But why did you come to begin with?"

"I think you know, Callum," she answered, embarrassed.

"Yeah, I think I do, but I want to hear it from you."

Why not tell him? This whole sequence wouldn't amount to much more than a dream tomorrow, anyway. "Because you're amazing, because you're a rock star, because you move me. There are probably a million girls on the planet who would do anything to be where I am right now." Luckily, she didn't tell him she loved him; that would have been really awkward. She made herself breathe. "But I took advantage of this ability I have. The real truth is that last night, I'm not sure I could have stopped myself even if I wanted to. I just never thought . . ." Sylvie trailed off, unable to continue.

"What?"

"I never thought you'd be able to see me. Most people can't."

"Really?" His expression was almost smug. "So why do you think I can?"

"I don't know. I don't think anyone really understands how this works. Most times I float around and go unnoticed. I thought if I could just see you, I could make a kind of peace with that." She looked down at her feet, feeling inexcusable. "I'm getting this all wrong. I just wanted to apologize, that's all. And now I really do sound like a stalker."

He laughed. "Hey, there are worse things in the world than being stalked by a beautiful girl who has this amazing ability to fly out of her body any time she wants to. What else can you do, Sylvie?" The question lingered in the air. She had a feeling that he wasn't talking about anything spiritual at all. In fact, she got the distinct impression that he was flirting with her.

"Don't you want me to leave? Aren't you pissed off?" she asked.

He laughed again, totally at ease. She wished she were as relaxed. "Listen, I'm a guy who likes his privacy. But there's something about you . . . something special. It seems crazy, but maybe I can see you because I'm meant to see you."

Sylvie didn't know what to say.

"Why don't you tell me something about yourself, why don't you tell me who you are?" Callum asked.

"I'm only seventeen, I don't really know who I am yet," she answered tentatively.

"Seventeen? Shit, that could be trouble. You seem so much older."

"I'll be eighteen next month. But my mom passed away this summer, and I think that's had a pretty big effect on me." Callum sat back down on the bed, and Sylvie did too, but sat so she was facing him.

"My mom died too, when I was twelve. She was in a car accident. How did your mom die?"

"Well . . ." Sylvie couldn't believe she was about to tell him. "That's a whole other story."

They talked for a very long time. And it felt like Sylvie had known him forever. Of course she did have the advantage. She had lived with his music and words for years. But the man she sat with that night was pretty normal; he was funny, he had a knack for being self-deprecating and egotistical all at once. He wasn't a diva; he didn't need attention all the time, or praise, which surprised her. She liked him. She would have liked him if he had a normal job; in fact, she was beginning to wish he did. It would have made things a lot less complicated.

That night had been a gift, and if she never saw him or spoke to him again, the memory of it would have been enough to carry her throughout her life. It would remind her about the power of belief and faith. But of course she hoped very much that she would see him again. She wasn't nearly that spiritual.

Just before she left, Callum said, "How can I reach you? I mean, if this isn't a dream. Can I call you or something?"

For a moment, Sylvie was tempted to simply leave without giving away anything else. The night had been so magical, she didn't think it could be recreated. She was afraid that the real her would somehow disappoint him. Then she chided herself. What kind of a moron wouldn't give her phone number away to the coolest guy she'd ever met because she was afraid? So she said the numbers and he wrote them down. Then she gave him what she hoped was her most seductive smile, and went.

Sylvie awoke feeling peaceful and rested. She did not remember floating back into her own body and she wondered, like Callum, if it had really happened at all. Her candle had burned away to nothing, and she felt a pang of guilt for being so irresponsible. That's all she needed on top of everything, to burn the house down.

It was early, and a school day. She would have to go and wake her father and sister. But maybe not just yet. Maybe she should sit in Piper's garden and tell her mother everything. Wherever she was, Sylvie was sure she would love to hear the story, and perhaps love even more the look on her daughter's face, and the music in her words as she told it. She got up and stretched, looking down briefly at the phone by her bed. He would call, when the time was right. She pulled on her dressing gown and made her way downstairs and into the morning outside.

2

Autumn opened her door that afternoon to find Siobhan Shigeru standing on the stoop, her fist raised to knock. "Come in, dear," Autumn said, wrapping her hand around that small fist like a mitten. "You're starving. Let me fix you a snack."

"It's OK," Siobhan told her. "I have to get home and finish my homework. I just wanted to give you this," she said, proffering a neat package of a stapled word processed document, which had been printed, childishly but endearingly, on rainbow printer paper.

Autumn was already leading Siobhan inside by the hand. "I just baked oatmeal chocolate chip cookies."

"Those are my favorite," Siobhan said, only half-reluctantly. Autumn already knew; that's why she'd baked them.

Once she had seated the girl at her kitchen table and put a well-stocked plate in front of her, Autumn decided to break the ice. "So this lovely essay here is your entry to my contest, I assume."

"Yeah." Siobhan swallowed a mouthful of chocolate.

"I'm very glad you're entering."

Siobhan blinked at her, clearly weighing something. "There is one thing."

"Your sister?"

Siobhan nodded vigorously. "I mean, I'm not trying to . . . you know, compete with her. It's just that . . . I know she's been practicing with you for so long, and, you know, she already knows she's got something special. So I thought, maybe . . . maybe if it, like, runs in the family, maybe I could learn to be special, too. So I thought, like, I should try." Her voice trailed off, but when she looked up from her plate, her eyes were sharp and fiery.

"You should almost always try, Siobhan." Autumn was impressed by the energy she saw in the girl's face. Siobhan might be a later bloomer than her sister, but she sure as heck was going to bloom.

"There's one more thing." Siobhan put down the half of a cookie still in her hand and looked Autumn intensely in the eye. "It's going to help me get to my mother, isn't it? Entering your contest. It's going to help me get to that place she said she was going, so I can see her."

Autumn shivered as a ripple of prophecy passed through the room. Yes, this girl was going to be very powerful. Someday. "Well, I can't tell you that. I simply don't know the answer." Autumn saw Siobhan's mouth set sulkily. "But I do imagine your mother would have wanted both your sister and you to enter the contest. I know that she believed, or rather, believes, that something would help you see her again."

Siobhan nodded again, her black ponytail swinging. "Thanks," she said. "I had a feeling you'd say something like that." She stood up. "I have to go home. Can I take some cookies, though?"

"As many as you want." Autumn smiled as Siobhan stuck a napkin full of cookies in her jacket pocket and waved good-bye. Inside, though, Autumn felt an inevitable swell of regret. There was a future great talent she would only be able to watch from a distance.

October 31: Samhain

I T TOOK AUTUMN ALL OF TWO SECONDS TO SURMISE that there would not be any rain today. Nor would there be sun. The clouds hung low over Avening, low enough to shelter the small town and gather it together so people would feel compelled to light fires, wear oversized clothing, watch old movies, and drink tea from cups that fit perfectly in their hands. She didn't know what to think about the weather's lack of ambition, today of all days. She also supposed it would have been rather tacky of nature to show off at her expense.

She glanced furtively over at her journal, lying open towards its middle on an old, high bookstand. There were so many mysteries inside, so many magical possibilities and riddles solved. But it was only because Autumn knew so very much that she could understand how little she really knew.

She was leaving today. Had to. Time had run out on her like a fickle husband. How appropriate that it should be today, Samhain. It was truly the end of summer and the beginning of winter, the end of one phase of her life and the beginning of a new one.

She knew there was no point in kvetching. She wasn't sure she would have ever been ready. Still, for someone as organized and thorough as Autumn, she hadn't done a single thing to prepare. Stupid, stupid. And she had an awful lot of life to gather up.

More than half a millennium ago she had been recruited by the Jaen. Six hundred years. The notion seemed preposterous to her, ridiculous even, like it didn't even fit anymore. She wasn't, of course, living in Avening when it began. Avening didn't exist; even the first settlers, the First Peoples, hadn't made their way over to the island until decades after. It was a time of kings (and perhaps a few queens). She had been born in what was now the United Kingdom, though it wasn't united then at all. She was glad she'd lived through that savagery, glad she could bear witness to how far humanity had come—in certain respects. In many others, she wasn't so sure that the human race had gotten that far along at all.

She had been all of twenty when the High Sister at Avesbury had come for her. Her name hadn't been Autumn then, of course; it hadn't even been Serafina yet. But that first name was the name that mattered the least, since it was the only name she'd had that she hadn't picked for herself. Back then, she was the only daughter of a wealthy merchant. She largely spent her time resisting the suitors her father paraded in front of her; she was determined not to be married off to some old letch. Her parents tried to get her to capitulate, believing she was wrongheadedly waiting for true love. How wrong they were. She was waiting, all right, but not for a man.

When she was in her late teens, Autumn had started to dream of Sister Dori. She saw her face, her long, tapered fingers, and her skin, so milky and translucent she could have traced the blue of her veins. Autumn saw this woman behind her closed lids almost every night for a year before she actually came. The dreams weren't sexual, but they were seductive. She knew that Dori would offer her something, though she didn't know what, and she didn't know when.

When Sister Dori finally arrived at her house, Autumn looked straight into her remarkable face and saw her future. She arrived in a retinue of Autumn's mother's extended family, and she was supposed to be some kind of a nun, but Autumn knew better. She never talked about Christ, let alone being his bride, and her behavior was far from pious, but no one seemed to notice her eccentricities. No one seemed to point her out or talk about her. Autumn wondered if anyone actually noticed she was there.

It wasn't as if Dori came out right away and offered her a place in the Jaen. She asked many questions over a period of days. Questions that, if overheard, would have been considered blasphemous, but between the two of them were just philosophical. It wasn't until Dori's very last evening there that she told Autumn the truth of what she was. She was one of the Jaen, an ancient order of women who dedicate their lives in the service of others. They train together in a cell of thirteen initiates at first, to learn the elemental basics. There were cells, which were called Khandas in the Jaen vernacular, all over the world, living, working, serving in absolute secrecy. Dori was the High Sister of her Khanda and now, after serving many lifetimes over, she was due for retirement.

The Jaen knew about Autumn, where to find her and what she was capable of (though at the time Autumn barely knew herself what that was). Dori wanted Autumn to take over as the High Sister of Avesbury. Dori warned Autumn how difficult it would be, how many years she would serve. She didn't make it sound glamorous or even all that exciting. But Autumn got a sense, a taste of something in her mouth and a faint smell of something familiar. And so she accepted Dori's offer with casual grace and a secret thrill inside her heart. Dori managed to convince Autumn's parents quite easily that she should join her nunnery, and off they went.

Together, Dori and Autumn, her new protégé, spent weeks combing the countryside for the new talent Dori knew was there. Within a fifty-mile radius they managed to find every woman the Vedea, the Jaen oracle, wanted. As Dori explained to Autumn then, the Vedea is always right. Always, even if it takes a while for its righteousness to unfold. The centuries since Autumn's first lessons had only proved this correct.

Autumn watched as women of all ages and social backgrounds joined their group. These women, once strangers, became her closest friends, Sisters in every sense of the word. Dori stayed with them a year, after each had been initiated formally into the Jaen. And then one day, she was gone.

As a High Sister, Autumn had many gifts and many talents; that was both her blessing and her curse, to be a jack-of-all-trades and a master of none. The rest of her Sisters specialized in one single ability. She could never be as good as they were, but she learned enough to do what was needed, when it was needed. Autumn's role in the community was as a source of wisdom; theirs, sources of magic.

The initiates stayed together at Avesbury for almost

twenty years before being called to apprentice in various places around the globe. Autumn remained behind, helping the local citizenry, central to the community, protected by her gifts. For some years, she wrote short, pleasant letters to her family, but eventually there was no one left to receive them. Time passed—it seemed like a few months, but it was more than a century. Then one day word came down from the Vedea that she was to leave Avesbury. She wasn't sad, and that surprised her. Maybe because she'd always had a feeling that she would be called to do more.

The Jaen were shifting their presence to the New World, as it was being called. There were Jaen already among the First Nation peoples and among their distant cousins to the south—Autumn herself had met the spirit of a traveler from the far west, from the great body of water Europeans would call the Pacific. But, after all, the Jaen philosophy was a Eurasian magic, a grassroots movement born of the Celtic spread through Europe and Central Asia. That other hemisphere had its own very ancient and well-established magical traditions—several of them, in fact—and in spite of some overlap in theory, the Jaen had not made any formal alliance with their counterparts across the Atlantic. There was, of course, always both curiosity and resistance when one met another practitioner of a slightly different variety of magic.

But by the close of the sixteenth century, Autumn had heard of the decimated populations in those other continents—even earth magic cannot overwhelm the disease and violence of which humans are capable. The message from the Vedea was clear: if the Jaen did not reach out now, broaden their horizons and open their minds, an entire chapter of Sisterhood would be lost. The order needed to set out, and quickly, for the New World, learn what they could, and ally with the shamans and wisewomen of those distant provinces. However, what was quick for the Jaen was usually more like generations for civilians.

Autumn herself wasn't sent across the world for another two hundred years, but eventually she was given a few months and a list of names. She needed to replace herself, and to recruit the experienced group of Sisters who would be making this huge move with her. She left Avesbury behind with affection but no regret, and boarded her well-provisioned ship with a very special collection of women who had been recruited from across the British Isles, and some from places as far as Anatolia, Bohemia, and the Arctic Circle. After a long, if largely charmed, journey over the stormy seas, Autumn and twelve other women were shipwrecked off the coast of a lush green island when a lightning storm split their hull clean in two. Autumn's instructions from the Vedea had of course been very vague, but as she watched the beams of her ship split and sink into the Pacific, she was pretty sure this island was their final destination. And the place on the island they would eventually settle was called Avening, an homage to Autumn's first Khanda in Avesbury.

She didn't love this group of Sisters any more or less than her Sisters at Avesbury, but she loved Avening. There was a practical reason the Jaen wanted a presence there. It was a powerful place, working on a different frequency it seemed, pulsing a steady undercurrent of magic that made it more than special. And how many people get to design a community? Autumn instilled her most intrinsic morals, maintained higher ground. A town grew up around her guided almost entirely by her own dearest principles, where the people weren't any better than people anywhere else, but where they wanted to be better, and were willing to work in order to get there.

Autumn was proud of what she had created nearly four hundred years ago, and even though it was now her turn to go, she understood why. Nature is a circle. It was somebody else's turn. The question was whose.

Autumn was, in truth, a little bitter about how the Vedea handled this whole situation. Most High Sisters got much more notice. And most of them didn't have to vet fifty different replacement candidates. But Autumn had done it— in one year, she'd narrowed down her list of fifty to twelve women she knew would become Avening's new Jaen sisters. She was absolutely sure about these twelve. She just wasn't so sure of the thirteenth, and had no idea which one could possibly be the High Sister.

Autumn thought on it this morning as, just like every morning before, she stood and squared her body on her purple yoga mat. In one fluid movement she began with the Sun Salutation. After all these years, yoga still hurt. But she breathed through the pain until her muscles let go and she was able to convince her body that, yes, it was meant to bend this way. Her body had been good to her, considering.

She appreciated her own reflection—she looked less than a tenth of her earthly age—but knew the years were bound to catch up. There had been a time or two when she had put a glamour on herself, to reverse those years, to remember and even to capture the attention of a young man so she could make the kind of vigorous love she had enjoyed before. But she wouldn't have tried to keep up the glamour permanently, or to create the violent kind of spells that she could have to remain in a state of perpetual youth. The crone cannot be a sage or wisewoman until she reaches beyond the shallow confines of her skin. Children of the earth must also change, like the seasons do. Autumn had seen herself in all these transitions: the tentative buds of spring; the heavy sensuality of summer. And now, like the fall, she was colorful and majestic but right on the verge of winter, to be stripped down to what was really important, the bare branches of what was true.

When she finished her final pose she sat lotus-style on her mat. She lit a white fire inside her ribs and let it spill out of her torso. To Autumn, the light symbolized the Goddess's love and protection. These quietest moments were a call to prayer: not for things, not even for direction. Rather, a call for acknowledgment of and gratitude for everything wonderful, and even things not-so-wonderful; for pain, too, because she understood that difficult times were ones in which she learned the most. This was the last time she would perform this exercise here, in her beloved house. But she knew it was only so hard to leave because the Goddess had given her something truly wonderful.

When she felt the weight of the impending day lift a little, she knew it was time to move. She needed to pack. Her successor would get not only the book, but also Demeter's Grove, the apartment flat above, and the guesthouse behind. Of course no one knew this; no one knew that she was leaving for good. This was in part because in her pride she still wanted to appear enigmatic and mysterious. The other part was that she didn't think she could bear to say good-bye to her friends. It was cowardly, and she bent a little with the knowledge of that.

Demeter's Grove had been her vision, and she knew that the future owner would want to change it, make it her own. So she was leaving behind enough money in trust for the new owner to do whatever she wanted with the space. Whatever it became, she was sure, would be wonderful.

The yoga session had dehydrated her, so she went to the kitchen, flicked on the electric kettle, and prepared a cup for tea. On the wooden counter, which was clean but lined with cuts and age, was the pile of entries. The contest had been the smartest way to go. Entries had trickled in over the last twelve months, particularly after Autumn's monthly announcements in the *Circle*, which always seemed to trigger a new crop of inspiration. Though the twelve she had settled on had all entered (some with a certain amount of prodding from Autumn herself), not all of them had been on the Vedea's list. She wasn't sure if this meant that the Vedea had, for the first time, been wrong, or if the vague nature of the list meant that it had only been a guideline anyways. She was, however, sure she had chosen correctly.

She flicked through the entries. She could almost feel each woman's intention through the paper. Ellie Penhaligan, who was so in tune with the earth and the elements that she could disappear into them. Stella Darling, whose suitability was a real no-brainer, especially now that she had opened her own natural healing practice. Stella was the only other person in Avening with formal magical training, and once time had mellowed her, she would be a true mistress of the elements. Nina Bruno, one of the most powerful candidates on her list, a real Charm Sister whose hypnotic personal energy would turn anyone her way. Eve Pruitt, who had no particular powers to speak of, but whose loving and giving energy radiated from her, putting everyone at ease—people magic. Maggie Moreau, who passed so effortlessly between worlds, and she hadn't even hit puberty yet. Her mother Mave—who would have thought Mave would have been interested? But she'd applied all on her own, and sure enough, Autumn had been forced to recognize her great untapped potential. Ana Beckwith, whom Autumn loved like a daughter born of her own womb, and who, whether she realized it or not, had already begun to tap into her ability to move through time. Ginny Emmerling, the lonely warrior who wanted to fight for a new piece of herself. Dottie Davis, the only applicant to understand the Book as a vehicle of spirituality. Charlie Solomon, that budding psychic reporter whom Autumn had all but coerced into settling down in Avening. Sylvie Shigeru, who was only just eighteen and had already made peace with her magic, and done so much to harness it. And last, her sister, Siobhan, who would be a prophet the likes of whom Autumn hadn't seen in many generations. Age wasn't a concern; Maggie and Siobhan wouldn't initiate for another ten years at least, and as for the older women, Dottie and Eve, initiation would change them the way it had changed Autumn so many centuries ago.

Every single woman was amazing, with incredible potential. But who would lead them? And who would she choose now to be the last one? Should she choose from the list given by the Vedea? Or her contest? And how in the hell was she going to get ready to go in time?

The water boiled. Autumn poured her cup almost full to steep and thumbed through the essays. The trouble was there was a good reason each candidate, no matter how wonderful, would not be suitable for High Sister. Ellie Penhaligan, obviously, was no leader—talented though she was, her skill lay in not being seen. Sylvie Shigeru would develop into a fantastic medium, but the High Sister needed to be more rooted with the living than the dead. Her youth aside, Maggie Moreau's magic, similarly, was too much about leaving this world and not enough about developing and helping it. Siobhan Shigeru was too much of a firecracker. She certainly wouldn't lack for charisma as she matured, but Autumn needed someone a little more level-headed and neutral.

Nina Bruno was too selfish, too magnetic; the Book would be nearly dangerous in her hands. Eve Pruitt, on the other hand, was the least selfish person Autumn had ever met, and so equally unsuited; the High Sister had to be able to turn away some cases without any guilt, or she would never survive her job. Mave Moreau, who might have been a good fit, despite her lack of training, had done well to confess in her letter that her family would always be her first priority, and Autumn couldn't ask her to make them secondary for such a demanding position as High Sister. Ana, despite her natural talent and her willingness to cultivate it, was simply not quite powerful enough. And while Ginny Emmerling couldn't have known Ana was a rival of sorts, her personality and her variety of magic were simply too aggressive; she wasn't nearly diplomatic enough.

Dottie Davis was a natural follower, not a natural leader. And however holy she had decided her interest in the Book of Shadows was, Autumn knew she would have a lot of negotiating with her Christian spirituality as the years unfolded. Stella Darling, if she could tone down her rage, would have been perfect, if only she hadn't had her intense affinity for earth. Stella had a natural-born specialization, and to ask her to give that up in order to become a less specialized High Sister would be to deprive the world of a consummate healer. Charlie Solomon, too, was a future specialist, and too much of a gypsy. Settling in Avening and never being able to leave would drive her nuts. Besides, it would never do to have a High Sister who was too psychic. A High Sister had to be able to listen to other things besides people's secret thoughts.

And now, with only hours to go before she had to finalize her decision, Autumn didn't have a candidate she felt comfortable selecting, never mind the thirteenth to complete the group. She got up, hearing her knees crack. She muttered a low curse to herself when the phone rang, but she picked up without thinking or remembering the genius of voice mail.

"Hello?"

"Autumn, it's Sylvie."

"Oh hello, my dear!" Autumn stretched this way and that before settling in an old wing-backed chair near the fire.

"I hope I haven't bothered you." Sylvie was nearly breathless. "I know it's your day off and everything."

"Not at all, Sylvie. I was just . . . puttering around."

"Oh good, because I have a small favor to ask. It's about a friend of mine."

Autumn laughed. "A friend, is it?"

"No, really. I'm not giving you the old 'friend' line, I promise. I really do have a friend who needs your help. I've been trying to get her over to you for ages, and she finally actually said yes. I realize it's Halloween, but I'm afraid I'll lose this momentum if I don't bring her over there. I wouldn't ask if it wasn't totally important. Could you just give us twenty minutes or so?"

Autumn sighed, but she tried to make it shallow enough for her young friend not to notice. The last thing she wanted to do was see anyone today. She really wasn't up for it emotionally, and she still had a lot to get done. If it were anyone else she would have said no, but it was Sylvie. When she considered what had happened with Piper, Autumn knew, with a little bit of dread, that Sylvie might be the one person she should say good-bye to in person.

"All right, hon. Bring over your mystery friend. But I'm right in the middle of something now, so can you give me a couple of hours? That will give me enough time to get everything finished."

"Absolutely. Thank you so much, Autumn. See you later."

"Bye, love," Autumn answered before clicking off the phone. Two hours would be barely enough time, but at least she could try to finish packing. Autumn sighed and returned to her room. All around her were tasks half finished, things left waiting and relics of her life. How could she simply walk away with so little? Walk away from her life and her friends? She wanted to cry, but her resolve denied her that weakness. No, this was the way it had to be. This was the next part of her journey and she had to take it. Besides, wasn't she always the adventurous one? Hadn't she resented her sisters and their far-off escapades to the most magical and mysterious places on earth? No, it was time to go and see what else her life and gifts had to offer. Her work in Avening may not have been completely finished, but it was done.

Soon, her trunk was almost full. Her Sister uniform, which she knew would be the only thing she'd wear going forward, her favorite volumes of poetry, some old philosophical manuscripts, and a few pieces of fiction. She pulled the quilt that lay folded at the foot of her bed; she would certainly take the quilt. All her Sisters had one; they had made them together. Hers was beautiful, a simple Celtic design of richly lush fabrics. What a quilting bee they had had! She remembered how much fun it was to sit together at the frame, each of them sharing stories of their lives. The steady pulling of the needle, the sound of it piercing the delicate fabrics had them all entranced, opened them up and bonded them, even before any of them had attempted any magic. What a smart way to begin things. Yes, it would be good to be with her Sisters again.

Even before she heard the faint press of her doorbell, she knew Sylvie had arrived. Quickly, she unlocked and opened the old oak door. There was Sylvie, looking as beautiful and serene as ever. Beside her was the most magnificent red-haired creature Autumn had ever seen. Who was this electrifying girl? Why had she never seen her before? It seemed impossible. Her skin, how simply marvelous! Light olive, Autumn supposed it would be called, but really, it was the color of bronze and gold combined. And then it hit her. This had to be Molly Moralejo, Sylvie's best friend, who had patently refused to meet Autumn for the last six months. But Autumn couldn't imagine how the girl had avoided her her entire life unless this moment, this particular encounter, was some work of fate. She supposed the shock must have registered on her face, because Sylvie's brow furrowed.

"Autumn? Are you okay? Are we too early or something? We can—"

"No no, come inside." Autumn ushered them through the door. "You must be Molly, right?" The girl looked surprised, and slightly embarrassed. "Sylvie's told me so much about you, you could hardly be anyone else. Come on, let's go to the kitchen and I'll make some tea."

Autumn could tell that Molly was impressed with her home as they walked through it. "I love your house, Autumn," Molly said, sure enough. "It's amazing. It's so much bigger than it looks from the street."

"Yes, I know, I was very lucky to have . . . found it. Let's have some caffeine, shall we? I've been drinking herbal all day, but I think I need a little boost."

"Thanks, Autumn. Should we sit?" Sylvie asked.

"Please," Autumn answered as she joined them. "So, Molly, Sylvie tells me you might need some advice. I know we don't know each other, but I can promise you that whatever you tell me will not leave this room, nor will it be likely to shock me. Sylvie can attest to that, right, love?" Sylvie nodded.

Molly didn't seem embarrassed, but she did look a little skeptical. "I've heard about you from Sylvie. She really likes you and trusts you."

"Well, the feeling is more than mutual. But I am surprised I've never met you before. We always seem to just miss each other. Which is odd, isn't it?" Autumn looked squarely at Molly, who, to her credit, did not back down from that look.

"Yeah, well. I don't know. The truth is, I don't really need any advice. And, well . . . I've kind of been avoiding you. I mean, that sounds harsh, I'm sorry. I don't mean to be rude."

Sylvie looked at Molly with a rather disapproving head tilt, but Autumn was more than intrigued. "Well, that's too bad. You seem like a very interesting young lady. I'm sure we would have found some common ground. But now you're here, and I suppose I'd like to know why."

Molly waited a beat or two. Autumn could tell the girl didn't know how she was going to say what she felt compelled to. "I know who you are, Autumn," she said finally. "I mean, who you are really. I never told Sylvie or anyone else. But I've dreamed about you."

Autumn ran cold with her words. It dawned on her suddenly exactly what was going on, and she threw a silent string of curse words up to the Vedea for keeping this from her.

"The thing is, see, I like my life, you know? I mean . . . um, okay. What do I mean?" She pursed her lips for a moment before continuing. "I've always known I was different. Like I would see things and dream things, and they would come true. And I knew that whatever this was was really big, you know? And I knew that it wasn't normal." Molly winced a little with these words. Autumn understood what saying them out loud meant. "I would dream about you," she continued, "and your group from, like, the olden days, and all your magic. But other weird things too, about lightning and clocks and being invisible and about Piper and where she went. It was like I was standing on train tracks, and you were the train, and you were coming. I could have walked down to meet you, but I wanted to wait as long as I could because I knew what would happen. I knew eventually I had to get on that train."

Sylvie was white, her breath rapidly moving her chest up and down. Molly was calm.

Autumn, more than anything, was relieved. "So, you know who I am. And you know what you will be a part of. I'm just not sure why you waited. I wouldn't have forced you to do anything you weren't ready to do." Autumn could have been annoyed, surely. But she knew enough to know that this was the plan. It had been all along and there was a reason for it.

"Well, I waited because I just wanted to be normal for as long as I could. Go to parties and drink too much and hook up with random guys and be irresponsible. I wanted to have as much of ordinary as I could before I joined the dark side," Molly said with a straight face.

"You don't really think I'm part of the dark side?" Autumn felt her eyebrows raise.

"No, no. I was kidding. You know what I mean. It's not just something you can stick a toe into. Right? I mean, once the curtain's lifted, you can't go back and pretend you never saw the wizard." Molly's face broke into a grin, which faded almost immediately. "In a few moments you're going to make me an offer, right? And then my life won't ever be the same. And it's cool, and I'm looking forward to what will happen. I just didn't want it to happen right away. I wasn't ready. And I don't think you were ready either. Or else why have this contest, right? I mean, if you'd been ready, you would have known all about me. You would have just come to get me." Molly leaned back in her chair. "Although I admit that I did as much as I could to make sure you didn't notice me. But it doesn't matter, right, because here I am."

"For fuck's sake, Molly!" Sylvie suddenly chimed in with enough anxiety to startle the both of them. "You could have told me, at least!"

Autumn felt for her at that moment. For all Sylvie knew, here was yet another person who was going ahead without her to a place she couldn't follow.

"No, I couldn't," Molly told her friend, her voice almost apologetic. "Because it would have gotten to you, and then Autumn would have picked up on it. I didn't tell anyone. I'm sorry. Don't be mad. Besides, you're—"

Autumn stood, stopping Molly in mid-sentence. She had said quite enough, and Autumn needed to talk to her to find out exactly how much she did know before she spilled anything else.

"Molly, I'd like you to come with me. Sylvie, help yourself to some tea. And go ahead into the store and get whatever you like, as much as you want. It's on me."

Sylvie frowned, looking at Molly, knowing she needed to leave her friend and clearly not wanting to. "Really?" she asked uncertainly.

"Absolutely."

Sylvie nodded and got up, and Autumn led Molly up the stairs and into her bedroom. Molly sat herself down on a chair in the corner of the room, but said nothing. Autumn sat on her bed, across from Molly, and closed her eyes, holding out both her palms. She felt a sudden slight breeze, and she felt Molly realizing it was she, Autumn, creating the breeze.

The whole world seemed to stop in that moment. Autumn imagined babies soothed and thirteen-year-old girls happy with their mothers and cars turning off and factory production lines slowing to a crawl. And then from the stillness, the sound of paper. Autumn's journal was floating off the tall bookstand and through the air until it rested comfortably in Molly's lap.

"Holy shit," Molly said.

"Holy, indeed. So you know already I'm going to offer you my journal?"

"Yes. I mean, I saw an offer, but I didn't see the book." She shook her head and her red curls tumbled. "That was insane! You, like, make things, like, move? Through the air?"

"So," Autumn said, feeling the need to invest the moment with some ceremony. "I give you this book. It goes through not only my life, but also the initiate lessons you will all need to master before moving on. By the time you are ready to begin, you will have a head start on the others, so don't worry. You'll be able to teach them."

At first the implications of what Autumn was saying went over Molly's head, and Autumn didn't blame her. "Autumn, it's really cool how you can move things with your mind and all, but what does that make you, exactly? What am I?"

"To be honest, Molly, I don't completely know," Autumn replied truthfully. "I mean, I know that we are a part of a group called the Jaen. Where the Jaen comes from, how it was started and when, I don't have an answer to these questions. We take a lot on faith around these parts." Autumn looked tenderly at Molly. She was a remarkable girl, with such incredible energy that it poured out of her like some kind of karmic tap. She understood why she would meet her now, just as she was leaving. More than any other Sister or friend she had ever had, this one special child would have become like her own. She would never have been able to leave her. Molly filled that hollow, childless place that had been empty for hundreds of years. Autumn would have lost her objectivity; she would not have been a good teacher.

"I get the feeling that you've seen quite a bit about what we can do and how we're set up. Am I right?"

"Yeah. No, I get it. Little groups, all over the place. But what I don't get is, why? I mean, why are you all in the closet?"

"Well, that is a discussion for another day," Autumn said, a little sternly. "You have to learn right away that we aren't leaders. We aren't heroes or daredevils or showmen. We follow orders; we serve for the greater good. This will frustrate the hell out of you, Molly. You'll have to do things that you don't agree with. And then, maybe years later, you'll understand why, and it will all make sense. The Jaen always have a plan, and annoyingly, it's the right one." Autumn took her journal and placed it gently in Molly's arms. "I can see you're not afraid. And that's good. You won't be alone. Mentors will be sent, and there will be a lot of time here in Avening for everyone to master the basics. You're brave, and a natural leader; you'll do a fantastic job."

Autumn read the look on Molly's face as what was about to happen began to dawn on her. "You are free to move in here," she went on. "Actually, as of right now, the house and everything in it belongs to you, along with a substantial bank account. Thank Goddess you're eighteen, as that solves one problem. The money is such that you can live off the interest alone. My lawyer arranged everything in advance; all we have to do is sign these papers together." Autumn pointed to a stack of papers on the desk.

"Oh my God, you're leaving, aren't you?" Her voice rose in something close to panic.

"Yes, my dear, I'm afraid I have to go." Autumn's very real regret came through in her voice. "If I had found you earlier, I suppose I could have been able to provide more training. But once the Book is passed on, officially, the previous owner has to step aside. It's a little like being thrown in the deep end. But I have all the faith in the world that you'll do just fine."

Molly drew the book up to her chest. Autumn could tell that already the pull of it was offering her a semblance of security. "But you can't just leave! You're probably the most important person in this town. People love you, people depend on you, and they sure as shit are not going to come to some snot-nosed kid for advice." Molly blinked twice, and sputtered, "Where on earth are you going to go? Where are you going to find a place where you're needed and wanted as much as Avening?"

Autumn put a hand on her knee to reassure her. "Long ago, more years than I could even begin to count, Molly, I met a woman who changed my life. What she offered me is much the same thing as I'm offering you. Together, we found twelve other women who, like us, like yourself, had a gift for magic.

When the group was complete, the woman went away to meet up with her own group of twelve. That's where I'm going now, to my sisters, for the next part of the journey. This may surprise you, but up until five minutes ago, I didn't have a leader for the twelve other magical women I've found here. I was going to settle, but the Universe corrects itself, so here you are."

Molly breathed in deeply, obviously trying to digest. "Are you absolutely sure about this? Because without you, I'm not. Aren't I too young or something? I'm pretty sure I need you here."

Autumn shook her head dismissively. "The first thing you need to do is go over to my desk and look through the essays of your new sisters. There is quite a diversity of talents here. There are charmers and menders and sentries and warders and psychics. But the most important thing I should stress is that you are the High Sister. You will lead these women. And you will eventually be able to do a fair bit of whatever talent they have. But that's ages away. For now, each one of them has something to teach you. You won't be alone. There will be thirteen of you, and among the lot, you'll be able to figure out the answers."

"Okay, okay, so we all do this together? That's comforting at least." Molly mulled for only moments, and then issued a series of precise questions. "But how long does it take, and will the Jaen send people to oversee us? How often will they come?" She was intent on remaining clear-headed and getting as many questions answered as she could before Autumn left.

"It takes as long as it takes. But once you formally initi-ate, the answers will become more clear, as will your direction. You will all live here together in Avening as initiates. Once that level is done, one by one, you will begin to leave. The others will be sent away to apprentice elsewhere in their particular gift. But not you, Molly; you will remain here, like I did, overseeing this community and the twelve others, wherever they are. And then it will be time to move on, just like I'm doing now."

"But where do you go? I mean, will I even be able to contact you if I need to?"

"Yes, and no. It's complicated. It's not really a location as much as a place between places. But I promise that I will be watching out for you, and the Book will be your guide." Autumn could see the relief in Molly's face, and was glad the girl trusted her, which meant everything at that point. "So, what do you say, Molly? I wouldn't ask this of you unless I absolutely knew you could handle it. Every bone in my body tells me you are the one. Shall we sign the papers?"

Autumn could tell that Molly was trying to connect to something. She was going down deep inside to listen to the visceral machinations of her body. She was looking, listening for an answer. Autumn was impressed that the girl did not jump to say yes. Molly got up silently, the Book still held against her chest. With her free hand, she picked up a pen and began to fill in her name on the stack of papers. A rush of relief poured through Autumn, and she found, surprisingly, that she felt rather light. The knot that had turned her stomach upside down turned into something else: anticipation. She was ready.

After she signed the papers herself, she turned to Molly. "I'm going to go now. Take some time to get used to all of this.

In a few weeks, I will help you address this to the others. Maybe then I'll even have some more information. Don't tell them I've been in touch, though. I want everyone to get used to my not being here. I think that after you read their essays, you will agree that they are all up to the challenge." Autumn made her way to the door, but Molly stuck out her arm to stop her.

"Wait, you're just going to leave? Like that? Without even saying good-bye? What about the store? What about Sylvie? She's right downstairs."

Autumn hooked her arm through Molly's and led her down the hallway until they were standing in front of the closed door to her room.

"I am so late already, Molly. I have to go now. The store was mine, now it's yours. You might want to wait until after you graduate, but you should turn it into whatever you want. Make it into a preschool, a library, a bar, whatever. Demeter's Grove was my vision. You have to find your own. As for Sylvie, well, you can tell her I'll be back. That's the very least that I should do. Good luck, Molly." Autumn kissed her soft, freckled cheek and opened the door. After she stepped through, the door shut resolutely.

There was a sound. A sound so piercing and so horribly wonderful Molly thought she might have imagined it. She gave it a couple of seconds and then opened the door Autumn had walked through. The hallway was empty, and Autumn was gone.

Alice, Alice, gone down the rabbit hole. That's how Molly felt. On one hand she was more a woman than she had ever been, in all her eighteen years, and on the other she felt barely eight. There was something about the Book, though, something about holding it close that gave her a kind of distance and strength. She felt connected in that moment, and in truth, she thought she might have the answers to all of the questions that were running around like maniacs in her brain right there, curled up on her tongue. Not that she could have said them out loud or anything. It was more that she just knew, which gave her a kind of courage that she had never felt before.

She made her way down the stairs. Sylvie, she was sure, would be shocked and saddened. Molly knew it would be difficult for her to lose yet another important woman in her life. But she was also sure that once she opened up Autumn's journal, everything would change. They would read the first page together. She would take her hand and whisper in her ear. She would show her that this was just the beginning. They would turn the dreaming world upside down and live the kind of life that people only imagined was possible. When Molly Moralejo got to the bottom of the stairs, she pulled the Book close to her, and smiled.

Acknowledgments

Many, many thanks go to my agents at Dupree Miller & Associates, Jan Miller and Nena Madonia, both of whom saw me as a real author before I ever saw myself as one. I feel so blessed to have these fierce ladies in my corner. On that front, thanks go to my dad, for introducing me to them.

To the amazing people at The Overlook Press, most notably Juliet Grames, editor extraordinaire, who was able to take the manifesto I gave her and turn it into an actual book.

To Kristin Barlowe, my gangstar. For the glorious pictures and amazing friendship.

Laura Holder, the Web mistress, who totally gets it.

Special thanks go to the many people that made the writing of this book possible. For location, I must thank Oprah Winfrey who suggested one afternoon on Desolation Sound that British Columbia was just as magical a place as New England. When Oprah offers up some insight, *you listen.* For mood, I have to thank all my girlfriends in the Monthly Dinner club: K-bar, K-russ, Buxy, and Shell—without you, I would have gone stir crazy, I'm sure. How lucky I am to call such strong, powerful women my friends. To everyone at Sanctuary for Yoga, for whipping my butt into shape and keeping me grounded.

For tone, I must thank my best friend and first editor (since 7th grade), Meghan Carter. Your advice and support has always been invaluable. My other best friend, Michael Buble, your loyalty and faith in me has never wavered. I have a career because of you. I have many sisters; there's a little bit of each of you in the women of Avening. My mother, who has always believed in me.

To my partner and not husband, Matt Freeman. Your love has made me the best me there is.

And finally to my girls, Mike and Eva, who taught me all about magic the moment you were put in arms.

About the Author

Amy S. Foster is an award-winning lyricist who has had multiple number-one hits around the world. Her most successful collaborations to date are the songs she has co-written with crooner Michael Buble. Although Amy comes from a musical background (her father is Grammy award-winning record producer and composer David Foster), her first love has always been writing. With her degree in International Communications from American University came a love of travel and exploration of different cultures that has taken Amy around the world, influencing both her song and fiction writing. She has written songs for Josh Groban, Diana Krall, Destiny's Child, and Andrea Bocelli. Amy lives with her family in Vancouver BC (not far from Avening). For more info, visit amysfoster.com.